The Origin of Enoch

Divine Trials Series
Book 1

MEGAN EINARSON

THE ORIGIN OF ENOCH

Contents

Prologue 1

Chapter 1 3

Chapter 2 11

Chapter 3 23

Chapter 4 32

Chapter 5 41

Chapter 6 52

Chapter 7 59

Chapter 8 66

Chapter 9 76

Chapter 10 86

Chapter 11 94

Chapter 12 100

Chapter 13 107

Chapter 14 109

Chapter 15 115

Chapter 16	124
Chapter 17	127
Chapter 18	133
Chapter 19	140
Chapter 20	148
Chapter 21	154
Chapter 22	161
Chapter 23	168
Chapter 24	175
Chapter 25	179
Chapter 26	185
Chapter 27	189
Chapter 28	194
Chapter 29	203
Chapter 30	207
Chapter 31	212
Chapter 32	218
Chapter 33	225
Chapter 34	232
Chapter 35	234
Chapter 36	241

Contents ~ *vii*

Chapter 37   246

Chapter 38   252

Chapter 39   259

Chapter 40   268

Chapter 41   276

Chapter 42   282

Epilogue   290

Glossary   293

Prologue

WHAT IS IT that decides our fates?

Before the events of that horrible day, this question had never plagued the young boy's mind. For children, grand questions of purpose and destiny are far less important than wondering what game would be most entertaining for the evening, or what their parents are making for dinner. While a child's dreams about the future may leap ahead decades and lifetimes, their concerns rarely consider further than the next couple days.

In a perfect world, the young boy could have lived in the present. Instead, he found himself trapped between the past and future, wondering what it was that led him to that fate.

Do our lives follow the whims of a higher power; chained to an ideal outcome by forces not of this world? Or are our fates riddled with possibilities; a branching web where our destinies are born from the connections we form with others? Threads cut and tied, creating and destroying futures that could or will be. Or perhaps, in a twist both cruel and liberating, fate doesn't exist at all.

Fate is a concept that allows us to deny that our suffering and our successes may simply be the result of our own actions. After all, is it not easier to blame a cosmic force for our misfortunes? Why choose to carry guilt and regret when you can simply claim the result was unavoidable?

That what happened when the young boy snuck onto the train was unavoidable.

That the crimson puddles in the rainy streets were unavoidable.

That what he saw, had been inevitable.

But... is it truly unavoidable? Are we chained to our destinies? Or can we save ourselves from fate?

Chapter 1

THIS STORY is a story of connections; of learning to love and to accept love. It's a tale of the bonds we form with others. How the threads of fate that tie us together take many forms. A lifeline, a snare, a stitch, a net that traps you, or one that catches you when you fall. It isn't just my story to tell. In fact, this story began long before my thread became entangled with the woven web that has ensnared me. However, I now find myself in a fitting position to share this tale, and after much thought, have found my beginning.

What better place to start a story of connections than a city connected to the rest of the world? Courciel, the capital city of the human realm Terrael, and the place where those two first met. The young Scribe with nothing to live for, and the man that, for better or for worse, convinced him to meddle with the threads of fate.

The capital slept beneath a blanket of morning fog. In the center of the city, the Grand Cathedral sat atop the hill that housed the higher-class districts. Its white, towering spire seemed to pierce the darkened sky. From this beacon, the warm glow of the streetlamps that lit the rest of the city trickled downward. Embers beneath the ivory fire. Canals lined the lower city, the shimmering water akin to a spider-web woven throughout the various districts before feeding into the moat that surrounded the Holy Wall, keeping the devout separate from those deemed unruly or undesirable in the outer areas.

Normally, Courciel was a bustling hub where people from all over the realm came to visit. Through the railways, it connected almost every part of Terrael. As the birthplace of the Church that swore to protect humanity, it was also one of the most defended cities in the human realm, with Priests stationed on almost every street in the inner districts. But at that moment, as they were every morning, the streets were quiet, a respite between the end of curfew and the day's beginning. In those hours, the Priests patrolled the cobblestone streets with heavy eyelids, the warmth of the streetlamps a poor replacement for the warmth of a bed.

Three such Priests watched groggily as a young man rode by earlier than usual. Though they'd never spoken, they knew the young man was Enoch, and that he was enroute to his job at the nearby cathedral.

From the awkward bend of his long legs, it was clear that he'd begun to outgrow his bike. The pointed gray detailing of the bottom of his black vest was reminiscent of a pen nib. He'd thought it fitting when he bought it, considering he worked as a Scribe, but there were many days where he wondered if it was perhaps a bit too on the nose. It was too late to return it now though.

The brown fabric of his calf-length pants stretched with each rotation of the pedals, revealing knee high socks beneath. His satchel, an accessory he never left home without, swayed with the movement of his body, the circular symbol of the Church embroidered on the side. On his wrist, a bulky gold bracelet gleamed like the Grand Cathedral spire in the sunlight now peeking over the distant mountains.

His face appeared almost ashen. It was a shade so pale that one could easily imagine it absorbing sunlight like a dry sponge in water if given the chance. It seemed even lighter when framed by his short, black hair, which he kept combed to the right. The dark, curled locks seemed to have a mind of their own, the occasional curls twirling away from the black waves draped over the right side of his head. The other side was trimmed short, needing far less effort to maintain, and exposing a sharp, yet delicate jaw, now clenched as the hill he was biking up proved more difficult to climb than expected.

The steepness of the street demanded that he return home to sleep just a little longer. But Enoch wouldn't dream of doing such a thing. These quiet mornings were his sanctuary. It wasn't that he enjoyed waking up early; quite the opposite in fact. But being able to avoid the crowds and obstacles that filled the commute during the day was well worth waking at an earlier hour.

Reaching the top of the hill, he gripped the bike more tightly, holding the heavy cloth bags hanging from his handlebars in place. The last thing he wanted was to lose their contents as he coasted down the hill's decline. Thankfully, despite the turbulent rattling of the cobblestone, the various snacks and baked goods stayed safely inside their cloth cocoons.

By the time Enoch passed over one of the many city canals, the familiar sight of other early risers began popping up around him. Street vendors setting up stands of books and trinkets by the edge of the water. Priests heading back to their assigned cathedrals to let the morning workers take over patrols. The owner of his favorite café wiping down tables in the outdoor eating area. Despite the early hour, the cafe already seemed to have a customer chatting up the owner. Though the man's yellow jacket stood out against the various reds, grays, greens and beiges of the nearby buildings, Enoch paid him nothing more than a quick, curious glance to the side. He had no time to waste on the bright break from the monotony, focusing solely on reaching his destination.

There was no need to stop and enjoy the view as Enoch passed through the polished metal gate. Even at an earlier hour, Penemue's Cathedral looked the same as it always did, standing proudly within the brick wall surrounding it. Like the other cathedrals scattered throughout the city, the large, central dome towered over all other buildings in the area. Four grand archways marked the front entrance. A decorative railing ran along the edge of the large balcony above them. The stained-glass windows lining the two branching wings hummed with warm light from the lamps within. The colorful glass, cleaned daily, depicted various angels and creatures from Spira, the divine realm.

The young Scribe walked his bike through the outer garden, passing beneath the lantern-lit buttresses arching over the path. The scent of flowers filled the air, an aroma that once knotted his stomach, but he had since grown accustomed to. Having parked his bike outside the usual window, he pulled out a small engraved pocket watch. With an approving nod at the time, he closed it with a snap, grabbed the bags, and headed inside.

For those of you unfamiliar with the human realm, the Church was once primarily an institute of worship, an organization formed by the Archangels long ago, intended to guide humanity. However, its responsibilities had broadened with time. The central hall of worship remained as the name implied, but the rest of the cathedral became dedicated to crime prevention, public service, and on occasion, education. Normally, Enoch would pass by the rooms used for matters unrelated to him, heading straight for the cathedral library to take care of his daily responsibilities. Today, he instead climbed the stairs to one of the many meeting rooms.

Click! Sssssssss Click! Through a series of switches, Enoch switched on the domed gas light, igniting it with a small spark. In an instant the room was lit, revealing various wooden tables and chairs, as well as a large chalkboard and the supplies he'd prepared the day before. Placing the bags on a nearby table, he rolled up his sleeves and got to work. Only a little over an hour had passed before Enoch had successfully transformed the room into a makeshift classroom. The chairs, sorted neatly into rows, faced the chalkboard covered in notes and diagrams on magic. An appetizing aroma overpowered the musty smell of gas and stone brick walls. Cookies, bread, fruit and lunch meat sat on the table, ready to tempt the guests that would soon arrive.

All that was left was a simple banner that read "Ability Tests!" that he'd painted the day before. Through no lack of effort, Enoch had managed to get one side to stay up, and was now precariously perched on a wooden ladder trying to hang the other. It was at this moment that the door opened with a slow *crreeeeeeeeak*, followed by the soft, yet surprised voice of an older man. A voice he recognized in an instant.

"Oh! Enoch! Are you finished already?"

"Hey Cyrus. Yeah, just finishing up." After a loud SLAM with the hammer, Enoch fastened the other side of the banner, turning to face the older gentleman when he heard the door click shut.

In a word, Cyrus' appearance could best be described as soft. Soft, chestnut hair; a soft, scruffy beard framing a round, somewhat aged face, with speckles of gray dotted throughout. Somehow always more than Enoch remembered. Even his body, despite his roundness being covered by the blue, militant Priest uniform jacket, looked soft. He was the kind of person you could look at for a moment and know he gave the warmest hugs.

His knee-high black uniform boots thudded on the wooden floor, followed by the soft tap of his cane, muffling as he reached the carpet. "I see... and here I thought I was getting here early," he said. "I came as soon as my patrol was finished, but– well, you must have left as soon as curfew ended." Cyrus rested a hand on one of the chairs Enoch had arranged before, wondering just how long they'd taken to set up.

Carefully, Enoch climbed down the ladder, sliding it into the corner behind a stack of extra chairs. "I figured it would be easier to get it done before people got here," he explained, unable to see the saddened smile on his mentor's face.

"I see..." Similar to a child meekly holding their favorite blanket, Cyrus lifted his wooden cane. "I'll admit, I'm a little disappointed. When you offered to help me set up, I was looking forward to spending some time with you."

Now that he'd emerged from behind the chalkboard, Enoch paused for a moment, caught off guard by the man's comment. He'd been so focused on simply getting the job done, that the thought of doing it together hadn't even occurred to him. Glancing over, he finally got a good look at his mentor. It was difficult to shake the feeling that the man had gotten smaller since the last time they'd spoken. Or, perhaps Enoch had simply grown taller. *Now that I think about it, just how long has it been?* he wondered. He rubbed the back of his neck, surprise shifting to guilt. Had he really been paying so little attention when Cyrus had asked him to help the other day? "Oh! Uh... sorry, Cyrus."

"No, no! There's no need to apologize!" Cyrus held up a hand to reassure his young friend, waving it frantically as if to wipe away the boy's guilty expression. "You're right, it was better to get this done sooner. You did a wonderful job!" Even if he'd wanted to help, the Priest couldn't deny that his sore feet were happy to skip setting up. With a movement more weighted than anticipated, he sat down in one of the chairs in the back row, cane resting in his lap. "And besides, there's still some time before the tests and presentation, so we can chat while we wait! How has your work been going?"

"Work is the same as usual, I guess." Enoch leaned against the back of one of the chairs, speaking to Cyrus across the dividing row between them. "I have a book delivery to do after the tests. Just need to finish transcribing the last few pages. After that I need to replace this. It expires today."

He lifted his arm, looking at the golden bracelet fastened to his wrist. Most of the time, he forgot he was even wearing it, the metal feeling more like an extension of himself than an accessory. As a child, he'd often stared at its design in curiosity and awe. How did they make the outer golden layers shine so beautifully? What was the purpose of the red runes carved into the indented silver layer between them? Why did the concoction within it smell like a garden after the rain? To his young mind, the tool was an enigma. A puzzle far beyond his capabilities to understand. Some questions were met with answers as he got older. Others, he simply accepted as mysteries that didn't need solving. All he needed to know was that the deceivingly simple item was the only defense he had against the rest of the weight he carried.

"It's not like you to leave that to the last minute," Cyrus commented, following Enoch's gaze to the accessory.

"I know. I just haven't had the time lately." Enoch lowered his arm, lightly gripping the bracelet with his other hand as he looked away. Cyrus glanced over, the older man trying to read the younger. He could see the bags under his eyes, unsurprising after Enoch had woken up so early. No doubt, he had some of his own after patrolling most of the night. Nevertheless, if Enoch was too busy to get around to something so important, Cyrus would have to see if he could convince the Consultant High Inquisitor to lessen his workload. "Well, I suppose you'll be fine as long as you replace it before tonight," he said, softly tapping his cane with his finger.

For a moment, only the nearby clock seemed interested in conversation, ticking away cheerfully through the silence. After rarely speaking for so long however, it seemed its two companions were both out of practice. Cyrus' worried stare shifted to one of sympathy. He stood up. "Why don't we practice the presentation?" he suggested, gesturing to the note-covered chalkboard. "Wouldn't want to seem unprepared in front of the kids. This is a big day for them after all!"

Chapter 2

DESPITE THE FACT he was standing in front of an audience of around a dozen young children, Cyrus' voice was calm and deliberate. He now stood next to the chalkboard Enoch had prepared. Compared to his earlier meekness, his warm smile and relaxed demeanor gave off an air of experience and comfort. Enoch, however, sat stiffly in his chair, very much regretting his offer to help. He had no problem staying seated and offering support, but in his mind, he begged the Archangels to grant him luck. *Don't make me talk. Don't make me talk. Please just let me sit here and be ignored!* As Enoch's mind repeated this on a loop, Cyrus continued the presentation.

"Magic exists inside every living thing in the Three Realms. How much magic a person has is called their magical capacity. All of you are here today because you've shown that your capacity is high enough for you to possess an ability." His words caused the children to stir excitedly. Though still rare in the bigger picture, having a magic ability was becoming increasingly common. Yet every child still feared the dreaded curse of normality. After all, in a world where magic could shape stone, summon beasts, or even transform its wielder into an animal, what kid would wish to be mundane? Clearly, such a desire would be absolutely insane.

"Now, a magic ability is a very big responsibility," Cyrus continued. "The test today will help us figure out what kind of ability you may have– but having one doesn't mean you can go around using it all willy-nilly." With the tip of his cane, Cyrus gestured to a somewhat crudely drawn stick figure on the board. The figure was surrounded by a powdery aura in the form of cartoonish chalk lines. "If you use your magic too much, it can make the people around you very sick. That's why only people in the Church are allowed to use their magic."

In the front row, one of the children's hands shot up with overwhelming enthusiasm. She had long, curly blonde pigtails, slanted as she raised her arm so high that she was practically lifting herself off the chair. With an amused smile, Cyrus pointed to her.

"Yes?"

"So– does that– are you magic then?"

Cyrus did his best to stifle a chuckle, the young girl's excitement both comical and infectious. Once again, he gestured to the chalkboard with his cane, this time to a neatly drawn diagram of the various kinds of magic abilities. Categories that, for the purpose of not overwhelming you, would be best explained later on as they become relevant to this tale.

"I do have an ability, yes," Cyrus replied. "I fall under the 'Converter' category, here."

As the first category to become relevant, the rules of a Converter's magic are quite simple. Through physical contact, a Converter can use their magic to alter the physical characteristics of a material. This change could be causing something to sprout fur, or perhaps making a rolled-up piece of paper become as durable as a metal pipe. With a single, maintained touch they can, as the name implies, convert the world around them.

To demonstrate such an ability, Cyrus lifted his cane. Kneeling down in front of the kids, he handed it to a young boy with dark, spiked hair. "Here, what does this feel like to you?" he asked. The boy inspected the cane, tapping the wooden surface and squinting his eyes in an attempt to see some sort of hidden secret behind its boring exterior.

"It feels like a stick," he replied bluntly.

Cyrus nodded, taking back the cane as he stood back up. "Yup! Just a normal, everyday walking stick!" Once he'd taken a few steps back, he held it firmly in both hands, palms facing the ceiling. "But when I use my magic on it..." He closed his eyes. The Priest's hands began to glow with a light green aura, his brow furrowed in concentration. Slowly, the light spread throughout the wood, the green glare reminiscent of a tree in the summer sun. In an instant, the cane lost all rigidity. It drooped in the man's hand like a loose piece of rope. Despite the trick being quite simple in the grand scope of magic abilities, in the innocent eyes of the children, he might as well have flown ten feet off the ground.

"Cool!"

"Again! Again!"

"Wow!"

The older man couldn't help but smile at their reaction. He and Enoch shared a subtle sense of nostalgia. He swung the cane in a movement akin to a ribbon dance, the wood bending and swaying freely, still covered in green light. As the kids began to settle down, he pulled the cane taut, the aura dissipating in the blink of an eye. It was nothing but a simple walking stick once more.

"My ability allows me to make objects more flexible," Cyrus explained as he moved back to the chalkboard, gesturing once again to the diagram. "But Converters are just one ability type out of nine. Your magic will fall under one of these categories, but that just determines how your magic interacts with the world. What you can do will be unique to you."

Eyes sparkling in excitement at the thought of having an ability of his own, the boy with spiked hair found himself curious about the abilities of others. He pointed to Enoch.

"Do you have an ability too?"

Enoch looked up in surprise at the sudden question, disappointed that the Archangels seemed to ignore his request for silence. He adjusted himself in his chair. Now that the rest of the children were staring expectantly as well, he rubbed the back of his neck.

"I have one, kind of. But it's not really something I can show you guys."

As if sent by the Archangels themselves, Cyrus positioned himself between Enoch and the children, doing his best to reclaim their attention. He gave them an apologetic smile. "Enoch is a Scribe, not a Priest. Though they still do work for the Church, Scribes unfortunately aren't high enough in the hierarchy to be allowed to use their abilities."

The children groaned in disappointment. "But aren't Scribes like, boring old people?" the pigtailed girl asked. The comment might as well have been a rotten tomato thrown Enoch's way. The Scribe's posture deflated behind Cyrus as the older man intervened once more.

"It's true that some Scribes are older, but there are many younger ones as well," he explained, his gaze wandering to the ceiling as he gave the topic more thought. "Though, Enoch is still a special case. He's always been a bright one after all, so I suppose 21 is still younger than normal." His hand began waving absentmindedly, the answer slowly becoming more of a ramble. "But he worked very hard to get to this point, so he's no less impressive than any Priest or Pilgrim or–"

"Cyrus."

As Enoch's voice pulled him from his tunnel-visioned tangent, Cyrus looked over in surprise. His cheeks flushed as he realized that he had, like many times before, chattered on about Enoch like a proud parent. He had to remember that he was there as an instructor, and that he had a job to do.

"Right! Sorry!" Cyrus cleared his throat with a volume only someone of his age could. Even as his mentor turned away, Enoch could notice the embarrassment in his posture alone. As much as he hated public speaking, he figured he should probably lend a hand. With a sigh, Enoch leaned forward in his chair, resting his elbows on his knees.

"Being a Scribe may not be the most exciting job in the world," he began, the children turning their attention his way. He fought the urge to hide his face. "But, having an ability doesn't mean you have to become a Priest. Some people are just better suited for safer, simpler work, and there's nothing wrong with that. Not everyone needs to be special."

Despite the truth behind Enoch's words, the kids, as children do, decided that they were going to accept absolutely none of them. The pigtailed girl slumped so far back in her seat that it was a miracle she didn't fall off the edge. "But Scribes are *booooooring!*" she groaned. Behind her, a young boy with a bandage on his face nodded in agreement, jumping up in his chair.

"Yeah! Priests do cool stuff like fighting demons!"

Enoch and Cyrus' bodies tensed as they heard that word. Demons. Like an icy drop of water landing on your neck. Quickly recovering, Cyrus forced a smile, hoping to get things back on track. Unfortunately, the rest of the children had no interest in dropping this new discussion topic. The pigtailed girl swung around to face the bandaged kid, pretending to shoot some imagined magic attack from her hands.

"Right!? They're like Pow! Pow! Take that demon!"

The bandaged kid turned to Cyrus. "Mr. Priest guy, have you ever seen a demon?" he asked. The other children stared in anticipation as well, all focus on the presentation now abandoned as they chased this far more interesting line of questioning.

"Ya! Have you?"

"Did you use a stick to fight them?"

More and more questions followed, the room buzzing with both conversation and curiosity, the words lost in the overlap. As the kids lost focus, Enoch instinctively reached for his bracelet, trying to find comfort in the smooth, metal surface. Each new outburst from the young audience made him regret being there more and more. *You have to keep it together. Cyrus is completely fine!* he told himself, *you can keep calm too.*

Even with a deceptive smile plastered on his face, Cyrus' discomfort was growing with each query. Enoch's whitened knuckles clasped around his bracelet were all too obvious out of the corner of the Priest's eye. He raised his hands, trying to calm the children down. "Now isn't really the time to–"

"Did you ever see one, Mr. Scribe?"

Enoch glanced up, his heart beginning to race. He'd already been anxious from being in front of a crowd, but now– *no. You have to calm down. This is ridiculous! All they did was say a simple word, so... why am I feeling so dizzy?* He couldn't even bring himself to answer their question, unsure which kid amidst the spinning crowd even asked in the first place. Thankfully, the kid with the bandage interjected before he could even try to speak.

"Probably just in books 'cause he's boring."

"I heard demons eat people!"

"That's not true!"

Enoch's hands began to shake. A sharp repetitive pain filled his chest. The chaos in the room grew and grew, the spiky haired boy pretending to loom over the others to scare them, hands curled and poised to attack.

"It is! My brother says they cut people open with big claws!"

Enoch closed his eyes, holding the bracelet so tightly that it felt like it could shatter in his grasp. The loss of sight did little to hide the images the child had sent flashing through his mind.

A rainy night.

A winged demon, silhouetted against the monotone sky.

Not a single sound to be heard.

"Children please, if you could just–" Cyrus tried and failed to regain control of the situation. Enoch did the same with his own mind.

Calm down!

A flash of a broken, wooden door; scratch marks carved into its surface.

Calm down!

A red splatter covering a recently swept floor.

Calm down!

"The demons are like AAaaarRgH! I'm gonna chop you up!

"Stoooop! That's too scary!"

Get a grip, Enoch! The Scribe thought to himself. *C'mon! Just calm down!*

Another flash.

A body barely visible in the light of an open door.

Calm down.

Calm down!

Calm down calm down calm down calm down calm down calm–

Panic. It's a frightening and powerful thing. Anxiety refuses rationality. Even something as small as a light breeze can roll a pebble off a cliff. That pebble can knock more and more stones out of place until it escalates into a devastating landslide. And so, no matter how many times Enoch begged his mind to calm down; no matter how much of an overreaction it would be to suddenly rush out the door in a cold sweat, leaving nothing but a clattering chair and confused children behind; he couldn't stop himself. The landslide had begun and all he knew at that moment was that he needed to escape. He could escape the room, the audience, begging the cool stone wall of the hallway to help stabilize his spiraling thoughts, but he couldn't escape the panic in his mind.

Enoch's back slowly slid against the dark gray wall as he crouched. He clasped his hands together. Disoriented, he desperately tried to regain his composure.

"C'mon, calm down, calm down. It's not real. It's not—"

Enoch could just barely make out the sound of footsteps through the swirling fog in his mind. A young woman, the golden Church emblem hanging around her neck marking her as a Pilgrim, stared down at him in concern.

"Hey, are you okay?" she asked softly. Before Enoch could answer, the meeting room door swung open, revealing Cyrus rushing into the hall. He hurried to Enoch's side the instant he saw him. Placing a reassuring hand on the young Scribe's back, he spoke in a calming tone.

"Deep breaths, Enoch. I'm here now. It's okay. You're safe."

Guided out of his thoughts by the calming voice and hand on his back, Enoch nodded, trying his hardest to slow his breathing. *In and out. In... and out...* His body still shook in panic, the slower breaths coming out as gasps. The torrent of traumatizing images in his mind found themselves competing against memories of his room, the pressure of a comforting hand, and reassurances that he was okay. That he was safe.

I'm okay... I'm safe.... It isn't real... I'm not alone.

As he had every other time, he focused on his surroundings. The cool stone he was sitting on. The comforting tone of Cyrus' voice. The golden shine of the Pilgrim's emblem. The musty smell of the carpet on the floor. As Enoch grounded himself, Cyrus looked up to the Pilgrim, gesturing to the door behind him.

"It's alright, he just needs a minute or two," he explained. "But, could you watch the children inside for a moment? I—"

"No!" Enoch interrupted. Both Cyrus and the Pilgrim turned to face him. "I'm fine, really. I'm..." Despite his reassurances, Enoch's face was still as pale as his whitened knuckles, his fingers a tightly clasped and tangled mess. Unsurprisingly, Cyrus wasn't convinced.

"Enoch, you don't need to push yourse–"

"I'm fine. I just... I'm going to the library. You can go back to the presentation, Cyrus." Enoch stood up with a sway. He gripped his sleeve, hugging his arms close to his body. Though he'd managed to calm down a small amount, he was still certain they could hear the rapid beating of his heart. "I just need to walk a bit... I'll be fine. It's fine."

Over and over, he lied. He seemed to be trying to convince himself just as much as the others. Cyrus didn't even have time to object before Enoch walked away, leaving the older man kneeling on the cold cathedral floor. The young Pilgrim woman helped him up without a word. Cyrus mumbled out a thank you, watching Enoch disappear around the corner into the circular hallway surrounding the hall of worship. The Priest took a step to follow, then stopped himself. Enoch needed space.

He always did...

A few hours later, the flickering flame of an oil lamp cast a cacophony of shadows around the modestly sized records room. Several large dust-covered cabinets lined the walls, each one neatly labeled with a decorative symbol. To the common man, these markings would cause nothing but confusion. However, any Scribe worth their salt would recognize it as the celestial script. Though it would do little more than buy some time, these letters acted as a failsafe of sorts. After all, the information stored within the locked drawers would best be kept hidden from those incapable of reading the script of the divine.

Enoch placed a file into a crowded box of dividers and folders, his mind not nearly as organized. With a sigh, he slid the box back into its proper drawer, locking it once he'd safely tucked it away. He headed towards the stairs leading back to the library above. The dust in the air assaulted his eyes, as his mind assaulted his confidence. *I thought I had the attacks under control...* With another sigh, he blew out the lamp.

Upstairs, Enoch shut the door to the records room. Even in his distracted state, muscle memory guided his hand as he locked up and returned the key to his bag. With a force heightened by the weight of his situation, he slumped into the desk by the window, grateful that the small library was empty. The rays of the morning sun passing through the window lit up the tidied bookshelves nearby, leaving the desk itself in a dim shadow. Enoch turned his gaze to the two open books sitting on the desk, but his attention was far from the pages in front of him.

I just wanted to help Cyrus with the ability tests, he mulled. Though, perhaps that wasn't the case. He hadn't *wanted* to do it. Things were far simpler when he just had to come to the library, work on his own, then return to his apartment to sleep and do the same thing the next day. But he also couldn't bring himself to say no to Cyrus. Now he wondered if things would have gone better if he had. *Even if I go back now, I'd just be a distraction after running out like that.* A heavy sigh shifted into heavy shoulders as Enoch dropped his head in shame.

"It was just some kids playing around! Cyrus wasn't even phased. How could I let that freak me out?" The empty library had no answer for him.

Enoch tried to shake away his thoughts as he turned back to the books. Regaining his focus, he began to copy the text of one into the other. There was work to do, and he was better off there, out of the way. As he wrote, his brace-let caught the light of the sun now slowly creeping towards the desk. Shimmering rays reflected onto the dark wooden surface. *At least I'll be able to get this replaced sooner this way* he thought; a golden, silver lining to the dark and gloomy morning he'd had.

And unbeknownst to him, not the only golden silver lining he'd experience that day.

Chapter 3

COMPARED TO THE ease of his morning commute, Enoch struggled to navigate the crowded afternoon streets. The whirring of his bike wheels mixed with the percussive clopping and rumbling of horse-drawn carriages. Carriages that irritatingly took up the entire road, forcing Enoch onto the sidewalk. The alternate path wasn't much better, now filled with pedestrians browsing stores or heading to and from work. Honestly, Enoch knew it would be easier to walk, but he didn't have time to spare. That, and he couldn't carry the delivery without the help of his bike's handles.

Transcribing the final pages had taken far longer than he'd expected. The bags of books the client had ordered pulled down on his handlebar, the metal creaking and bending under the weight. His trusty bike had managed to carry far heavier in the past, so he did his best to stay optimistic. *It just has to hold out until the Hart District,* he reassured himself, *if I take Cavalier, then maybe I could still make it to the House of Healing in time.*

He signaled for a left, taking a sharp turn towards one of the many inclined streets he had to choose from for his delivery route. Sweat began to form on his brow as his pace slowed. Pedestrians passed by on foot. With a hushed grumble about taking up sidewalk space, he swerved around a man in a yellow coat flirting with a nearby woman as he handed her a package. Once he finally reached the top of the hill, the young Scribe sighed in relief. The bike coasted down the decline as he checked the street signs ahead.

"Cavalier... Cavalier.... ah! There it is!" Enoch signaled for a right turn, happy the street here was open enough for proper steering. But as he leaned his weight on the handlebar...

CRACK!

"Crap!"

One second the handle bar was there, the next, only the cracked metal remained. Between the speed from the hill, and losing his ability to steer, he had no choice but to ride the momentum down, the wheels of the bike teetering before fully falling over. His satchel protected him from some of the friction until the cobblestone snatched it from his shoulder. After that, his leg burned from the unforgiving battering of the street as he skidded downward with no escape. Nearby pedestrians leapt out of the way. The wooden bench on the side of the road, on the other hand, made no attempt to dodge Enoch as he and his bike crashed right into it. A crowd began to gather, staring as the Scribe laid beneath the crumpled mess that was once his bike; his head and the crooked bike wheel both still spinning.

"Ow..." Enoch winced, trying to regain his bearings. As he noticed the crowd, his pale face grew noticeably flushed. He focused on removing himself from the bike, ignoring the all too noticeable stares to the best of his ability. The cobblestone had torn his pant leg to shreds, the leg beneath scraped enough to make even the bystanders wince.

Using the bench for support, he struggled to lift himself up. It was the least the wooden structure could do after coming out of the impact without a scratch, unlike the now very much in pain Scribe. A woman emerged from the crowd, reaching out her arm to assist as well, but Enoch raised his own in return, palm out to stop her.

"I'm fine, tha– Ah!" Enoch's leg fought against the attempt to stand, giving out and sending the Scribe back towards the wreckage. He braced himself for the impact, instead feeling a warm arm wrap around his torso.

"You sure? Looks to me like you could use a hand."

Looking up, Enoch saw who had caught him. The man was smiling brightly, the expression emphasized by his orange lipstick. In fact, he was wearing a surprising amount of makeup. Warm toned eyeshadow just a tad lighter than his amber eyes. Two small, orange triangles painted beneath them. Expertly applied contour emphasized the curve of his jaw, the jaw itself a perfect combination of strong and soft, giving his face an almost androgynous look. Adding to the androgyny was his soft, silver hair. Though many loose strands hung gracefully around his face, the rest was pulled back into a mid-length, scruffy ponytail, revealing the fact that he was also wearing turquoise, heart-shaped earrings. Overall, though Enoch wasn't the best judge when it came to such things, he was an incredibly beautiful man. A man now holding him as if they'd just finished an intricate dance with a dip.

With surprising ease, the man lifted Enoch up, offering his arm for support. Though he preferred to be self-reliant, Enoch reluctantly relented, knowing he couldn't reach the bench himself. Once he was seated, Enoch got a better look at the man's outfit.

Though Courciel was filled with a wide variety of clothing styles, Enoch had never seen a jacket quite like this one. From a distance, it appeared to be a simple yellow long coat. Up closer, the hems and various detailing looked almost metallic through the dark gray coloring and reflective texture. Even if that was simply a trick of the eyes, there was no doubt that the belt dividing the top and bottom halves was made of some kind of solid metal, leaving Enoch wondering how exactly the man went about removing the garment.

Overall, the jacket's shape gave off the feeling of armor, with the shoulders covered by fabric pauldrons, and the torso feeling like a tight-fitting chest piece. The lower half was open at the front, the metallic stripes on the sides akin to divided armor plates. Even the cuffs could easily be compared to gauntlets from the right angle. Aside from the jacket, he wore a dark, turquoise dress shirt, as well as a white cravat with a decorative ruby to add a sophisticated feel. His hands were decorated in variously colored rings, a necklace of some sort also tucked into his jacket. Somehow, despite expertly emphasizing the athletic build of his legs, his knee-high brown leather boots and his black riding pants were the least interesting part of the ensemble.

Enoch looked down, trying his hardest to hide from the attention coming from all sides thanks to the crowd. The man's silver brow furrowed in confusion before he realized what was happening. With no hesitation, he turned to the crowd, pulling out the necklace that had been tucked into his jacket. To Enoch's surprise, it was the circular emblem of the Church, given to all Pilgrims under its employment.

"Alright, move along everyone!" the man said, holding the emblem up for the crowd to see. "I'm with the Church, so I'll handle things from here. Give the kid some space for now."

The crowd reluctantly dispersed, a few people still glancing over at a distance, far less inconspicuously than they were clearly trying to be. Once they had some space, the man turned back to Enoch. The Scribe was noticeably more relaxed without the burning gazes of the gathered audience.

Now that he could think more clearly, Enoch looked down to his bike, lips curled into a frown. While it was certainly unfortunate to lose his means of transportation, what hurt more was that the bike had been a gift from Cyrus. Now that happy memory was nothing more than a mangled heap of scrap metal. As he mourned the loss, he noticed the yellow-coated Pilgrim still staring.

"I'm fine, really," Enoch reassured.

"I'm sure you are, tough guy," the man replied. "But I'd still like to take a look just in case." He knelt down next to Enoch, taking a closer look at the scraped-up leg like an appraiser with a strange antique. "Out of curiosity, what's your definition of fine? I usually use it in a more positive way like a fine wine, or fine partner, but I'm always up for learning new interpretations."

"I, uh..." Enoch could only look back in confusion, completely baffled by how direct and immediately comfortable the man was. He was so used to the shielding powers of the phrase *"I'm fine"* that he wasn't sure how to react to someone immune to it. After a moment, he rubbed the back of his neck, looking away from the Pilgrim. "You said you're a member of the Church, right? I don't think I've seen you around."

"Expertly deflected," the man replied with a cheeky smile. "I'm not from Courciel. Just here to make a delivery and pick up some jobs. Typical Pilgrim work, y'know?" He took a closer look at Enoch's ankle, causing the Scribe to wince despite the delicate nature of the touch. "Well tough guy, the good news is that your pants can probably be patched up. Bad news is your ankle seems pretty swollen already. Not to mention the scrapes and cuts. So, injury-wise, you're probably not as fine as you claim to be."

Enoch's posture slouched somewhat as he realized he couldn't argue with that. It was more than obvious that his leg was in bad shape. He turned his gaze away again, scanning the street with his eyes. Nearby, a group of young girls were staring dreamily at the Pilgrim, with the occasional more nightmarish glance of jealousy in Enoch's direction. Passing them by, he finally found what he was looking for. Along with a guiding nod of his head, he pointed in the direction of his satchel still laying on the side of the street. "I can actually bandage it up on my own," he said, "I just need my bag."

The man sat up so quickly that Enoch could swear he felt a rush of air. "Alright then, sit tight!" he exclaimed. "I'll go grab it for you!" With another bright smile, he headed over to Enoch's bag. As he did, Enoch looked down to his injured leg with a pained expression. *I should probably clean it first, considering how dirty the street can be. But unless I decide to use canal water, I don't think I have anything to rinse it.* With a sigh, he made a mental note to start carrying a bottle of some sort.

At the very least, or from what he could tell from a distance, the books he needed to deliver seemed to be okay. It was a small victory though, since without his bike there'd be no way to make the delivery in time now.

"Here!" The man's voice pulled Enoch from his thoughts. He held out the bag triumphantly.

"Thanks." With no hesitation, Enoch pulled out some bandages, causing the man to raise his eyebrows in surprise.

"I'm impressed, tough guy! You're pretty prepared!"

As he removed his shoe and sock, Enoch gave the man an irritated glance. He'd let it go the first few times, but the nickname was starting to annoy him. "My name is Enoch," he replied.

"Enoch, huh?" The man smiled, seemingly oblivious to the irritated stare that had been sent his way. "Don't think I've met an Enoch before." With a cheerful shrug, he moved over to the bike as Enoch unrolled the bandages. He leaned over the wreckage, subtly inspecting the bag of books still tangled in the center. "As for me... well, you can call me Gregory."

Enoch had been placing his shoe and sock into his bag, but paused for a moment at the man's words. *Gregory, huh? That doesn't seem right for some reason. Feels too normal for a guy like him.* "Well, uh... nice to meet you Gregory, I suppose," he replied.

"Same to you, Enoch!"

The Scribe began to bandage his leg. After the morning's chaos, Gregory's well-intended words drained more and more of Enoch's dwindling energy. *When did socializing become so difficult?* he wondered. Oblivious to Enoch's inner struggle, Gregory ran his finger along what remained of the bike's broken handlebar. "Is this made of steel?" he asked, breaking the silence.

"Uh... yeah? Probably?"

Gregory nodded in approval, turning his attention back to the bike. Confused, Enoch watched for a moment, waiting for an explanation that didn't seem to be coming. With a shrug, he finished patching himself up, returning what was left to his bag.

"Well, Gregory, I appreciate the help, but I really am good now."

The disbelief in Gregory's expression was painfully obvious.

"You sure about that?"

"Yes."

"Really sure?"

"Mhm."

Gregory stood up, turning his attention to the street. He seemed to be looking for something, though Enoch had no idea what that would be. "So, if I leave right now, you'd be completely fine?" the man asked. "The good definition of it?"

"Yep!"

"Alright! Best of luck to ya then!" With the carefree attitude of a leaf drifting down a stream, Gregory walked up the hill, gaze glued to the ground. Enoch propped himself up using the bench, hesitantly putting some weight on his injured leg. The resulting pain sent a jolt through his entire body.

This'll be harder than I thought.

"Still completely fine over there?" the Pilgrim shouted, continuing his search a fair distance away.

"Yeah! I'm good!" Enoch shouted back.

Gregory gave him an encouraging thumbs up, as if to say *"you've got this!"*. The thumbs up Enoch gave in return translated to more of a *"please just let me go home"*. Gritting his teeth through the pain, Enoch untangled the bag of books from the wreckage. They were heavy, but perhaps he could simply tough it out. Steeling himself, he pulled on the straps, letting out a sudden gasp at the immense pain he felt as a result.

In the distance, Gregory finally seemed to find what he was looking for, crouching down to pick it up as the lingering members of the earlier crowd returned to watch Enoch's struggle. Noticing this, Enoch sighed. *Did the Archangels decide to punish me? Is that why my day keeps getting worse and worse?* He racked his brain for a way out of this, but could only find one solution that would spare him immense pain. Physical pain, at the very least. He sighed, not even turning as he finally spoke. "Okay fine. I need help."

As if he'd been waiting for a cue, Gregory practically appeared out of thin air next to him. He smiled sweetly, twirling the broken handlebar of Enoch's bike in his hand as he pretended not to notice Enoch's flushed cheeks.

"Well, when you ask so nicely, how can I refuse?"

Chapter 4

A S HE HAD several times since he'd met the man minutes ago, Enoch eyed Gregory in confusion. The Scribe was once again sitting on the bench, the two bags of books he had to deliver sitting safely by his side. Next to him, Gregory dragged Enoch's bike away from the crash site.

"Okay," the man muttered to himself. "Just gotta move this here, and..." He crouched down next to the scrap pile. With the delicate and deliberate movement of a surgeon, he held the broken handlebar piece up to where it had snapped off. Gripping the other part of the handlebar as well, he nodded his head. "Perfect!"

The Pilgrim's cheery expression shifted, the sparkle in his eyes morphing into a determined spark. As his demeanor grew more serious, a light appeared around his hands. A dazzling, golden glow spread from his fingertips to the cool metal held between them. Overpowering the faded reflective shine of the bike's steel frame, the light continued to grow and grow, engulfing it all. The wreckage began to ripple and stir. One might expect it to creak and groan, fighting against the movement, however, there wasn't a sound as the frame shifted like water suspended in the air. The bent bars straightened effortlessly. The broken handlebars reconnected like two merging raindrops. Enoch stared in awe. After only a few hypnotic seconds, the bike was in one piece, as smooth and pristine as the day he'd first got it.

Once Gregory let go, the golden light vanished, pulling Enoch out of his trance. The Pilgrim dusted off his hands, admiring his handiwork with a smile. "There! Good as new!" Turning to Enoch, he rubbed the back of his head with an embarrassed smile. "You probably can't ride it yet with your ankle all messed up, but I did reinforce the handlebar. It should be able to hold the weight of those books without breaking now."

It took a moment for Enoch to pull his gaze away from the bike. Snapping out of his shock, he looked over to Gregory. "You're a Sculptor then?" he asked. *He mentioned that he worked for the Church, so I guess it's not surprising that he has a magic ability,* the Scribe realized. True as this thought was, it didn't leave Enoch any less startled to see the ability in action, or bewildered by the fact that Gregory was able to roll the once destroyed bike over to him.

"I am!" Gregory replied. "My magic resonates with steel specifically, so I guess we're pretty lucky I'm the one that stuck around to help you out!"

As stated by Gregory, a Sculptor's magic resonates with a specific material. When in contact with said material, a Sculptor just needs to picture what form they would like it to take, and they can then use their magical energy to mold it like an artist shaping clay. Unlike Converters who can, within the rules of their personal ability, affect and alter any non-living object, a Sculptor can only sculpt their resonant material. However, past this the only limits to the forms they can give it are their own imagination, the amount of material, and how well they can focus on the shape of their recreation.

With the bike now in working condition, Gregory lifted the bags of books onto the handlebars. "I'm not too familiar with bikes myself," he admitted, lips curling into a proud smile as the bike effortlessly held the weight. "But thankfully it wasn't broken enough that I couldn't figure out the proper shape." He swiftly turned to Enoch, pride replaced with worry. "Wait! Just in case, I should probably check before we try really moving it. It looks okay to you, right? Nothing out of place?"

Enoch leaned back, caught off guard by the sudden intensity. "I– I mean, yeah. It looks fine to me."

The release of tension in Gregory's body was nearly palpable. He let out a sigh of relief, smile returning to his face as he held out an arm to Enoch. "Great! Let's head out then! I can move the bike while you use me for support!"

The Scribe's gaze shifted between the Pilgrim and the outstretched arm as he tried to process what was happening. *Is he offering to walk me the whole way?* he wondered. The thought moved from Enoch's mind to form a pit in his stomach. He was already much too tired for this. "Thanks, but I can probably just use the bike for support. I'm sure you have better things to do than walk with me all the way to the Hart District. I'm fine, really."

"There's that word again." With a warm smile, Gregory moved to the other side of the bike, using his hands to balance it. "If you're heading to the Hart district, I'm actually staying at the Ivory Inn over there. So, we can just look at this as you walking me home."

The pit in Enoch's stomach doubled in size at his response. He'd hoped mentioning an outer city district would be enough to convince the man to abandon his offer, but his poor luck seemed to have won out. *What are the chances of a Pilgrim of all people staying in an outer city inn?* he wondered. Though Enoch was admittedly curious of the motivations, he shooed the thought from his mind. *No, it's not my business. I shouldn't get involved.* That being said, it was becoming more and more apparent that trying to argue with this guy would get him nowhere, so...

"Fine."

Careful not to put too much pressure on his injured foot, Enoch lifted himself up, resting his elbow on the seat of the bike for support. With his other hand, he grabbed the handlebar, watching Gregory do the same on the other side. After exchanging nods to signal they were ready, they began to slowly make their way. Surprisingly, with Gregory clearly being such a quiet individual, the silence lasted a whole three seconds.

"So... Based on the fact you own a Church-issued book bag, I'm guessing it's safe to assume you're a Scribe?"

"I am, yeah."

"At such a young age!? Seems like there's an interesting story there."

Enoch shook his head, eyes glued to the road in front of them. "Not really. Just a normal guy living a normal life."

As Enoch looked forward, Gregory's gaze drifted to the golden bracelet on the Scribe's wrist. "I dunno..." he replied, "That magic-suppressing bracelet of yours says otherwise. You a Shapeshifter?"

Enoch glanced down to his wrist, releasing the handlebar for just a moment to pull his sleeve over it. "That's just to help with my sleep."

Gregory tilted his head to the side, brow furrowed in both confusion and suspicion. "Your sleep?" he repeated, finding no more clarity hearing it in his own voice. "I don't follow."

Finally peeling his gaze away from the road, Enoch turned to Gregory, his dismissive tone giving way to a subtle vulnerability. "If it's all the same to you, I'd rather not get into it."

To most people, Enoch's expression would have appeared defensive and asocial. However, Gregory couldn't help but notice the frailness hidden in the boy's eyes. It was enough to overpower his curiosity. "Alright," he said with a sigh. "I won't pry then, even if you're making it *really* hard not to."

The two of them continued to make their way through the city streets. Having decided to leave Enoch to his thoughts, Gregory waved to some children playing at the side of the street, the two waved back just as cheerfully. Enoch, however, was feeling far less lively. His gaze wandered back to his bracelet, the gold peeking out from behind his white dress shirt cuff. *Even with Gregory's help, getting to a House of Healing before curfew would be impossible now. Seems like I'll just have to take my chances tonight.*

At such a slow pace, it took the two of them nearly an hour to reach the towering Holy Wall that divided the inner and outer city. The entire area was filled with the scent of wet stone and mildew, as well as several other questionable odors, the origins of which would be best left to the imagination. Grand arches in the wall acted as gateways between the districts, each one towering over the bridges passing through them below. The bridges themselves allowed pedestrians to safely cross the moat lining both sides of the wall, each one split down the middle so the bridges could be raised in emergencies.

Though the Priests here were tasked with monitoring the people passing through the wall, most of them were simply leaning against the bridge's railing, discussing recent events. Others were eyeing up pedestrians they considered threats, or perhaps aesthetically pleasing. The Church symbol on Enoch's bag, as well as the one hanging from Gregory's neck, were enough to get the two of them through without trouble once the Priests half-heartedly checked their authenticity. Now the duo stood beneath the somewhat rusted street sign marking the edge of the Hart District.

Enoch's gaze wandered as he took in the people and buildings. The outer city, while not quite filthy, wasn't as well kept as those under Church control. It wasn't due to negligence, however. Perhaps, the best way to describe the outer city would be that they saw no value in matching the performative cleanliness of the rest of the city. The tall, crooked buildings gave the streets charm and identity. The shouts, conversations and sounds of people at work were a lively melody, accompanying the locals throughout their days. The laundry hanging from clotheslines above offered glimpses into the lives of their owners. Owners that, at that moment, were eyeing the Church symbol on Enoch's bag with distrust.

Enoch lowered his head somewhat. He tried to hide his bag, and by extension his profession, beneath his arm. He knew that many, if not all of the people here were on poor terms with the Church. Those that disagreed with their way of running things; those that had gotten on the wrong side of the laws they enforced, or even those that just didn't like the constant feeling of being watched. Thankfully, due to there being fewer Priests stationed in the outer city, that was far less of an issue there. Their opposition lost them their protection, condemned to life beyond the Holy Wall.

Next to him, Gregory tucked his golden pendant back into his jacket, his face more confident than the young Scribe's. "I'm surprised the Church is making a delivery here of all places," he said quietly, his face growing pale once he heard the words aloud. He quickly turned to Enoch. "Not to imply people out of the Church aren't the reading type! I just figured they'd get their books somewhere else."

"Yeah, we don't usually accept requests from this side of the wall," Enoch replied. "But the client was willing to pay extra, so the High Inquisitor let us make an exception." His brow furrowed as he looked at the lump of jacket concealing Gregory's pendant. "Now that I think about it though, you said you were staying here, right? Don't Pilgrims get to stay in inner-city inns for free while working?"

For once, Gregory had nothing to say. Ironically, that made Enoch all the more interested in what his answer might be. After a moment of silence, the Pilgrim blushed, shrugging with his free hand. "Honestly, I'm just out here for the food!"

The silence had built up an air of suspense. Like a swift gust of wind, that air disappeared. Unfazed by the look of disappointment on Enoch's face, Gregory's own expression lit up, the bike swerving slightly as he sped up out of sheer excitement.

"The chocolate chip cookies the Ivory Inn serves with breakfast are to die for! I say this about a lot of places, but I really mean it for this one. They're the best in Courciel! One bite and you fall in love!"

Enoch let out a sigh, questioning the credibility of the Pilgrim's seal of approval. He got the feeling that the man was understating how often he gave it out. "I see..." Enoch turned away from Gregory, once again watching the road. "I think the best cookies in Courciel are actually at Lamech-son's though."

His response caught the attention of the excitable Pilgrim. Not that that was too difficult a task to do. "I don't think I've heard of that café. Is it new?"

"It's a store, actually." A look of pride filled Enoch's eyes, though the young Scribe was undoubtedly unaware of this fact. "They sell homemade toys and furniture. The co-owner is the best baker in the capital. She'll usually offer what she makes to the customers if they're nice enough. Doesn't matter what she's making, it'll always look and taste better than anything you'll find at a café.

Somehow, Gregory's already glowing smile brightened even more at this new information. "I'll have to go there sometime!" He playfully poked Enoch's shoulder, the warmth of his smile growing just the slightest bit smug. "Especially since that's the most you've spoken since we met. It must really be as good as you say!"

Realizing the man was right, Enoch's cheeks went red. Somehow, it seemed Gregory had managed to get through his attempts to keep conversation to a minimum. He turned away in a futile attempt to hide his embarrassment. "Right..."

What small fraction of pride Gregory was feeling for getting Enoch to say more than a sentence quickly shifted to a smile of warm admiration. Enoch had been trying his hardest to seem distant and dismissive, but it seemed he was just a socially awkward kid after all. Not wanting to push too far, Gregory turned his gaze back to the road, enjoying Enoch's company in silence.

Chapter 5

WITH A SOFT thud, Enoch closed the inn door behind him. He held a small bag of coins in his hand, the two empty book bags hanging loosely off the other. Despite having completed the job, the Scribe's demeanor was dejected and deflated. To put it lightly, the client had been less than happy about how long the delivery had taken, and felt it was important that Enoch knew this. So important in fact, that he'd felt the need to keep Enoch at the door for ten whole minutes to talk about it. Or rather, talk at him about it.

Leaving the delightful client behind, Enoch tucked the book bags into his satchel, jealous that their work was done. From the other side of the bike, Gregory smiled so genuinely that you'd never suspect the two had only known each other for a few hours.

"Now that that's done, would you like me to walk you home Enoch?"

"No, I'm fi–" Enoch caught himself. *I really do say that word often, don't I?* "I'm alright," he corrected, "Without the books throwing the bike off balance, I should be able to get there on my own. And besides, based on where you said the

Ivory Inn is, if you did walk with me, you wouldn't be able to get back there before curfew begins."

The Pilgrim sighed in disappointment. "True..." He did his best to shrug off the rejection, but still seemed like a puppy that had its treat taken away. As a Pilgrim, he could technically still be out and about past curfew, but it certainly would be nice to avoid proving his employment to every Priest that would stop him along the way.

"Well, I don't like the idea of letting you walk alone while you're hurt, but I guess I don't have much of a choice, do I?" With a quick, dance-like step back, Gregory gave Enoch a deep, graceful bow. "It was a pleasure running into you today, Enoch! Hopefully our paths will cross again some time!"

Faced with a goodbye pulled straight from the pages of a romance novel, Enoch rubbed the back of his neck in confusion. "Uh... yeah, same to you." As he went to place the small bag of coins into his satchel, he froze, turning back to Gregory. Realization slowly dawned on him. *Is that why he was so insistent?* he wondered. He pulled out a handful of coins, holding them out to the Pilgrim.

"Here, I didn't sign a commission form, but I should probably split this with you since you helped with the delivery." Suddenly, Gregory's actions made more sense. Pilgrims earned money by helping people, so clearly the man was simply waiting for compensation. Gregory reached out in return. Admittedly, Enoch felt his heart sink somewhat as he did, though he couldn't place why in the moment. As Gregory's hand reached the coins, he gently curled Enoch's fingers closed with a smile. Both the expression and his continued touch were quite warm in contrast to the evening air.

"There's no need for that," Gregory replied. "I offered to help after all."

"Are you sure?"

"Of course!" Gregory nodded, his grip tightening ever so slightly. "It's a Pilgrim's job to help people! And besides, doing good things for people is just what I do! One good deed a day keeps all the bad at bay!"

The sheer positivity radiating off of Gregory was infectious. Even Enoch couldn't fight the slight smile on his face. Or rather, that's what he believed the cause of the smile was. Why else would he be feeling so warm in his heart? Admittedly, the gesture was a small kindness, but even a slight warmth can feel scalding to numbing ice. That same smile shifted from involuntary to forced, however, as he began to wonder just how long the Pilgrim was planning to hold onto his hand.

The city was nearly asleep by the time Enoch reached the alley beside his apartment, just as it had been when he'd left in the morning. Exhausted both physically and mentally, he leaned his bike against the wall, swapping one support for another. The brick was rough and cool to the touch. Enoch did his best to focus on that and ignore the pain shooting throughout his body. He was so close to being back home. His apartment, his bed, he wanted so badly to climb into the comfort of his soft sheets and pretend the day had been nothing but a bad dream, but...

Bad dreams. That was the problem. He lifted his arm up, staring at the golden bracelet on his wrist. After all the chaotic events of the day, he'd never made it to the House of Healing to replace it. Perhaps sleep wouldn't be the sanctuary he so badly needed after all.

The bracelet practically glowed in the light leaking into the alley. Light that Enoch only just realized wasn't usually there this time of day. The nearby streetlamp wouldn't be able to reach that far. As he turned the corner he found its source, a candle sitting on the steps of the store Enoch knew quite well; Lamechson's.

Enoch had first learned of Lamechson's existence through an ad in the paper. Though his connection to the Church could get him a simple home in the upper-class districts, the young Scribe preferred the freedom and solitude of having his own place. Or rather, the apartment located above a family run woodworking shop. The store itself sold a wide variety of items. Furniture, toys, frames, whittled knick-knacks; if it could be built out of wood, then Noah could build and sell it at the highest quality. He ran the store with his wife Namaah, the aforementioned greatest baker in all of Courciel.

For the most part, they respected his privacy. They'd share the occasional greeting or small talk as Enoch paid his rent, or as he passed by the store to reach the gated stairs that led to his apartment. At times, Enoch's work or journaling would be interrupted by a knock at the door, followed by offers of leftovers when they somehow managed to "accidentally cook too much" with recipes they'd been making for years. Even the furniture in his home had all been provided by Noah at no extra cost. The two of them were good people, and Enoch respected that, even if at times he found it hard to accept it.

And now, Noah sat on the front steps of his store. The usual welcoming warmth behind his tired, hazel brown eyes was accompanied by a sparkle from the candle next to him. The candlelight, though not all that strong, was still enough to illuminate the large front window of the store. Above the various wooden wares on display, the word "Lamechson's" sat atop a shelf, spelled out with painted wooden blocks. The rest of the store lay hidden in the darkness of the evening, aside from a small stripe of light beneath a door in the back, no doubt accompanied by the wonderful smell of whatever Namaah was currently cooking in her home behind it.

In addition to the candlelight, the streetlamp behind the middle-aged man silhouetted his face, giving his dark brown hair and face a slight glow. The light also emphasized the crooked shape of his nose, never fully recovered from an unfortunate hammer mishap long ago. The carpenter looked up to the second figure he was currently speaking to. Even partially silhouetted, Enoch could recognize them with nothing more than a glance. As he limped around the corner of the store, Noah and Cyrus both turned to face him.

"Enoch! There you are!" Cyrus exclaimed, before feeling a light slap on his arm from Noah.

"See, told ya he'd come back before curfew," the carpenter said. "You cut it pretty close though, kid."

Enoch switched from his hand to his elbow for support as he reached the store's front window, not wanting to smudge up the glass. "I know. Sorry Noah," he replied, noticing Cyrus fidgeting with his cane out of the corner of his eye.

"You've had us worried sick, where–" The Priest's words caught in his throat as he noticed Enoch's injury and what remained of his pant leg. "Heavens! What happened!?"

"That's a bit of a long story."

As Noah and Cyrus listened intently, Enoch explained the events that transpired after he'd left the cathedral. He now sat at the bottom of the staircase between Lamechson's and the clothing shop next door. The same staircase that led to the painfully close comfort and isolation of his apartment. Both Cyrus and Noah nodded slowly as he finished his story.

"Well, you're lucky you ran into that Gregory guy," Noah replied. "Seems like he was a big help."

Enoch responded with a slight nod of his own. "Yeah, but even with his help, I didn't get to replace my bracelet in time."

Hearing this, Cyrus gave Enoch a sympathetic look, knowing fully well what that meant for the young Scribe. Noah, on the other hand, simply placed his hands on his hips.

"Shouldn't be too bad though, right? Just gotta not use magic for a night. It ain't a full moon, and from what I can tell, y'got the self-control for it."

"Right..." Enoch's gaze shifted down to his expired bracelet as the uncertainty in his mind stole away whatever words he might've said. Noticing Enoch's discomfort, Cyrus placed a hand on Noah's shoulder.

"You're right, I'm sure he'll be fine," he agreed, "For now, why don't you head inside before curfew starts, Noah. I'll help Enoch get upstairs."

In his usual relaxed demeanor, Noah shrugged in response. "I'll leave him in your hands then, Cyrus," he turned to Enoch with a small, two finger salute. "Glad ya got home safe, kid. Well..." He nodded to Enoch's injured leg. "Safe enough, at least. If ya need anything, just give a holler."

Once again, Enoch nodded in return. After they heard the soft click of the store's door locking, Cyrus held out a hand to Enoch. "Alright, let's get you inside."

Amidst the chaos, pain and confusion of the world, there's a peace of mind found only in the safety of one's home. Small as it was, Enoch's apartment was just that, a home.

Under normal circumstances, his evening routine would begin the second he passed through the front door. He'd hang his satchel on the coat rack next to the entrance, and head right for his desk, falling into the seat in a slump. Yes, he spent most of his day seated at a book covered desk already, but there was something special about it being his own rather than his work. The textbooks on the attached shelf were his. The jar of interesting pens and pencils left unclaimed in the library were his. The journal sitting comfortably on the wooden surface, as well as the words within it, were his and no one else's.

Once he finished sharing the details of his uneventful day to his paper companion, he'd use the aptly named washroom and get ready to sleep. Sometimes, he might even put together a snack in the cozy kitchen located just a short distance away from the foot of his bed. Though more often than not he'd simply pick up some food from a café on his way home. And if he was feeling restless or bored, he'd end the day sitting halfway down the bed, people-watching as he leaned on the windowsill. The pedestrians below were familiar strangers, unaware of the curious stare above imagining what secrets they might be hiding. The secrets themselves differed depending on the day, at times exciting and imaginative, and other times beautifully mundane. Today, however, Enoch's usual routine had been interrupted, the events of the evening far from beautiful or mundane.

Currently, Enoch was seated at the round wooden table across from the front door. A once clean bowl of water sat in front of him, a damp washcloth and crumpled pile of bandages in a pile next to that. The young Scribe had swapped his torn, dirt-covered outfit for his far more comfortable night clothes. Dark, soft, and much more intact pants, accompanied by a loose-fitting white blouse. The exhaustion of the day finally began to catch up to him, and his heavy eyelids seemed intent on dragging his head down to the tabletop. Thankfully, the following *thud* came from Cyrus placing a freshly made mug of hot cocoa on the table instead, the sweet scent pulling Enoch out of the numbness that had begun to overtake his mind. Cyrus took a seat across from him, barely able to hear the boy's mumbled thanks.

"I hope I'm not imposing," Cyrus said, watching Enoch rub his eyes to wake himself up somewhat. "I just wanted to check in on you after this morning."

"No, it's fine," Enoch replied. He picked up the hot cocoa, catching himself before adding a burnt tongue to his list of injuries. Carefully, he began to blow on it to cool it off. The action gave him an excuse not to speak. Cyrus seemed to have the same plan of action, the two of them sitting in a nervous silence, wondering how their once cheerful interactions had become so awkward. They both knew the cause, of course, but that didn't stop their minds from asking regardless.

Cyrus was the first to take a sip, perhaps a little too early based on the subtle wince that followed. As he glanced over to Enoch to see if he'd noticed, he caught the Scribe staring at his bracelet, gaze so distant he might as well be staring through it. The Priest lowered his cocoa with a frown.

"How long has it been? Since you've slept without it, I mean."

"Long enough that I don't know the answer to that."

"I see..." Cyrus took another sip of cocoa as Enoch's remained untouched. The Scribe stared into the swirls drifting dreamily through the drink.

"I could just stay up," Enoch suggested after a moment. It was difficult to tell if he was speaking to Cyrus or himself. Either way, the Priest shook his head.

"You look exhausted already. I don't think that's a good idea." Despite Enoch's slow nod in response, Cyrus wasn't sure if his words made it through. Or perhaps past experiences were simply making him skeptical. Thankfully, Enoch's mind seemed to return to the apartment. The distant look in his eyes, still glued to the bracelet, faded somewhat as he finally took a sip of his cocoa.

"True... I guess I'd be too tired to get to the House of Healing tomorrow if I did that." Enoch let out an exhausted sigh. Cyrus matched it with one of relief. The older man leaned back in his seat.

"Well, you could just try to sleep with it on. There's always the chance that whatever they put in there lasts a little past the expiration, right? You can hardly be the first person to miss the replacement date."

Finally pulling his gaze away from the bracelet, Enoch gave Cyrus a proper nod, accompanied by a nervous smile. "Yeah... It's worth a shot at least." The confidence felt more forced than faint, but it was still a step in the right direction as far as Cyrus was concerned.

"That's the spirit!" He smiled in return, but the expression quickly reversed as he noticed the clock on Enoch's wall. "Heavens, is it that time already? I should probably start my patrol before it gets too late." Regretting it shortly after, Cyrus quickly chugged the rest of his cocoa before heading to the door. He grabbed his cane leaning next to it as he turned the handle. With one foot out the door, he stopped, glancing Enoch's way one last time. "I'll be at work tomorrow afternoon if you need me. Try not to stress about this too much, okay? I'm sure you'll be fine."

"Yeah..."

"Goodnight, Enoch."

"Night, Cyrus."

Relieved that the conversation had ended far less awkwardly than it began, Cyrus closed the door behind him, leaving Enoch alone at the table. The Scribe watched the door in silence for a bit, the exchanged goodnights adding a bitter aftertaste to the sweetness of the cocoa. *He always looks so much smaller than I remember...*

After he'd tidied up the mugs, Enoch collapsed into bed. He rolled onto his back with a wince as the friction of the fabric managed to reach through the new bandages. At the thought of fabrics, he turned to look at the torn pants draped over the chair at his desk. He wasn't fully tired yet, or at the very least he could manage to convince himself that that wasn't a lie. *Maybe I could try patching those up tonight?* he considered.

"No." He shook his head, hoping the verbal disagreement would help him ignore the troublesome thoughts sneaking into his mind. "Cyrus is right. I need to rest." He lifted his arm, holding the bracelet in the faint light making it through the curtains of the nearby window. "All I can do is hope you'll last one more night."

Lowering his hand with a sigh, he tried to find comfort in the smooth surface of the accessory. His fingers ran along the metal, only interrupted by the button next to where the bracelet would split open, and the small hinges on the other side. He slowly polished the metal with his touch until he was sure he'd rubbed clean through it, as if the action might somehow grant him the good fortune he'd been lacking throughout the day. *After everything that went wrong today, my bad luck has to have run out, right?* With this less than convincing thought in the back of his mind, he drifted out of consciousness, sinking into something far worse.

Chapter 6

THERE ARE MANY people in the world that believe magic is alive. That it's more than just a mindless energy residing in, and connecting all things. They believe it has a will, and that it chooses its own path as it flows throughout the Three Realms.

Enoch had never given much thought towards the nature of magic. He had no reason to wonder if it had hopes and dreams of its own, or if, like him, it was moving mindlessly with no set goal or direction. Regardless of motivation, however, there was no denying that it was in fact moving. Though it may seem to slow or hasten at times, life doesn't grant us the luxury of stagnation until it ends. And magic, the essence of life itself, is not spared this inevitability. It is ever changing; ever shifting; moving in all directions in a dizzying web both chaotic and calculated. But to Enoch, magic always seemed to pull him in one very distinct direction.

Down.

Like sinking through an inky, black ocean, he drifted ever downward; lower and lower, beyond the binds of time. In the depths of this abyss, threads of light began to cut through the surrounding shadow. Shooting stars weaving a tangled net until the darkness appeared almost shattered. Enoch fell backwards between them, eyes closed in his dream-like state, the light reflecting off his dark, wafting hair and clothing.

Slowly, Enoch's body began to right itself as his eyes flitted open. His foot landed gently on one of the strings, ending his descent. As if strummed by a musician, the light vibrated, the waves creating ripples that sent all other threads back into the darkness. The light from the thread flowed into Enoch's body. Forming intricate patterns, it passed through the soles of his feet, up to his chest, and finally reached his eyes, which now glowed like an azure lantern in the dark.

Revealed by this new source of light, Enoch's surroundings began to change. A cobblestone street beneath him. Crooked buildings emerged on either side. An alley? The architecture seemed similar to the familiar streets of Courciel; or what he could see of it, at the very least. Outside of the glow centered on the young Scribe, the scenery faded back into shadow. Curious and confused, Enoch walked forward, his silent footsteps causing the image to ripple as if he were walking through a thin pool of water. He tried his best to find some sort of sign; any indication of where he might be. Hadn't he just been in his apartment? How did he get here? Why did this silent abyss fill him with both a chilling dread and a familiar warmth?

Before he could find any answers, a blinding light overpowered his vision. His body tensed, reflexively taking a step back as he saw the figure that had just walked through him. A humanoid silhouette continued walking forward, a thin cane in their hand, their body made entirely out of dazzling, turquoise flames. Despite standing in said flames only seconds before, Enoch couldn't feel any sort of heat, nor could he hear the crackling tongues of fire. A second figure passed to his left, joining the first. This figure seemed somewhat bulkier in comparison, the flames a deep green instead.

The two figures stopped a short distance away. They had no faces, but based on their movement Enoch assumed they had been startled by a sound. Following what he believed was their line of sight, he looked upwards. The cold dread from before escalated into a bone-chilling fear at what he saw. Perched on the edge of the rooftop, just within the range of Enoch's light, was yet another silhouette of flames. Two large, fiery wings extended out from the dark purple blaze, a tail swaying back and forth as it looked down at the figures below. There was no mistaking the shape. This was a demon.

The winged figure swooped down, landing in the cobble-stone alley on all fours. Like a nervous stray cat, it crawled towards the green and turquoise figures before tilting its head. The turquoise figure knelt down, holding a hand out in the demon's direction. Then, in an instant, their bodies tensed. All three figures turned to face Enoch. The green silhouette moved in front of the others, not that its defense was needed. Behind them, a monstrous shadow emerged from the demonic silhouette, rushing towards Enoch and engulfing him in darkness.

In a futile attempt to defend himself, Enoch raised his hands. His vision went black as the shadow passed through him, the light leaving his eyes and retaking the form of a glowing thread; the vision's origin.

Enoch turned back to the light, surprised to find several other threads diverging off of it. Curiosity overpowering his reason, he reached out, grasping the closest branch. Just as it had before, the light passed through him. The same otherworldly patterns appeared on his fingers, up his arm, returning his sight to him as his eyes glowed once more. This time, however, there was no scenery to see. Instead, the light simply revealed a single figure standing alone in the abyss.

Dark, chaotic, red flames made up the figure's body, the inferno filled with an intensity that was almost overwhelming. Unlike the others, however, this figure was not entirely featureless. Moving to the figure's front, Enoch was surprised to see a sharp metal mask covering their face, the slitted eyes glowing menacingly from the light of the fire behind.

The masked figure began to move forward, eyes fixated on something beyond Enoch's perception. With nowhere else to go, Enoch joined them. He followed in silence. Absolute silence. Even their heavy footsteps were swallowed by the resulting ripples. Even the familiar figure emerging from the darkness ahead made no sound at all.

The newcomer, much to Enoch's surprise, was Gregory. The masked figure seemed just as surprised to see the man, as their flames grew wilder and brighter for a moment at the sight of him. Slowly, they crouched down, engrossed by the oblivious Pilgrim facing away from them. Their fingertips brushed against the ground; the water unaffected by the flames' heat. Enoch found himself fascinated by the reaction, wondering what exactly the masked figure was trying to accomplish. The answer caused his heart to leap from his chest, as two spikes of raging red fire shot out of the ground beneath Gregory. The Pilgrim barely dodged; his side skewered despite having avoided a lethal blow. Crimson blood splattered outward, far darker than the red of the fire.

Now that he was aware of the attacker, Gregory managed to dance around the continued barrage of spikes. The Pilgrim reached for something on his hip, suddenly bathed in a light so bright that Enoch had to shield his eyes. Once the flash had disappeared, a sword had taken its place in Gregory's hand. Moving swifter than Enoch thought possible, the Pilgrim rushed towards the masked attacker.

Desperate to defend themselves, the attacker summoned another spike in front of them as they backed away. The makeshift shield staggered the man's attack. Though Gregory had aimed for the masked figure's arm, it seemed his attacker had expected a killing blow. In a cruel irony, the newly formed spike redirected the off-center blade towards the fleeing attacker. For once, Enoch was relieved this place was silent, as the resulting sound of metal through flesh, or rather fire, would be a difficult thing to forget.

In an instant, the flaming spike melted to the ground. The masked attacker grasped at Gregory's jacket collar as they collapsed towards him. Gregory caught them, lowering them to the ground as he tried to process what had just happened. Holding the figure in his arms, he removed their mask. Though Enoch could only see the same crimson flames, Gregory's face grew as pale as his silver hair, eyes wide in absolute horror. The figure's body went limp. The flames softened and dimmed. Enoch held his breath, before realizing he hadn't been breathing since he'd arrived here.

Then... silence. Silence far deeper than the abyss Enoch had sunk through. Nothing but Gregory tightly gripping the red flames growing darker and darker. Then, the body erupted into a turbulent hellfire. A storm of flashing light.

The ferocity of the heat distorted the world around them. Once again, Enoch moved to shield himself, before realizing he couldn't feel the flames. Both he and Gregory sat in the eye of this maelstrom, unaffected by the blaze. Well, perhaps not entirely unaffected. As Enoch looked down, he saw that his body was once again covered in unnatural intersecting patterns, now the same red as the masked figure's flames. These marks lingered, even after the fire faded away into sparkling embers.

Gregory hadn't seemed to notice the sudden burst. Or perhaps he hadn't cared. As the inferno dissipated, he remained on his knees, staring in shock at the mask in his hands. The body of its owner was nowhere to be seen. All that remained was the man that had ended their life. Broken, just like the cracks forming in the air and ground around him.

They were so small at first that Enoch hadn't noticed them, but there was no denying that reality itself seemed to be crumbling. Spectral white hands burst from the fissures, grabbing Gregory's body. The man struggled against their grip for a moment before glancing once more at the mask. He stopped fighting, holding the mask tightly as the hands dragged him down into the crumbling darkness. The ground continued to crack beneath Enoch's feet until he fell through as well, plunging into the abyss once more; the glow fading until nothing remained.

Enoch sat up in a cold sweat. The darkness was gone, replaced by the faint amount of sunlight sneaking through the closed curtain. His breathing was heavy. His heart beat so quickly and loudly that it was nearly deafening after the silence of his dream. He checked his surroundings, his hand instinctively moving to his bracelet.

His stomach sank, perhaps still plummeting from the dream he'd awoken from. It seemed the bracelet was now nothing more than a simple accessory. Exhausted, he pressed the button to release it, carefully taking it off. He winced as the acupuncture needle inside slid out of his wrist. He'd never enjoyed that part.

With a sigh, he fell back onto the bed, the pillow cold, damp, and as unpleasant a feeling as what he'd just experienced. It seemed the Archangels really were punishing him.

"Damn it."

Chapter 7

I F YOU'VE EVER been awoken by a nightmare, you should already know that it can ruin your entire morning. A bad enough one may even linger for the rest of the day as a foul taste in your mouth. Normally, when Enoch was bothered by an unpleasant dream, he'd distract himself with other matters. He'd remind himself that the images were simply the product of an over-imaginative mind, or on especially bad nights, the result of cruel reminiscence. However, the unfortunate truth was that what he'd experienced the night before, while similar in effect, couldn't be brushed aside as just a troublesome nightmare. Or at the very least, not without an accompanying foul flavor of guilt to compliment the lingering bad taste.

As he limped through the streets of Courciel, using his bike for support as he had the day before, Enoch's brow furrowed. Even the crowded streets, full of inconsequential commotion, weren't enough to disperse the thoughts fogging his mind. His movements were slow, feeling aimless despite his clear goals. Get to a House of Healing. Get his leg healed. Replace the bracelet that failed to offer one final night of blissful protection. These subconscious goals pushed him forward as his surface thoughts wandered to Gregory.

There was no doubt that meeting the yellow-coated man had triggered his vision. The memory of shaking Gregory's hand, so warm and comforting, suddenly shifted to a skewer of crimson fire piercing the Pilgrim's side. *Gregory is going to be attacked. But why? Is it because he works for the Church? Or maybe it's a personal grudge... Should I go warn him?* Enoch shook his head.

You don't know him. Don't get involved.

Even if Enoch did decide to warn him, what could Gregory do? If he tried to change the outcome by not defending himself, he'd simply succumb to the spikes instead. Not to mention the fact that Enoch had no way to know when it would happen, or the attacker's identity, or even the origin of the spectral hands. There were far too many missing facts. It would be best to simply forget he saw anything. If that was Gregory's fate, then so be it.

Don't get involved.

Two Priests passed by Enoch, paying him little mind as they patrolled the edge of the plaza. Up ahead, the House of Healing towered above the people below. The golden cross and circle, the emblem of the Church, shined atop the building's highest stone spire. Arched windows lined the walls, metal bars covering the smaller ones on higher floors. A black, metal fence followed along the base of the building, keeping pedestrians off the small, colorful garden behind it. The flowers sparkled like stars, recently watered by a Church worker making their way along the fence, with a watering can far too small to complete their job in one trip.

A short distance away, the front door of the building stood propped open by a brick to let in the fresh air. Even on the inside, the Healers emblem was carved into the door. A pair of garden shears in front of a four peaked star. It was the same symbol marking the apron of every Healer employed by the Church.

With his destination so close, Enoch limped with more determination. Once he finished his business inside, he could finally leave the events of the day before behind and go back to his normal life. Perhaps, even the vision could become nothing more than a forgotten dream.

As he pushed forward, leaning his bike against the fence, Enoch barely noticed the commotion happening just a few paces away. Near the entrance of the House of Healing, a man and woman with desperate expressions were speaking to a Priest. They were both pale, their appearances disheveled enough to raise questions about their wellbeing. No doubt they were among the many people seeking asylum from the demon attacks out in the more rural areas of Terrael.

"Why won't you take this seriously?" the man asked. "We really did see demons outside the city! A group of them, all wearing masks!"

Enoch had intended to simply pass by the commotion, but now he couldn't help but glance over as he propped himself up with the fence. From where he was, he could hear the Priest's faint sigh, and see the stern look he sent the couple's way.

"Look, I'm sure you two have been through a lot, but you don't have to worry about demons here in Courciel." With a sweep of his hand, he gestured to the many other Priests patrolling the square. "The capital is one of the most well-guarded cities in Terrael. The demons aren't stupid enough to attack the communities this far in. If you saw some demons outside the city, then that's where they'll stay." The Priest ignored the growing frustration of the couple and pointed down one of the roads branching off the plaza. "Now, why don't you two go and get registered into a shelter. I have work to do."

The disheveled man opened his mouth to argue, but the woman cut him off, gently grabbing his shoulder and shaking her head. Defeated, the two of them walked Enoch's way. Had they chosen any other direction, Enoch likely wouldn't have heard the man's muttered words.

"Their blind faith in the Church's protection is gonna get them killed."

"Not so loud! Are you trying to get us arrested?" The woman glanced around in fear. Enoch turned away just in time, unable to see her relief that no one had heard. They hurried away, leaving the plaza. Their words lingered behind.

"Masked demons..." Enoch whispered. *The mask in the vision looked different, so I didn't even consider that they could be linked to that group...*

The Soldiers of Lilith. For Gregory's sake, Enoch hoped the potential connection was nothing more than paranoia. He turned back to the House of Healing, his expression even more distraught than before.

A decent crowd filled the House of Healing's lobby. No doubt the people inside had ironically hoped to beat the busy hours by getting there early. Now, most of them sat on the available benches, waiting for their turn. Two Priests stood guard at the door, scanning the room with little interest. Across from them, a wooden door in the corner swung open as a patient left the back area. Enoch glanced up at the sound before turning his attention back to the form in front of him. He hardly had to think as he filled it out, other than a moment of hesitation as he tried to recall the date. With a slight wince, he stood and limped over to the front desk, handing over the paper as he had every time before. The receptionist smiled as he did, just as she had every time before.

"Thank you, sir!" she said with a forced sincerity. "You will be authorized only one magic-suppressing bracelet for this prescription period. Being in the possession of multiple bracelets is punishable by a fine of 1000 gold." She pulled out another form from what Enoch could only imagine was a nightmarish number of files beneath her desk, turning it to face him. "If your bracelet is lost or damaged, you'll need to file a request for a replacement. Distribution of the bracelet, or use of it on any other people is considered a felony and will be punished accordingly. If you understand these terms, please sign here."

Enoch took the pen she held out to him, signing at the bottom of the form. As he finished, the door in the corner swung open once more, a Healer entering the lobby. Her long green robes swayed somewhat with the movement of the door, the fabric covering her head to toe thanks to the golden-hemmed hood. With her neck and lower face covered in white fabric to protect against disease, it was impossible to gauge her appearance. Though, based on her posture and movement she was likely getting a little long in the tooth. Even her eyes were hidden behind the round goggles she was wearing. Despite this, it was still easy to tell she was scanning the room as she called out "Enoch Augnium?"

At the sound of his name, Enoch waved. The Healer did the same in return, gesturing with a fitted, brown, leather glove for him to follow her. The receptionist looked up with a practiced smile. "Perfect timing!" she exclaimed. "We'll have your bracelet ready for you by the time you're done! For now, please head to the magical treatment wing."

Enoch did just that, allowing himself to be led through the various tidied halls of the treatment area. They passed through the crowds of patients and Healers in the general clinic. The identical uniforms of said Healers created an almost uncanny atmosphere over time as it became difficult for Enoch to tell if he was simply limping in circles.

After that were the emergency rooms. Though each door was tightly sealed shut, Enoch couldn't help but sense the muggy, lingering cloud of magic building behind one of them. It seemed that the Healers' efforts hadn't been enough to save the patient, or prevent their final burst. *Must have happened recently if I can feel the magic through a closed door,* Enoch deduced. His lips tightened, and he pushed through the pain to limp faster down the hall, hoping to leave the tragic scene behind him.

Eventually, he reached the magical treatment wing, where those with a high enough tolerance to magic could be treated through an ability. Convenient as these treatments could be, the risk of magic exposure to those with too low a tolerance meant the wing had to be tucked far away from the general clinic. By the time he reached his destination, Enoch realized his jaw had begun to hurt as well. He hadn't even noticed how tightly he'd been clenching his teeth to fight the pain. Before long though, he found himself sitting on a comfortable metal bed with a soft mattress and white sheet.

The Healer removed his bandages as she spoke. "My magic will reduce the pain and inflammation. The scratches will still be there, but you'll at least be able to walk." With the bandages removed, the Healer gently placed her hands on Enoch's ankle. Not sure what else to do, Enoch focused his gaze on a nearby shelf of medical supplies to make the situation feel less awkward.

"Right," he said meekly. The Healer likely felt far less anxiety than him as a green glow emitted from her palms, moving to surround Enoch's injury. The swelling and discoloration slowly lessened, as if absorbed by the magical energy. Despite his apparent fascination with the nearby shelf, Enoch glanced over, reminded of the similar glow that had fixed his bike the day before, as well as the man responsible. He let out a defeated sigh, and after a soft curse in the back of his mind, he looked down to the Healer.

"Hey, uh... do you know the quickest route to the Hart District from here?"

Chapter 8

T HE CROOKED BUILDINGS of the Hart District covered the alley in a lopsided shade. Enoch carefully walked his bike between them, his new bracelet sitting safely on his wrist. He would've loved to simply coast through what the Healer had described as a shortcut to the Ivory Inn, but the uneven cobblestones caused such a bumpy ride he'd likely have to return to the House of Healing for bruising if he tried to use his bike any longer.

On either side of the alley, the occasional pile of discarded junk forced Enoch to tread carefully. One such pile grabbed hold of his bike's front wheel, the torn sheet tangling itself with the spokes. Enoch let out a sigh. *If this trip breaks my bike, I'm making Gregory fix it again.* When tugging the bike failed to work, Enoch knelt down, carefully untangling the sheet instead. *I'll just head to where Gregory said he's staying, tell him about the vision, then go back home. What he does with the info is up to him.*

After doing his best to remind himself why he was putting up with this, Enoch finished freeing his bike. He let out his frustration in a sigh and continued on his way.

Whooosh! Thump Thump Thump

A sound above caused Enoch to jump. Looking up, he saw nothing but the evening sky. *A bird, I guess?* he tried to rationalize. *A... really clumsy one?* More alert, he passed by a small wooden structure built into the wall. Bags of garbage sat neatly inside it. Though it was better than the sickeningly soggy piles he'd passed by before, Enoch still fought back a gag. He was glad the inner districts didn't have to worry about their garbage sitting out for so long.

Thump Thump Thump

The distracting smell was interrupted by another sound on the rooftops. Once again, Enoch turned to look. As he did–

THUD

A rush of air behind him sent a physical and mental chill down his spine. Slowly, Enoch turned to face the source, seeing the shadow that had jumped from above.

A lavender skinned demon crouched on the path in front of him, perched on all fours like a hunting cat. Long, tangled, dark purple hair covered his face. Two black, chipped horns escaped through the strands, following the curve of his head before curling up at the end. Though, the tip of the right one seemed to have been broken off long ago, smoothed over time.

A pair of angelic, indigo wings protruded from his back, still outstretched from his landing. Had it not been for the terror Enoch was feeling, he would have found the wings quite beautiful. After all, he'd only ever seen the scaled, bat-like wings demons were known for. However, at that moment he was instead focused on the demon's hand, the sharp claws catching the fading sunlight for just a moment as he moved forward.

A million thoughts ran through Enoch's mind. *What's a demon doing in the capital? Why is it targeting me? What should I do? Is it with the ones that couple saw outside the city?* Though Enoch had more questions than explanations, he found one answer when the demon lifted his head. A large, faded scar ran down his cheek and neck. His two golden irises seemed to glow in the darkness of the alley, surrounded by the blacks of the demon's eyes. Despite the demon's intimidating, animalistic demeanor, the face seemed surprisingly soft in shape, other than their pointed nose and ears. Most importantly, the face was completely exposed. Not a mask in sight. So, unless he'd simply forgotten it, he likely wasn't with the Soldiers of Lilith. But in that case, what was he doing there?

Enoch took a shaky step back, gaze locked on the newcomer. Again, the demon crawled forward, freezing Enoch with his unbreaking stare. The movement seemed almost familiar. Enoch's mind scrambled for an answer, finding it in the memory of his vision the night before. *A winged demon that moves like an animal; an alley in the capital; I've seen this before!* Finally willing himself to move more than a terrified step, he glanced behind him, searching for the other two figures he'd seen. Instead, he found nothing but an empty cobblestone alley. He and the demon were completely alone.

"*Shiny...*" The demon's voice was quiet and hoarse, as if it had been some time since he'd spoken. It had a surprisingly young tone to it. Enoch turned back to face him.

"Shiny?" he repeated. "My... My bike? Or–"

The demon stopped his advance as Enoch replied, his thin, pointed tail swishing slowly behind him. He tilted his head as he raised a clawed finger to point at Enoch's wrist. *"Your hand."*

Enoch lifted the aforementioned limb, noticing the new, polished bracelet fastened to his wrist. "My bracelet?" he asked. The demon tilted his head the other way.

"Bracelet?"

Enoch nodded, grateful that this conversation seemed to be buying him some time to find a way out of this. His relief was short lived though, as he suddenly found himself flat on the ground, air pushed from his lungs, bike clattering onto the cobblestone next to him. He could hardly breathe with the demon now pinning him to the street, but he still attempted to let out one final, desperate cry.

"Hel–!"

A clawed hand cut off Enoch's plea. The Scribe's rapid breaths barely made it through his fingers as he stared up in absolute terror. For some reason, however, the demon seemed just as frightened, unable to make eye-contact in return.

"Shhhhhhh," he said, his voice growing somewhat sturdier with use, despite the hushed tone. "No noise. Just want the bracelet." Holding Enoch's body down with his leg, one hand still clasped over the Scribe's mouth, the demon lifted Enoch's hand, examining the golden accessory. His tail swished happily as he did. Now that the demon was so close, Enoch finally noticed his surprisingly elegant outfit.

The demon's black dress pants were torn at the bottom, revealing his clawed feet, one still pressed firmly against Enoch's torso. His long, red, velvet tailcoat was in a similar state. Slashes and tears were scattered across the fabric, some clearly from claw attacks, others possibly from various kinds of blades. However, it had undoubtedly been quite high quality before taking damage. Decorative embroidery covered the tails and torso. Faded gold lining added a touch of flare as well, dividing the red fabric from the black vest beneath. The color scheme, aside from being aesthetically pleasing, also served to hide the faded bloodstains covering the garment. Had Enoch not been close enough to smell them, he wouldn't have thought to look at all. Now, he wished he hadn't.

It... It's killed people! Am I next? Maybe I'll be fine if I just kept quiet, but... He glanced at his attacker's sharp claws, currently poking at the bracelet hinges. *What if it kills me anyways? Is this really how I'm gonna die? Clawed to death in a dark, disgusting alley?* The demon finally let go of Enoch's mouth, using both hands to try to slide the bracelet off. Though the acupuncture needles inside released a numbing agent while piercing the wrist, the movement still caused Enoch to wince.

"There's a—" Another frightened expression from the demon cut off the Scribe's words. His tail swished forward, the sharp tip digging ever so slightly into Enoch's throat; a reminder of his earlier warning about noise. Enoch flinched before looking at the bracelet, making sure to speak in a softer tone. "A button. There's a button to take it off." The demon turned back to the bracelet; lips pursed in confusion as he searched for this button. Based on the reaction, Enoch wasn't sure if he even knew what a button was.

Maybe I could fight it off? he considered. *No, probably not. With the strength and speed it used to tackle me, I clearly won't win in a physical fight. All I can do is wait for the demon to kill me.* With less fear than would be expected, Enoch closed his eyes. *Maybe this would be a fitting way to go. Actually, it would almost be poetic justice, in a way.* As he left his fate in his attacker's clawed hands, the demon suddenly turned behind him.

"New... smell?" he said curiously. Equally confused, Enoch's eyes flew open, following the demon's gaze. To his surprise, Gregory was standing in the middle of the alley a short distance away. The Pilgrim frowned at the demon's words.

"That's disappointing," he said, "I really thought I used the perfect amount of perfume today. But I guess I must've overdone it." He tapped the side of his nose with a smile. "You have a sharp sense of smell, my friend."

Gregory shrugged with far more casualness than acceptable for the situation. As he looked over, his movement stuttered a moment as he recognized who the attacker had pinned to the ground. Quickly recovering, he turned back to the demon.

"Anyhoo, I'm not sure how long you've been in Terrael, but up here, most people aren't okay with being tackled in the streets without consent." He slowly gestured to Enoch, careful not to startle the demon. "So, I'm going to have to ask you to let him go."

Like a scolded animal, the demon lowered his head. He pulled his wings closer to his body. "I... I didn't..." Noticing the change in the demon's demeanor, Gregory took a step closer. Almost instantly, the demon's wings extended once more in a defensive stance. Gregory stopped.

"It's okay," he said softly. "All you have to do is step off of him and we can sort this out." Slowly, Gregory knelt down, matching the demon's eye-level with a comforting smile. "What's your name?"

For a moment, the demon's posture softened. The question seemed to catch him off guard, and his gaze lowered, a slight furrow in his brow as he pushed himself to remember. "It was, um... Eighth... Circle?" He swiftly shook his head. "No. Um... Mahway. I'm Mahway."

Gregory's smile grew warmer. "That's a very nice name, Mahway," he replied, placing a hand on his chest. "I'm Gregory. Do you think you could step off my friend there, Mahway?"

Mahway's gaze darted over to Enoch and his bracelet. The Scribe glanced between the demon and Gregory, still frozen in fear. Though there was still a sliver of defensiveness in his tone, Mahway's voice felt far softer than before as he turned back to Gregory.

"He's scared."

"Yes, he is," Gregory replied with a nod. He held his hand out once more, slower than he had the first time. "But if you–"

"Is everything okay? I heard–" The three men had been so focused on their conversation, that not a single one of them had noticed the redheaded woman approaching Gregory from the shade behind him. From the dull, worn coloring of her dress, it was clear she was an outer city resident. Her footsteps and voice were both soft as she curiously peeked past the Pilgrim. That is, until her eyes went wide at the sight of Mahway. Her mouth quickly followed as she let out an ear-piercing scream. In a frantic attempt to back away, the woman tripped over the uneven cobblestones. Enoch could feel Mahway's body tense once more. Gregory turned back in surprise, wondering how he'd failed to hear her approach.

Faster than Enoch could process, Mahway leapt off Enoch. Had the action not knocked Enoch's head against the stone, the Scribe would have seen the demon rebound off the wall, passing by Gregory to rush at the woman with his claws. Despite the demon's speed, Gregory reacted just as quickly. Almost reflexively, he grabbed a metal button on his right forearm, dashing between Mahway and the woman. His jacket sleeve began to glow with his golden, magical aura.

CLANG!

Just before Mahway's claws could reach their target, Gregory's sleeve changed shape, forming a smooth, steel shield that blocked the attack. He'd used his other arm to brace against the impact, but the force still pushed him back towards the woman. The surrounding dirt and debris were blown away as Mahway used his wings to retreat backwards, staring in shock and confusion at the shield that had suddenly appeared. Gregory shook out his free arm.

"Humans also don't agree with shredding up beautiful women," he said, voice as smooth as the shield he had sculpted. The Pilgrim moved a hand to the metallic lining of his jacket collar, hands glowing once more. "That's twice now that you've attempted to attack innocent civilians. I'm afraid I'm going to have to take you in, Mahway."

Like a cornered animal, Mahway crouched lower. He shook his head. "No cages," he growled.

"Sorry, but it's one of your better options." As the reply left his lips, the light surrounding Gregory's hands spread throughout his jacket. In the blink of an eye, his body was cloaked in the same golden glow. The woman shielded her eyes. Curiously, seeing how the Pilgrim's magic only worked with steel, the fabric of Gregory's jacket shifted. The silver details expanded, spreading over the garment like melted metal filling a mold. Once the light faded, the woman could barely believe what she saw. Gregory's jacket had transformed into beautiful, shimmering armor. Even in the shade of the alley, it appeared almost incandescent, the polished steel shining with a sun-like hue from the yellow threads mixed throughout. The man's face was both focused and relaxed as he used his magic, an ease in his expression that betrayed the years of practice he must have gone through to achieve such a complex reconstruction.

With a similar familiarity, he reached down to his hip, as if to grab some unseen weapon. Instead, he gripped the metallic belt hidden beneath the hanging armor plates, drawing it forward like a sword. To the woman's surprise, that's exactly the shape it took! The curve of the belt straightened and sharpened into an elegant, decorative blade, the weapon shining gold until fully free. Careful not to get too close to the woman he was protecting, Gregory swung the blade dramatically. Sending a quick wink in the woman's direction, he ended the wondrous transformation with a heroic pose.

"It's time for me to steel the show!" he said proudly. The woman blushed, perhaps due to the ridiculous pun, or perhaps out of admiration. Mahway felt far less impressed. He crouched lower still, rapidly looking over this new threat. Gregory turned the blade in his direction. His words, however, remained directed at the woman.

"I'll keep him here. Go get somewhere safe." The woman nodded, scrambling to her feet. Unfortunately, though reassuring to her, Gregory's words only served to push Mahway over the edge. The surrounding black nearly swallowed the gold of his eyes. His rapid breathing grew dizzying.

"No..." he said quietly. "Can't get caught!" Once again, he leapt off the ground, flying high to avoid the dangerous reach of Gregory's blade. He moved swiftly, cutting off the woman's retreat with a panicked landing far less graceful than the one Enoch had heard before. The woman stopped. Gregory quickly caught up, gently pulling her behind him. Body tense and on the verge of shaking, Mahway stared through them, speaking in a frightened growl.

"Guardian!"

A dark, purple aura began to emerge from Mahway's body, growing larger and larger. As it did, it began to take the form of a massive, winged creature, evidently named Guardian. The shape was similar to that of a wyvern; a fantasy beast that at that moment, Gregory wished had remained on the pages of storybooks.

Aside from the edge of the outline, the form lacked solid details. The creature itself almost seemed to be made of black and purple smoke, despite its very palpable weight and solidity. It expanded until it was nearly as tall as the buildings surrounding the alley, looming above the two below it, as well as the unconscious Scribe behind them. The summon's glowing red eyes glared down, its deep, rumbling voice filling the air.

"You won't escape."

Gregory's heroic pose deflated somewhat at the sight before them. He stared at the creature in disbelief.

"Are you kidding me!?"

Chapter 9

T HOUGH THIS SEEMS a somewhat inopportune time
to do so, as the current focus of the story lays unconscious in an alley, I would like to use this moment to describe the next relevant kind of magic ability. Summoners.

Magic is an energy that resides inside all living things,
and Summoners are able to shape their energy into conjurable objects. This form will be something unique to the
Summoner themselves. For example, a summoned weapon,
an element of some sort, or perhaps even a creature capable
of thought.

However, the most peculiar aspect of a Summoner ability
is that the physical nature of the magic will adjust to fit the
form. A summoned wolf's fur may feel soft. Fire made from
magic will be hot to the touch. And a large, wyvern-like
monster will certainly break more than a few bones should
it manage to land a hit. Knowing this, Gregory focused on
dodging Guardian's attacks to the best of his ability, prefer-
ring his bones as they were.

Enoch, on the other hand, focused on sitting up. A
throbbing pain was beginning to form in the back of his
head where Mahway had accidentally slammed it into the
street. "Damn it. That's gonna bruise," he muttered to him-

self. Looking around, he noticed the woman from before crouched behind the wooden structure built into the wall. The smell of the garbage within it hadn't improved, but there wasn't much else in terms of hiding places.

Further down the alley, he saw Gregory fighting a large monster that hadn't been there before. The Pilgrim's sword was doing little damage, and Enoch got the sense that he was likely only still alive due to the alley's narrow width limiting the creature's movement. Enoch rubbed his eyes, wondering if he was seeing things.

Is Gregory wearing... armor now? he realized. *Wait, no. More important, what's that thing he's fighting!?* He couldn't pull his gaze away from Guardian, a wide-eyed stare as he tried to figure out what had happened after he'd lost consciousness. *Either the demon transformed, or this is a summon of some kind,* he deduced. Based on the form, it was likely the latter. In fact, as he thought back to the winged demon in his vision the night before, he realized that this was likely the shadow that had emerged and passed through him. Panicked, he turned to Gregory, his aching head still spinning even after the movement stopped. "Gregory!" he called out. "If someone in a mask shows up, don't kill them!"

Gregory stabbed his sword into Guardian, the action seeming more akin to a pinprick as far as the creature was concerned. He glanced over in confusion. "What!?" he called back. Before Enoch even had the chance to explain, Guardian swung down at Gregory. The Pilgrim ducked, having no choice but to wait for an explanation. He couldn't afford to be distracted right now.

Enoch watched the fight in horror, trying to figure out what to do. *There's no way Gregory could defeat a huge monster like that! Should I try to find a Priest?* He glanced down the alley. *No, there won't be any close enough this side of the wall. And I don't know where the demon is either.* Panic began to fog his mind. *What should I do? What... What can I do? Can he even win this?*

"Hey!" Despite the fact he shouldn't divide his attention, Gregory glanced back at the panicking Scribe. The Pilgrim's gauntlet morphed into a small shield that barely blocked an attack. He struggled to keep his balance as it knocked him back several feet across the cobblestone. "It was Enoch, right?" he continued after recovering. "Grab the girl and get out of here! It's not safe!"

Enoch looked up in surprise, "R-Right!" he shouted back. *That should be doable, I think. If I can get myself and that woman away, then Gregory could focus on the fight!* He scrambled to his feet, heading over to the woman's mostly ineffective hiding place. *I don't have to beat the monster; I just need to get away from it. I... I should be able to do that much at least.*

"C'mon, we gotta run while he's distracting that thing!" Enoch said, more fear in his voice than he'd like. The woman shook her head, fingers tightly gripping the fabric of her dress as she held her knees to her chest. She couldn't even bring herself to look at Enoch as she spoke.

"The demon is still out there, if we run it'll attack us!" she whispered. Though she did have a point, Enoch couldn't help but glance over to Gregory dodging Guardian's swing-ing claws. "Yeah, but we'll probably end up killed if we stick around too," he argued. With a panicked look in his eyes, he turned back, holding his hand out to her. "C'mon, he can't keep that thing busy forever."

The woman hesitated for just a moment, scanning the rooftops around them with darting eyes. She reached out her hand before glancing towards the fight. "Look out!"

Enoch had barely processed the woman's words before feeling a strong push from her direction. As he landed on his back, the space in front of him became a storm of dust and debris, filling his lungs and eyes. He coughed out what he could as things settled, before gasping the air right back in at the sight of the aftermath.

Guardian had slammed Gregory against the wall, holding the Pilgrim tightly in its monstrous hand. A large broken dent had replaced the wall of bricks, which now sat in a crumbled pile below. Once the dust cleared, Enoch let out a small scream at the sight of the woman pinned by the beams of wood that had offered her safety moments before. *Her eyes are closed,* he realized, *Is... Is she dead?* Like a needle piercing his mind, a memory forced its way into Enoch's consciousness.

A corpse. The body laying just as the woman was now, drops of rain collecting on the tip of its unmoving finger.

Another scream began to build in the back of the Scribe's throat, but before it could escape, Guardian's tail crashed into his side, sending him flying into a pile of garbage farther down the alley with an unpleasant, heavy squelch.

"Gah!" Gregory used what limited movement he had to take a swing at Guardian's arm with his blade. The summon responded with another slam into the wall, the force sending the shining sword clattering to the ground. Disappointed in both the situation and his grip strength, Gregory watched it land. "Oh, come on!"

The Pilgrim took in his surroundings. Below him, he could somewhat make out the woman buried in debris.

Further down, he saw Enoch attempting to regain his bearings in a nice bed of trash. *Well, this rescue has been nothing but successful so far,* he thought to himself. With a sigh, he turned his attention back to his opponent. It was difficult to tell through the ringing in his ears, but he was sure the destroyed wall had been loud enough to attract attention. *I have to wrap this up before more civilians get involved.*

The creature had to have some sort of weak spot; an opening he was failing to find. Strangely, Guardian's attacks had stopped. Now, it simply held Gregory firmly against the wall, glaring menacingly. *If it isn't attacking, maybe I could still try talking my way out of this,* Gregory theorized, *I don't know where Mahway ran off to, but with a summon this big he still has to be close.*

Under normal circumstances, Gregory's eyesight was quite impressive! Unfortunately, a gigantic wyvern blocking most of your field of vision could hardly be considered normal circumstances. *Now, if only tall, dark and edgy wasn't blocking the view. I'll have to lure him out instead.*

"Y'know, I love your ability, Mahway!" Gregory called out. "Very broody and aesthetic! But– *Ack!*" Guardian growled and tightened his grip. With a strain in his voice, Gregory continued through gritted teeth. "It was a compliment! Loosen up a little!" His diplomacy plan and several bones crushed, Gregory shut his mouth, mind now occupied with the realization that ribs probably weren't supposed to pop like that.

Once he regained his sense of direction, Enoch turned his attention back to the fight. Both Gregory and the woman were where they'd been before, so he probably hadn't passed out again. His panic returned with his bearings as he sat up in the trash pile. *I have to help them!* he told himself.

Unfortunately, the sight of Guardian's form... the claws, the size, the monstrous tail; what little courage Enoch tried to build up was dwarfed by the creature before him. *But... there's no way I can get past that!* he thought, *I can't just sit here and waste time like an idiot either though.*

"Damn it!" He slammed a fist into the garbage pile before glancing over as he felt something disturbingly damp on impact. He quickly regretted indulging his horrified curiosity, looking away from the unknown substance. Though it seemed a trivial action at the time, had Enoch not done so, that day likely would have ended quite differently. After all, had he not glanced away, he never would have noticed the small space between two buildings down the alley. A break just wide enough for someone his size to sidle through.

A whirlwind of thoughts flew through Enoch's mind. *I can get away! I could go get help! But I'd just put more people in danger, right? Should I fight then? No, I can't. I'm not a hero. I can't save people. I... I'm just in the way.* Without even realizing it, Enoch leaned closer towards his escape, *I should leave... I should run... I have to run!*

Behind him, Gregory let out a pained gasp as Guardian tightened its grip. Enoch's fist tightened as well; the Scribe frustrated by his own cowardice. *What choice do I have!?* He argued against his own guilt. *Even if I did try to fight, the demon would probably attack me again before I could even get close!* He glanced back to the fight, once more noticing the unconscious woman that had said the same warning to him. Once more thinking back to the corpses that plagued his dreams. If he tried to fight, then...

As he did every time anxiety assaulted his brain, he turned his attention to the bracelet on his wrist. A comforting, golden sanctuary amidst the insanity he had stumbled into. He felt the smooth surface with his fingers. The sharp ridge of the hinges. The curves of the release button. His mind began to clear. He couldn't just sit there.

I have to run.

Face wracked in panic, Enoch ran from the fight, gaze glued to the narrow escape he'd seen before. He'd hardly stepped out of the slippery puddle surrounding the garbage before the sound of flapping wings filled the air behind him. Feeling the force of the wind, he turned around mid-step. Enoch faced Mahway, the demon once again pinning him to the ground. For a moment, Mahway hesitated, as if he hadn't planned what to do past this point. The look in his eyes appeared as panicked as Enoch's as he stared down at the Scribe.

"I... I just wanted–" Though he didn't say the word, Mahway glanced down to the accessory that had started the encounter, only to find Enoch's wrist completely bare. "What!?"

Without wasting a second, Enoch raised his free hand, grateful he'd moved it out of the demon's sight when he'd been tackled. Acting completely on reflex, he clasped the bracelet onto the arm pinning him down. The needle inside pierced the demon's wrist as the accessory clicked into place. The Scribe's eyes went wide in surprise that his plan had actually worked! Mahway's eyes went wide in pain and shock at the unexpected attack.

In an instant, Guardian faded away like smoke dispelled by the wind. At the same time, Mahway collapsed off of Enoch in exhaustion, unable to reabsorb the immense magical energy used to form the beast. Gregory fell to the ground as well, catching himself on the cobblestone. "Nice one, kid!" he shouted, turning to Enoch and Mahway. The praise went unheard as Enoch scrambled back, wanting to put some distance between himself and the demon.

His movements slowed by fatigue, Mahway clawed at the bracelet. "No... No! No-no-no-*no-no!*" Each failed attempt to remove it was followed by another, more and more frantic despite his weakened state. Enoch backed away further, surprised by Mahway's reaction. He'd hardly expected him to be happy about it, but behind the growing terror in the demon's eyes was a look of... betrayal?

Unable to remove the bracelet, Mahway staggered back somewhat, drunk on fear and adrenaline. The spark of betrayal flared into a burning rage as he lunged at Enoch. Even as time seemed to slow around him, death flying towards his throat in the form of sharpened claws, Enoch's mind couldn't keep up with the demon's speed. All he could do was freeze in place, just like the world around him, petrified by the fear and ferocity in Mahway's golden eyes.

THUD!

Before the attack could land, Gregory tackled Mahway to the ground, the two laying in a mess of feathers and limbs. The Pilgrim's armor was nowhere to be seen; his heavy jacket left behind for the sake of celerity. "C'mon, we talked about the shredding people thing already!" Gregory said. Mahway struggled against the Pilgrim's hold, clearly weakened by the loss of Guardian. Despite his pained winces, Gregory gave the demon a look of sympathy. "I didn't want it to come to this, kid. I swear. I honestly didn't want to see you locked up."

In an almost imperceptible moment, Mahway froze at Gregory's words. His fear and anger reached a climax, and he pushed off the ground with hysterical strength, knocking Gregory back. Like before, he rebounded off the wall, his wings blowing dust into Enoch's face before he skidded to a stop behind Gregory. The Pilgrim had no time to react as Mahway grabbed him, digging his claws into the man's now defenseless chest.

Gregory let out a scream of pain that sent chills down Enoch's spine. Or perhaps, the chills were caused by the sight of Mahway spreading his wings once more, lifting Gregory into the air. Horrified, Enoch rushed forward, too slow to grab hold before Mahway lifted the Pilgrim above the rooftops. All Enoch could do was stare, watching them ascend higher and higher until there was no way Gregory could survive the drop.

Faced with such an uncommon disaster, Enoch's mind offered no shortage of illogical plans. *Can I catch him!? Or throw something? Or... Or maybe I could...*

"Cough Cough" The Scribe's gaze had been locked on the scene above him, but he now turned to face the rubble. *She's alive!* He realized. Enoch sent one final, guilt-filled glance to Gregory and Mahway, noticing another disaster teetering atop the crumbled wall.

A large brick that had managed to hold out after Guardian's attack was now on the brink of falling, the unconscious woman its unfortunate target below. Enoch rushed over, attempting to push the rubble off of her. However, his years of library work had done little to help his strength, and the mess of bricks and beams proved too heavy for him. Instead, he grabbed a plank of wood from the edge of the pile, pushing it beneath the beam supporting the rest of the debris.

"C'mon, c'mon, c'mon!" Using the plank as a lever, he managed to tilt the beam enough to send the bricks above rolling down the pile, away from the two of them. Having lessened the weight, he carefully pulled the woman out, propping her up on his shoulder once they were far enough away from the wreckage. Heat was radiating off her body. Now that he was close, he noticed beads of sweat on her face. The sun had nearly set, the alley cold enough to cause Enoch to shiver. So, why was she overheating?

The teetering brick finally joined the others, breaking the beam Enoch had lifted moments before with an unsettling *CRUNCH!* Enoch jumped somewhat at the impact, looking up to the rooftop once more. When he did, he noticed just how high Mahway had lifted Gregory. The two were little more than specks, barely visible against the darkening twilight sky. Enoch sighed in frustration. "Damn it!" he cried, carrying the woman down the alley. There was nothing he could do, and if he wasted too much time then they'd be next.

"I'm sorry, Gregory."

Chapter 10

THERE'S AN indescribable beauty to the colors of a sunset. The gradual contrast of the darkened night sky with the fading radiance of the sun. A meeting of two worlds. Light and dark; dreams and consciousness; the ethereal sky above and the immovable land below. In Terrael, sunrise and sunset were sacred times. The moment where the lingering souls of the Celestials Adoil and Archas were closest, both sun and moon visible in the heavens.

Gregory's experience with sunsets was bittersweet, yet he could never deny their magical allure. Even fighting for his life felt all the more charming when faced with the elegant flare on the horizon, warming the capital below with its lingering light, like a final kiss goodbye. He just wished he could give the breathtaking view the attention it deserved. Unfortunately, he was preoccupied with the claws digging into his chest.

He struggled against Mahway's grip, the demon continuing to lift him high above the city. High enough that pleas for help would go unheard. Far enough from the Holy Wall that no Priests would see the man in peril against the darkening sky. Gregory could see a small crowd forming in the outer city streets below, likely lured by the sound of Guardian smashing the wall.

Hopefully none of them look up.

Calming his movements, Gregory did his best to look to Mahway, the movement difficult as his back was held tightly against the demon. Or, as close as it could get, at least. "C'mon Mahway, talking is still an option," he said calmly. Hearing his words, the strength of Mahway's flapping wings lessened, maintaining the height they had reached; not that a few more feet would matter as high up as they were.

"Stop lying!" Mahway growled. "Demons. Humans. All you do is trap and hurt." Gregory held back a cry of pain as Mahway moved his claws, tearing through the Pilgrim's shirt. The size of the wounds in his chest were growing more concerning and painful by the second. Gregory couldn't afford to let Mahway slice any further. He'd rather not deal with the consequences. Mahway didn't seem to care though, the claws digging so deep you'd think he was trying to break right through the man.

"*Agh!*" Gregory couldn't hold back the cry of pain this time, knowing that final movement had crossed the point of no return. He'd have to get out of this quickly. To his surprise, however, Mahway loosened his grip somewhat, his anger fading ever so slightly.

"Even up here... I'm alone," the demon whispered. Though Gregory felt that the words weren't directed at him, that didn't make them any less painful to hear. He hesitated for just a moment. *Almost wish he'd stayed angry,* he thought to himself, *would've made this next part hurt a little less.* Closing his eyes, he focused on the decorative bracelet hidden beneath the teal sleeve of his dress shirt. *Sorry kid.* He repeated this apology in his mind with a heavy heart. Though one would expect his heart to feel lighter, as the cool tone of his shirt began to shift to a crimson red around the tears in the fabric. Mahway's eyes went wide.

"Your blood..." he gasped. "Smells like mi–"

In his moment of distraction, Mahway was cut off by a sharp, digging pain in his side. He let out a cry, a small, steel dagger stuck in his skin where the man's hand had been a second ago. Shocked by the pain, he let go, sending Gregory plummeting towards the city streets.

Down in the alley, Enoch muttered an apology to the Pilgrim he'd had no choice but to abandon. With the unconscious woman propped up on his shoulder, he made his way towards the end of the alley. Now that the fight had died down, he could make out the sound of distant, panicked conversation. It seemed that the residents of the Hart District had finally noticed the commotion.

Would they have been able to help if they'd gotten here sooner? If I'd shouted a little louder... he wondered. *Or would they have been crushed by that monster too; splattered on the cobblestone, just like Gregory is going to be?*

Though he told himself not to, hoping to spare himself the guilt and trauma, he couldn't help but glance up one final time, just as Mahway let the Pilgrim go. Enoch's grip on the woman tightened, and he found himself unable to turn away. He knew he should, but perhaps he felt it a fitting punishment for getting the man involved in the first place. He'd saved Enoch's life; now, the memory of the fate that led him to would stay with him, whether he wanted it to or not.

As for Gregory, he cleared his mind, feeling the wind flow around him like a stone in a gentle river. The cool current danced across his skin, and he slowly moved his fingers through it, the sensation sending a comforting shiver through his body. His clothing and silver hair fluttered up behind him, and though he could see the ground approaching, all he could think in that moment was how beautiful the sunset was. From so high up, he could see the mountains to the north; the flat, shifting desert far in the south. Even the ring of ocean mists at the edge of the world gave the horizon an almost fuzzy appearance.

Behind him, the air began to shimmer and dim. A glittering starlight, like a paper burning away into embers. The fading sunlight, clinging to the final seconds of the day, began to reflect off of something behind him. The wind cleared the fog in his mind caused by the loss of blood, and he realized how close the ground truly was. Adjusting himself, the Pilgrim turned his attention to the approaching rooftops. *Just a few more seconds.*

As the city rushed up to greet him, the ember-like glimmer behind him gave one final, dazzling burst, revealing two beautiful, bright angel wings on the man's back. At the last possible moment, just before colliding with the rooftop, Gregory spread the wings, using the momentum to swerve through the chimneys in a graceful swoop. As he did, he noticed movement out of the corner of his eye. Below, in the alley that had nearly been the death of him, Gregory saw a young, familiar, awestruck Scribe staring back. Though the woman he was carrying was still unconscious, it seemed there had been a witness after all.

Enoch watched Gregory disappear behind the cover of the rooftops, a distant thud followed by footsteps proving that he'd landed safely. The young Scribe tried to make sense of what he'd just seen, before hearing the woman cough again. "Right," he said, returning to reality. "I need to get her somewhere safe first." His fear replaced with confusion and curiosity, Enoch glanced upward to the empty evening sky before finally leaving the alley.

It didn't take Enoch long to find help. Just as he'd thought, the sound of Guardian's destructive attack had attracted a group of curious bystanders. People ready to join the fight that was now over; people wondering what it was that had destroyed the back of their home; as well as a man looking for his wife, their young daughter close behind him, both rushing over in fear and relief at the sight of the woman. As they reached Enoch, the young girl took her mother's hand in hers. What followed was a long explanation from Enoch to the crowd as he described what had happened. The demon attack, the monstrous summon, the Pilgrim that had come to help before chasing the demon on foot. Admittedly, he still wasn't sure if Gregory's angelic form had been real or not. Until he knew more, he felt it best to keep that particular information close to his chest. If he shared it now, they'd no doubt think he was completely insane, and his story was far-fetched enough already.

The sight of the destruction, the answers he provided, as well as Enoch's disheveled appearance were enough to convince them he was telling the truth. Eventually, the interrogation ended and Enoch was able to leave behind the site of the attack. With Gregory's surprisingly heavy jacket draped over his arms, he began to wander back down the alley. Unfortunately, his bike had been a casualty in Guardian's attack, the twisted handlebar sticking out from within the pile of rubble. Enoch did his best to fight back tears at the sight of his trusty traveling companion. This time, there was no one there to fix it.

The outer city citizens were focused on the destruction Guardian had caused, but Enoch's focus led him elsewhere. He'd heard the distant sound of Gregory's landing, and though his rationality begged him to simply make his way back to his comfortable home, his feet continued forward towards the unknown. The feet themselves felt heavy. If Enoch stopped to rest, he was certain he wouldn't be able to continue again. To distract himself, and keep himself awake, he thought back to the woman's unusual fever.

Even if she wasn't a magic user, the amount of magic used in the fight shouldn't have been enough to cause symptoms of magical overflow. But, why else would she develop a fever so quickly? Was she just sick already? Enoch adjusted his hold on Gregory's jacket, surprised by how heavy it was. It was now quite clear that the gray embellishments were made of metal, explaining the armor from before. *Or was it Gregory? If I didn't imagine those wings, maybe it was because he's an angel? Or, scary as it'd be, maybe that demon was strong enough that she was affected that badly just from the magic leaking from his summon.*

Enoch sighed, shaking his head. Though it was a curious topic, he'd have to solve that mystery later. It had been a while since he'd heard Gregory's landing, but if the Pilgrim hadn't left, Enoch was certain he'd reached the location of the earlier distant thud.

"Gregory?" he called out. He checked every nook and cranny, even using his foot to dig through the bags of garbage at the side of the alley. He'd managed to wash his hands off with some water, but he'd laid in a pile of it long enough before that the smell no longer bothered him. Just as he decided to give up the search, he heard a rustling above him. The initial relief he felt at possibly finding

Gregory was cast aside by the invasive realization that the sound could be Mahway back for revenge. Just in case, he picked up a broken rolling pin from the trash, holding it in front of him.

"If you're the demon from before, you better stay back! Or I'll, uh..." He thought back to the strength of Mahway's tackle, the Scribe's ready stance losing some of its vigor. "Okay, I'll admit this probably won't do much, but still!"

With far less grace than his earlier recovery, Gregory landed in front of him. Enoch jumped back, feeling his heart leap into his throat. Though he couldn't make out many details in the dark of the alley, even without light he could see the very real wings folded against Gregory's back. While part of him was glad he hadn't lost his mind and imagined them, the dizzying number of questions running through his brain almost made him wish he had.

Swaying on his feet, Gregory began to fall to the side. Enoch tossed the rolling pin away, rushing forward to steady him. The angel's chest felt wet and hot to the touch. Enoch's stomach churned at the painfully familiar smell. The torn fabric clung to the Scribe's fingers as he adjusted his grip, not wanting to cause the Pilgrim more pain. *No wonder he can barely stand!* Slowly, Gregory looked over to Enoch's tossed aside weapon.

"A rolling pin, huh? Guess you didn't... grab my sword too then..." Gregory tried to gesture to his jacket, still draped over Enoch's arm. Instead, he lost his balance once more. Enoch held him tighter, the events of the day and the shaking of his arms making him wonder if he should start to train again.

"You've lost a lot of blood. We need to—" Enoch's legs buckled somewhat as Gregory grew heavier. Both of them dropped to their knees, the Pilgrim's strength beginning to fade. "We need to get you to a House of Healing."

"No!" With a rush of panicked energy, Gregory gripped Enoch's shirt, weakly turning his head to make eye contact. "No Church..." The man's other knee finally reached its limit. Enoch's own fatigued muscles barely kept Gregory from falling to the ground completely. The Pilgrim's words drifted off along with his consciousness. "They can't... Church can't see... me... like this."

As Gregory's eyes slowly shut, Enoch lightly squeezed his shoulders, desperate for a reaction. "Gregory?" he asked, stomach knotting as the angel replied with only faint, struggling breaths. Gently, he lowered the man onto the cobblestone. With no hesitation, he reached into his bag, pulling out a hot water bottle and cloth to clean the wound. He needed to work quickly if he wanted to slow the bleeding, and so he found himself working in a focused panic, oblivious to Death's gaze, drawn to the night-chilled alley.

Enoch had spent much of his life haunted by death; the ghosts of his past, and the phantoms of the future. Gregory's life wasn't the first he'd held in his hands, and it was far from the last. But as he watched that life in particular begin to fade, he made a decision.

He didn't need any more ghosts.

Chapter 11

IN A WORLD filled with chaos and uncertainty, some can find serenity in allowing the threads of fate to ensnare them; accepting the knots that bind them to their destiny. But as the angel's bloodstained thread began to fray, Enoch wondered if he could possibly mend it. The thought filled him with an unfamiliar adrenaline. He'd been numb for so long that even the small curiosity felt as though it could tear through his entire body. If he was cursed to see the threads of fate, then perhaps he could weave a new future into destiny's web. Perhaps he could save him.

After all, at that moment he was the only one that could even try.

The sun had set. Enoch could barely make out the bandages he'd wrapped around the man's chest. With the severity of the wound, they were as effective as a bucket collecting a rainstorm, but at least they would buy him some time. Hopefully they'd keep the rest of Gregory's blood where it was meant to be for now. At least until he could figure out what to do next.

Enoch placed what was left of his medical supplies back into his bag. *The smart thing to do would be to bring Gregory to a House of Healing,* he thought to himself. *My limited medical training isn't enough to save him. He needs a Healer, not me.* It was long past curfew now, but perhaps helping a Pilgrim would be an adequate excuse... He shook his head, the man's words echoing in his mind.

"They can't... Church can't see... me... like this..."

The Scribe's jaw began to hurt as he clenched it in frustration. *He just had to make things complicated.* With a sigh, Enoch relaxed, his determination growing. "You better not die on me, Gregory," he warned. "I have enough on my conscience already."

"Azazel."

"Huh!?" Enoch had been working in a tunnel-visioned silence for so long that the sudden response caused him to jump. He leaned away from the man he'd thought had been unconscious, just as Gregory managed to get his eyes open, a weak smile forced onto the angel's face.

"My real name is Azazel," Gregory, or rather, Azazel replied. "You've seen the wings, so you might as well know."

Having never interacted with an angel before, as was the case with most people in the human realm, Enoch wasn't sure how to react to that. All he could manage was a confused stare in response, a weak "Azazel, huh?" managing to push through the stupor. A quiet voice in his mind nagged at him. *Why does that name seem familiar?* he wondered. But, as he often did with perturbing thoughts and questions, he pushed aside the inquiry. Now that Azazel was awake, there were more important things to take care of.

"Well, Azazel," he said, grabbing his bag and the man's jacket. "I um... I patched you up best I could, but your wounds still need to be stitched up. If we can't go to the Church, is there anywhere else I can bring you?"

Azazel tried to sit himself up, wincing somewhat from the effort. Enoch's hands rushed forward, grabbing the man's shoulder to support him. His back would no doubt be a better bracing point, but the young Scribe wasn't sure if it would be rude to touch his wings without permission. Azazel weakly lifted an arm, pointing up to the night sky. "Not unless you can help me fly up north," he replied.

"Fly?" Enoch glanced at Azazel's wings. "Oh uh... right. That's a no then. But what about the inn you're staying at? Or a doctor in the area?"

"What about you?"

The Pilgrim said the words with such a matter-of-fact tone that they managed to catch Enoch off guard. After the day he'd had, Enoch hadn't thought that was possible anymore. "Me?" he asked. Azazel nodded.

"Yeah. You clearly have some medical training. And since I'm not technically supposed to be here, I'd rather not risk any other humans seeing me like this if I can help it."

"I... I don't think I could." Reflexively, Enoch sought comfort in his bracelet, finding only his bare wrist instead. The hesitation he was feeling blended with a sudden sense of vulnerability. Before this could escalate to a state of panic, a gentle touch brought him back to the present. Looking down, he saw Azazel's hand resting on his own. The angel gave him a reassuring smile.

"And I think you're selling yourself short," he argued. "But I also don't want to force you. It's your choice."

The following silence felt heavy despite Azazel removing the weight of his hand from Enoch's. The Scribe took a moment. His neutral expression hid the conflict in his mind. At the end of his internal battle, he held out his hand to the injured angel, compassion victorious against his self-doubt and fear. "Alright. But I don't have the supplies here. Can you walk?"

"No idea. Where do you have in mind?" With more effort than ideal, Azazel managed to take the offered hand. Enoch helped the man to his feet, supporting someone on his shoulder for the second time that evening. His legs groaned in protest, but he pushed through it, turning to face the inner city.

"I'm gonna take you up on that offer to walk me home."

Though there were far fewer Priests patrolling the streets in the outer city, the duo stuck to the alleys. Azazel's injuries considerably slowed their progress. On the bright side, this allowed Enoch to step carefully, feeling the jagged cobblestone with his feet to avoid tripping. Unfortunately, it also meant that the Pilgrim leaning over his shoulder felt heavier and heavier as the small, miraculous spark of strength Azazel had found faded with each sluggish step. Their breathing cut through the hushed surroundings, the only sign that Azazel was still alive. That is, until the angel let out a small chuckle, followed by a pained wince.

"This is pretty embarrassing actually," he said, the whisper shattering the silence. "I'm usually better in a fight than that, I swear."

"I can't judge. I just froze up for most of it." The guilt tied Enoch's stomach in knots. He couldn't help but wonder, *if I'd been faster, if I'd helped him in the fight, would things have gone differently? Would I still be carrying a dying man in the middle of the night?*

"That was probably your first time seeing a demon, right?" Azazel replied. "Of course you'd freeze up."

The knots tightened. Though he could barely see it, Enoch's gaze remained glued to the ground. *Right... I was frozen in fear at just the sight of the demon. It's stupid to think that I, of all people, would've been able to do anything to help... Saving people is hardly my strong suit, after all.*

"And what about your family?" Azazel asked. The question nearly caused Enoch to trip, wondering if the angel had somehow peered into his mind.

"What?" he asked in a panic.

"We're heading to your home, right? Won't they be worried to hear you get back so late after curfew?"

It took a moment for Enoch to recollect his tumbling thoughts. That's all the angel had meant? After a deep breath, Enoch shook his head. "I live alone," he replied. "The only people that might notice are my landlords Noah and Nammah, since they live one floor down." The Scribe shrugged with his free shoulder, the movement already feeling stiff from fatigue. "But if we're quiet, they'll probably just assume I came back in the morning after sleeping at the cathedral."

"I see." Azazel nodded; his subtle frown hidden by the alley shadows. "A bit of a workaholic then, huh?"

"Not really," Enoch argued. "I just lose track of time. And it's easier to sleep at a library desk than it is to ask a Priest for an escort home."

The light of a streetlamp leaked into the alley as it connected to a proper street. Carefully, Enoch glanced around the corner. Not a single soul could be seen. As they crossed the street as swiftly as Azazel's injuries allowed, the angel gave it a passing glance as well. "Right, well... at least there's not many Priests this side of the wall. Should help us avoid an unwanted escort tonight."

Hearing the angel's words, Enoch turned towards their current goal. Above the crooked rooftops, the Holy Wall towered over them, the torches lining the top giving the stone an orange, fiery glow. Even from the alley, Enoch could see the distant silhouettes of the Priests patrolling overhead.

"Yeah, but it's the wall itself I'm worried about."

Chapter 12

AZAZEL'S FOOT sent the gutter water splashing onto the cobblestone. Nearby, a cat quickly jumped out of the way, offended by the soggy interruption to its nap. Though far from the puddle, Enoch's brow was equally damp, sweat beginning to form as they finally reached the base of the Holy Wall. Or, an alley next to it at least. Faced with the immense challenge of getting to the other side, Enoch realized just how towering the wall truly was.

Gently, he helped Azazel to the closest building, leaning the man against it. Now that they were closer to the lights illuminating the Holy Wall, he noticed the angel covering his chest. His hand did little to hide the red stain soaking through the bandages. The Pilgrim's silver hair clung to his face. The sweat on his skin almost sparkled in the dim light. Azazel may have been putting on a brave face, but they were clearly running out of time.

His motivation rekindled, Enoch moved to the edge of the alley, peeking around the corner. A fair distance away, he could make out the archway he and Azazel had passed through the day before. Now that cheerful, yet somewhat awkward walk felt like a different life. Though most of the bridge beneath the arch was hidden behind the stone, he could still make out several Priests standing guard. If there were that many at the edge of the arch, he shuddered at the thought of how many were likely still hidden from view.

"There's so many!" he whispered. Next to him, Azazel moved his shoulder in what Enoch could only assume was his attempt at a shrug.

"Makes sense. They don't want the criminals and riff raff of the outer city sneaking into the Church-run areas at night."

Nodding in agreement, Enoch frowned, holding his chin as he began to think. He'd been so focused on getting to the wall that he hadn't considered how they would get past it once they did. *It's only a matter of time before Greg- I mean, Azazel loses consciousness again, so we have to be quick,* he thought. *But Azazel also can't move quickly, so sneaking by or distracting the guards would probably get both of us caught.* The Scribe looked further down the wall, judging the distance to the next bridge before shaking his head. *Even if we try a different arch, there's probably just as many Priests stationed at each one!*

No matter how hard he thought, he couldn't think of a single plan that wouldn't end in disaster. "I'm sorry, Azazel," he said, nails digging into his palm. "I thought I could do this, but–"

"Hey. No need to give up yet!" Azazel smiled warmly. "I'm sure we can think of something." Despite the pale shade of the angel's face dampening the effect of the smile, Enoch's expression did soften at the reassurance.

"I doubt it. But the optimism is appreciated."

"I've been told it's one of my best features!" With his free hand, Azazel gave a shaky thumbs up. "But either way, the Priests are staying over there for now, so we have time to thi–"

CRASH!

There are times in a person's life where the world simply decides to make things as difficult as possible. Perhaps it's divine punishment. Perhaps it's poor luck. Or in the case of Enoch and Azazel, perhaps it's simply a cat seeking revenge for a rudely interrupted nap.

The neatly stacked paint cans sitting by a half-painted alley wall fell to the ground with a clatter and crash! Enoch and Azazel jumped, turning to see the fleeing feline that had shattered their small glimmer of hope. After exchanging a worried glance, they turned back towards the Holy Wall. Two Priests were now approaching, sabers at the ready.

"Neeevermind," Azazel said. Enoch propped him up on his shoulder once more.

"Let's head back. We can circle around to another alley." Far faster than the comfortable pace they had taken up to this point, they rushed back down the alley. At the half-way point, they skidded to a stop, seeing the faint glow of a lantern approaching around the far corner. Two voices accompanied the light.

"Came from over here, I think."

"Could be the kids that vandalized St. Owena."

With both escape routes cut off, Azazel and Enoch stood frozen in the center of the alley. Enoch's eyes darted about, searching for an exit. Azazel's expression was calm and determined.

"You hide, I'll distract them," he said sternly. "You shouldn't get a criminal record for my sake."

Though Enoch did appreciate the sentiment, he nodded towards the angel's wings. "I thought the Church couldn't see you," he asked. Azazel paused in realization.

"Right." He glanced down at his bandages. "The whole not letting them know angels walk among them thing. I think the blood loss may be getting to me."

Two Priest-shaped shadows appeared in the light ahead of them, the bodies casting them still hidden around the corner. Enoch begged his brain to focus. *Think! Think! What can I do? We're gonna be caught! I'll be arrested for breaking curfew! I'll lose my home, my job! Cyrus won't ever speak to me again! Not to mention the fact that Azazel will be discovered, which he seems to be willing to die to avoid.*

The angelic Pilgrim glanced down, noticing Enoch's pale, panicked expression out of the corner of his eye. "Where do you live?" he asked.

"Huh?"

"Your home, where is it?"

The unexpected question seemed to ground Enoch to an extent, breaking through the rush of thoughts in the boy's mind. "The, uh... The Waterside District," he replied. Azazel nodded in response; his lips pursed somewhat as he did some calculations.

"Yeah, that should be doable," he said with a nod. "Probably." With a smile, he turned to Enoch, giving the Scribe's shoulder a reassuring squeeze. "Alright, I have a way to get past them."

In an instant, the color returned to Enoch's face. "You do?" he asked excitedly. "What do you need me to do?"

"Hold on tight and don't scream."

The angel gritted his teeth as he lifted Enoch in his arms, supporting the Scribe's legs and back. Before Enoch had even taken a breath to protest, Azazel spread his wings. Fully open, they nearly filled the width of the alley. The knocked over paint cans rolled across the stone from the force of the wind as Azazel took off into the air. The two groups of Priests turned the corner, finding only a cat settling down to resume its nap.

Far above this, several Priests leaned casually on the edge of the Holy Wall's peak, no doubt discussing the strangely personal topics that only surface in the late hours of the night, when the guarded walls of one's mind decide to slumber. It would seem that their eyes had decided to rest as well, as none of them noticed the source of the sudden breeze that passed them by. Nor did they notice the angel that appeared far above them shortly after, the distant white wings lost amidst the drifting clouds.

Enoch, however, was well aware of the angel and his wings, as they were the only thing keeping him from a sudden, painful and brief encounter with the city below him. He gripped Azazel's arms tightly, his eyes glued shut.

"Aaaand we're over!" Azazel said cheerfully, leaving the Holy Wall behind them. "How're you doing?"

"T-Terrified! But you said I couldn't scream!"

The angel chuckled. "Fair enough! Don't worry, I won't drop you!" Azazel's tone softened somewhat. It had been some time since he'd flown with a passenger. It admittedly hurt more than he remembered, but he'd just have to tough it out. "You should open your eyes and take in the view! The city is beautiful tonight."

There was a moment of hesitation as Enoch wondered if he could bring himself to do it. Part of him worried that seeing how high up they were would end with him passing out in fear. But the comforting warmth of the angel's voice seemed to guide him out of this uncertainty. Slowly, Enoch opened one eye. In an instant, his tense, worried expression softened into awe.

Beneath them, the city glowed like molten gold. The haphazard hills and streets that had grown so dull and familiar over the years were nearly unrecognizable from above. So beautiful. So small. So quiet and peaceful from this far up in the air. Even as high up as they were, the Grand Cathedral spires still reached further, beyond the reach of the warm, candescent streetlights. Instead, the pale stone reflected the moonlight, blending with the thin clouds drifting lazily past the stars.

The sight took Enoch's breath away. He wondered if this was how it felt to dream. A weightless, otherworldly wonder bringing both a hopeful warmth and chilling awe. In that moment, all his fears, anxieties; the weight of the world, it felt so trivial. He was so caught up in the moment, that he nearly didn't hear his own voice as he softly whispered "It's beautiful".

Azazel smiled, simply watching Enoch as the Scribe continued to stare in wonderment. "See!" he said. "What did I– *ack!*"

With a sudden wince, Azazel's graceful glide wavered. The two lost some altitude. Enoch's tight grip returned as he turned his attention to the angel.

"Are you okay?"

"J-Just a few broken ribs! I still got you though! Don't worry!" Another drop challenged the man's words. "Okay, m-maybe worry a little." Being held against the angel's chest, Enoch could see Azazel's bandages growing redder by the second. Their flight grew turbulent. Azazel did his best to stay conscious, gliding closer and closer to the ground.

His heart racing, Enoch looked beneath them. He could make out Lamechson's a few streets away, as well as the patrolling Priests nearly close enough to notice them.

As the angel reached the limits of his strengths, he managed to find a place to land. Or, perhaps their sudden impact with the trees in the local park would be better described as a crash. Branches and leaves snapped and broke, cushioning the fall somewhat despite hurting them in other ways. But at the very least, the duo was still alive as they landed in a heap at the base of the trunk. Enoch groaned, untangling himself from yet another crash.

"Ow..." Once he regained his composure, Enoch quickly turned to Azazel, the angel's clothes and hair covered in broken leaves and bark. "Azazel!" he called out before covering his mouth, realizing there could be Priests nearby. Crouching down, he noticed the bloodstained bandages beginning to drip. Despite his clear fatigue and pain, Azazel forced a smile.

"I did my part!" he said weakly. "Don't let me down... tough guy..."

With Enoch knelt beside him, Azazel finally allowed himself the respite of sleep. The brief dream Enoch had experienced in the sky was once again a nightmare, and Enoch wished desperately that he could simply wake up.

Chapter 13

FOR THE SECOND night in a row, Enoch trudged past the front of Lamechson's late into the evening. Unlike before, there was no one waiting to meet him. Noah and Cyrus had likely gone to sleep hours ago. Enoch was grateful for this small stroke of luck. After all, how would he explain carrying a half-dead angel up the stairs to his apartment? How would they react to seeing him lay the bleeding man on his bed? How would he explain the drops of blood on his floor, his sheets, on his face as he moved his hair out his eyes, fully focused on stitching up the man's wounds?

The entire series of events blurred together. It felt as if Enoch was viewing his actions from the back of his mind. Looking through a window as his body worked on its own. He was fully aware of what he was doing, but thankfully not in control. If he had been, he was certain he wouldn't have been able to stomach it. By the time he slowly came back to his senses, he found himself by the sink in the bathroom, Azazel's jacket in his hands.

He'd collected all of the angel's belongings together. A key and Pilgrim license from his jacket, a red stained cravat, as well as a torn, blood-soaked paper that had been tucked into an inner chest pocket of his shirt. Now, he scrubbed at the jacket, trying to wash out the red that had dyed the yellow fabric. He had no clue how long he'd been scrubbing, but after a while he slowed to a stop, staring at the blood on his hands. Letting go of the jacket, he lifted them up. His neutral expression slowly twisted, lips curling into a slight, terrified smile.

"Huh... they won't stop shaking..."

The room around him seemed to darken, focusing in on the blood covered hands. He frantically scrubbed at the skin, tears forming in his eyes. As he did, the memories of earlier events assaulted his vision. The sharpness of Mahway's claws; Guardian's terrifying glowing red eyes; Azazel's torn and bloody chest. The weight of these memories broke through the dam in his mind, the panic and adrenaline causing others to cascade into his consciousness. A street filled with bloodied corpses. Reddened puddles rippling like the water in his sink. A wooden door torn to shreds with claw marks uncomfortably similar to those he had patched up moments before. A blood-stained hand, laying limp against a familiar floor.

As if trying to escape his own mind, Enoch pulled away from the sink, his back hitting the wall with a heavy thud. He slowly slid down, hugging his shoulders as he tried to calm his panic. Unlike before, there was no one coming to help him. The sink continued to run. The tears continued to fall. His hands continued to shake. All he could do was sit on the floor, alone with the pain and trauma, too afraid to allow himself to faint and escape it all.

Chapter 14

THE CURTAINS WAFTED in the morning breeze, light and carefree, oblivious to the events of the night before. Though the wooden shutters were closed, beams of sunlight still found their way through the cracks, painting stripes across the bed sheets, as well as the angel sleeping beneath them. As the light reached his face, Azazel's eyes twitched. Pain radiated through every part of his body. For a moment he considered simply drifting back to sleep. Just for a moment, before he realized this wasn't his room at the Ivory Inn.

In a state of confusion one can only feel when caught between sleep and consciousness, he took in his surroundings. His shirt and jacket were gone, replaced with fresh, clean bandages. Thankfully, it seemed the jacket hadn't made it too far. The garment, still torn from the fight but no longer covered in crimson stains, was hanging above the kitchen sink a short distance from the foot of the bed. The curtain rod supporting it curved under its weight. A light repetitive dripping sound was enough to tell him it hadn't been hanging there for long.

Ironically, a rich and delicious smell drew his attention *away* from the kitchen. On the desk next to him, he noticed a plate of cookies. The plate itself didn't seem to match the ones neatly stacked on the counter, but Azazel didn't give that much thought. All he could think of was how the aroma caused his mouth to water. Before he could succumb to his impulses, he froze, noticing Enoch sitting across the room. In an instant, he realized where he was.

Enoch, on the other hand, had yet to notice the angel had woken up. Currently he was sitting at the table, his tired eyes focused entirely on the needle and thread in his hands. With his bed taken, he'd decided to use the time to patch up the pantleg he'd torn when his bike broke. He pulled the stitch tight, caught in a trance as he'd nearly repaired the entire tear. Azazel let out a sigh, lowering his head back onto the pillow with an amused smirk. "Did you steal my shirt?"

Enoch looked up in surprise, stabbing his finger with the needle as his trance was broken. "*Ack!*" Pulling back his hand, he tried to wave away the pain, glaring at the pants. With a betrayed sigh, he set them aside, walking over to Azazel. "Please don't make it weird. I had to take it off to treat your wounds. It was too torn to repair anyways." Once he was closer, Enoch pulled out the seat at his desk, sitting down next to the angel. He couldn't help but glance at Azazel's wings. Noticing this, the angel smiled.

"They're soft, if you wanna touch 'em."

"N-No thanks!" Enoch tensed, turning to face the desk. Azazel let out a chuckle at the response, quickly regretting it as his wounds protested the movement.

"Alright, your loss!" he replied after recovering. A long, somewhat awkward silence followed the exchange, neither sure of how to start the conversation after everything that had happened. Far more subtle than before, Enoch watched the angel. Azazel was still taking in the room, currently focused on the curtains with a slightly distant stare. Realizing he'd likely have to be the first to speak, Enoch nervously tapped his legs with his palms.

"So, uh... how're you feeling?" he finally asked. It was hardly the first question on his mind, but it felt appropriate.

"Like your definition of fine," Azazel replied, staring up at the ceiling. He smiled wryly before turning back to Enoch. The playfulness lessened, replaced by warm-hearted gratitude. "But I'm alive, and I have you to thank for that."

"Right..." Enoch glanced away once more. For some reason, the gratitude felt almost uncomfortable. Azazel raised an eyebrow.

"And what about you?" he asked. "You seem to be handling all this surprisingly well." Enoch shook his head, forcing a smile at the angel's comment.

"Not nearly as well as you think."

Hearing this, a sympathetic sadness snuck into the angel's smile. He began to sit himself up. "Well, that's— *ow!*" He winced, body freezing up in pain. Unfortunately, he'd already committed to the movement, pushing through the discomfort until he was sitting against the headrest. Once he'd recovered, he began counting on his fingers as if nothing had happened. "That's to be expected. You were attacked by a demon, encountered an incredibly handsome angel, and then had to save said angel's attractive butt, all within a few hours!" He carefully shrugged, not wanting to hurt himself again. "I'd say you've earned the right to freak out a little."

All Enoch could do was smile softly, unable to agree or disagree with the angel's words. With no response, Azazel furrowed his brow, thinking back to the incident. "I was actually pretty surprised to see you were the one I heard call for help though," he continued. "I didn't expect to run into you again after the book delivery." The Pilgrim sighed, smiling wistfully. "I'm happy I did though! Whatever your reasons were, it seems we were fated to meet again!"

At the mention of fate and motivations, Enoch's eyes went wide. In all the chaos, he'd nearly forgotten his reason for going there in the first place! "Oh right!" he exclaimed. "Actually, I was there to find you!"

"Really?" Azazel raised an eyebrow, sending a flirtatious smile Enoch's way. "Did I win you over with my charms during the book delivery?"

"Uh, no." The flirtatious smile vanished as quickly as it had appeared. Azazel's posture deflated at the blunt rejection. Enoch, on the other hand, simply rubbed the wrist where his bracelet had been, oblivious to the effect of his words. "I..." He hesitated. He knew he'd decided to warn Azazel, but he couldn't help but have reservations about sharing how he'd gained the knowledge in the first place. *How would he react if he knew?* Enoch wondered. *Can I trust him?* The angel looked over, an innocent curiosity building in the silence. With a sigh, Enoch made his decision. Azazel had trusted him, so he might as well do the same in return. "It's actually because I'm a Seer."

In the short silence that followed, Enoch could swear he heard the gears in Azazel's mind turning, processing the information just given to him. After a moment, a spark of excitement filled his eyes as he put two and two together. "Wait! You're a Seer!?" Before Enoch even had a chance to reply, Azazel lightly smacked his own forehead, amused by the realization. "Of course!" he exclaimed. "So, that's why you needed the bracelet without an ability! Y'know,

I probably should've realized sooner!" He turned back to Enoch, smiling like a kid at the Winter's End Festival. "This is so exciting! It's been so long since I've run into a Seer! What form do your visions take? How long have you had them? What's–"

Enoch held his hands up. "J-Just hold on a sec!" he sputtered. His face flushed red. It turned out telling him was a mistake after all, but not for any of the reasons Enoch had expected. Thankfully, Azazel nodded, clearly having to make an effort to hold himself back. Enoch let out an irritated sigh. "Seriously, you'll tear the stitches if you get all worked up like that." The Scribe leaned on his desk with a more somber expression. "I don't really use my ability if I can help it, but... I had a vision about you being attacked, so I was on my way to warn you."

Concern snuffed out Azazel's excitement. He thought back to the fight with Mahway. Enoch had shouted something at him during the encounter, but he hadn't given it much thought at the time. "I see," he replied. "So that's why you were shouting about people in masks?"

"Yeah. But before I say more, I have some questions of my own." Enoch crossed his arms as he leaned back in his seat. They'd been talking for a while now, so it was about time he got some answers. "I'll tell you everything I saw, but I think it's only fair you explain your, uh..." Unsure of how to phrase his words, he gestured to Azazel's wings. "Well... all this. If that sounds fair?"

It was hard to read the angel's expression as he considered the offer. After nearly a full minute, he let out a sigh. "Can't say I like the idea of agreeing without knowing what you're gonna ask, but I guess that I owe you that much after how much trouble I've put you through to keep my secret." Carefully, he folded his hands on his lap, resting his head against the wall. "But there are certain things I'm not allowed to talk about, even if I do owe you for patching me up."

"Yeah, that makes sense." Enoch leaned forward, resting his elbows on his knees. No one had seen an angel in hundreds of years. He wasn't dumb enough to think someone from Spira would share their secrets like an open book. In fact, if it hadn't been for Azazel's friendly nature, he likely wouldn't have been bold enough to ask in the first place. After all, Enoch was only a human. Even if Azazel was clearly mortal enough to bleed, his very nature meant he was far more important than Enoch could ever dream of being. If the Pilgrim was willing to share even a shred of information, that was good enough for him. "Well, I guess I'll go first then," he began. "In the vision–"

Grrrrrrrrgle.

Just as Enoch began, the sound of Azazel's stomach rumbling filled the apartment. The duo shared a moment of surprise, the sound shattering the serious atmosphere. Enoch's shoulders slumped at the organ's unfortunate timing. "Right..." he said, "I guess I forgot about breakfast. Do angels eat eggs?"

Azazel smiled, nodding with flushed cheeks. "Eggs sound wonderful, yeah."

Chapter 15

Ssssssssssssssssssss!

A satisfying sizzling filled the room as the eggs hit the pan. They mixed with the savory juices of the sliced ham already frying next to them. Enoch sprinkled in some spices, adding to the delicious aroma drifting throughout the apartment. As he stared from the bed, Azazel could feel himself drooling. He watched Enoch cook with pleasant interest.

"That smells good!" he complimented. "Certainly smells like you know what you're doing." He watched Enoch grab a clean cutting board and knife, moving from the stove to the counter with a confident familiarity.

"Well, I've lived on my own for a while, so knowing some basic recipes is pretty important." Enoch kept his back turned to Azazel, grateful the angel couldn't see him blushing. *He doesn't need to know I can only cook one or two dishes,* he thought. After all, why would he risk failing to cook something fancy when he could afford to just buy a dish made by someone that knew what they were doing?

Oblivious to the Scribe's embarrassment, Azazel's expression softened, a hint of sadness in his eyes. "I see... That sounds pretty lonely."

"Yeah, I guess so..." Enoch replied. He grabbed some apples from a basket on the counter, moving them to the cutting board. "But it's also a lot simpler to be on your own."

"Simpler isn't always better," Azazel argued. Without a word, Enoch began to slice the apples into wedges. Noticing the silence, Azazel shrugged, deciding to change the subject. "So, you were saying? Before my stomach so rudely interrupted."

The chopped apples slid from the cutting board onto an empty plate. Lowering the knife, Enoch turned to look at Azazel. "Right," he began. "I should probably explain how my visions work first. That way you have a bit more context. I get them at night, when I'm dreaming."

"Dreams, huh? So that's why the bracelet helped you sleep?"

The Scribe nodded before turning back to the cutting board. The second apple let out a crunch beneath the knife. Though he was focused on ensuring he kept all his fingers, Enoch couldn't help but feel his gaze drift to the patch of paler skin on his wrist, usually covered by his bracelet. "Yeah. It helped me avoid having them, but it expired the day I had the vision."

Azazel furrowed his brow, admittedly somewhat confused. "I see, kinda. But how do you tell the difference between your visions and normal dreams?"

With both apples sliced, Enoch returned to the frying pan. "It's actually pretty easy," he replied. "The visions always have three distinct traits." He lifted his free hand, raising a finger for each explanation. "First, they always start in darkness. I fall through it, like I'm sinking in a deep pool of water. And at the end, I always end up in what looks like a giant web." Carefully, he shifted the contents of the pan, watching steam and smoke rise into the air. "Second, unless I know them, the people in them will be silhouettes. Sometimes they'll have distinct shapes or clothing, but usually they're just walking shadows."

He lifted the pan for a moment, the sizzling of the food growing quieter from the sudden change of temperature. "But the biggest tell is that the visions are always completely silent. Even I don't make a sound as I walk through them. If the dream meets all three of those criteria, then it's a vision. Or, that's what I thought at least. In the vision I had about you, the silhouettes were strange." With an approving nod, Enoch slid the food onto the plates, happy that it seemed to have turned out alright.

"Oh? Strange how?" Though Azazel had leaned forward, eagerly absorbing every word with excited curiosity, he found himself distracted by the sight of Enoch plating the food. He was glad the Scribe was too far to hear his stomach rumble again as the younger man placed the pan on the cooler part of the stove.

Enoch grabbed a fire iron, opening the front of the stove. Inside, the fire flickered fiercely. "Like I said, the silhouettes are usually like walking shadows," he explained. "But this time, they were burning."

Instantly, shock and worry replaced Azazel's curiosity. "It isn't because they'll be set on fire, is it?" he asked in a panic. Enoch shook his head, using the iron to spread out the wood and ashes in the stove. With each poke, the blaze dulled.

"No, I don't think so. They didn't seem to notice the flames. It was more like they were made of them. I've never seen anything like it before." Once the flames were dull enough, Enoch covered them with a metal lid, using a thick glove to protect himself from the heat. It didn't take long to extinguish, and once it had he turned back to Azazel, tossing the glove back onto the counter. "Either way, that's the basics of how the visions work."

Azazel nodded several times, visibly relieved by Enoch's reply. "I think I got the gist of it. Darkness, silence, shadowy and sometimes fiery people." He watched Enoch carry over the plates, accepting his with a smile. "Thank you."

"No problem." Enoch sat at the desk once more, watching Azazel dig in. The angel shoved a forkful of egg into his mouth large enough to choke someone. Enoch raised an eyebrow in both judgment and a small amount of disbelief. Noticing this, his mouth still full of food, Azazel looked back in innocent confusion.

"Hm?"

"Nothing," Enoch replied. He casually turned back to his own food, hiding his slight smile with a bite of his own. Azazel shrugged off the exchange and went in for a second bite.

"Shothevish–" The angel covered his mouth, realizing just how full it still was. After swallowing, he gave Enoch an embarrassed smile. "Sorry, uh... The vision you were talking about. What happened in that one?"

Enoch scooped up some eggs onto his fork, thinking back to the vision that had started all of this in the first place. He carefully explained each detail to the angel. By the time he finished, the empty plates sat neatly stacked on the desk. They clattered slightly as Enoch leaned on the wooden surface, watching Azazel mull over the information. Having finished his late breakfast, the angel was now focused on the plate of cookies that had caught his attention before.

"So, the masked figure exploded after I attacked them?" he asked.

Enoch nodded, "That's what it looked like, yeah. Then colored patterns appeared all over my body."

Hearing this, Azazel's face darkened, the words extinguishing the light in his eyes. The change was so drastic that even Enoch couldn't help but notice. "Those patterns sound like late-stage symptoms of magical overflow," Azazel said. "Once they're there you're as good as dead." Noticing Enoch's concerned stare out of the corner of his eye, Azazel quickly recovered, forcing a soft smile onto his face like a mask. Though Enoch was curious, he decided to leave it be for now. He already had enough questions to ask.

"That's what I thought too," he replied, crossing his arms. "The explosion was probably the masked figure's final burst, but there's no way that alone would be enough to cause such severe symptoms."

"That isn't necessarily true," Azazel argued. Again, Enoch looked over in confusion at the angel's response. He watched Azazel lift a cookie off the plate. There were a few chocolate chips scattered throughout, but for the most part it felt almost depressingly bare. However, the angel didn't eat it, instead holding it out for Enoch to see. "A final burst is when a person releases all the leftover magic they have when they die, right?" the Pilgrim explained. "For a human with an average capacity, this amount is pretty low. At most, someone near the burst would get a fever if they stuck around awhile."

He replaced the first cookie with another. This one was more normal, the chocolate evenly spread. He held it up just like the first. "But for demons and magic users, the amount of magic released goes up. It doesn't take long for a person to start showing symptoms if exposed."

Gently tossing the second cookie aside, he picked up the bare cookie again, as well as one other. Through what Enoch could only imagine had been some kind of mishap with the batter, this final one was almost more chocolate than cookie. Azazel held the contrasting cookies close together. "And if a strong magic user dies with most of their magic, they could cause severe overflow symptoms in someone with a low enough tolerance." With far more flare than necessary, he lifted the chocolate filled cookie high. "So! If this burst immediately caused late-stage symptoms, it's safe to say our mysterious masked figure is either a demon, a strong magic user, or both!" The angel held his triumphant pose for a beat before shrinking into himself. He rubbed the back of his neck. "But I guess that doesn't really help narrow it down, huh?"

"Not really, no," Enoch replied. Now that he knew Azazel was an angel, the Pilgrim's carefree nature was even more surprising to him. He'd always assumed that the divine denizens of the heavens would be more stoic and proper. Perhaps even somewhat condescending. But Azazel's energy and optimism felt almost child-like at times. As if trying to further prove this, Azazel pouted, taking a disappointed bite out of the chocolate filled cookie. The sweet taste chased away his embarrassment, now replaced with joyful surprise.

"Oh hey! These are really good!" he exclaimed, turning to Enoch. The Scribe couldn't help but smirk.

"I told you, Lamechson's has the best cookies," he replied. "You should try them when they're fresh." As Azazel eagerly went for another, Enoch stood up, grabbing a textbook titled "The History of Terrael" off the shelf above his desk. It had been some time since he'd flipped through the pages. A few stuck together, the ink of his carefully written notes forming a makeshift glue after mixing with the pressure of being tucked onto the shelf for so long. Thankfully, the page he was looking for had been spared. Though, Enoch certainly wouldn't have minded if it hadn't.

"Back to the vision though," he continued. "You're probably right about the demon part." Enoch turned the book to Azazel. The page was discussing demon hierarchies, as well as known influential demons in the demon realm, Diapogeum. Azazel skimmed the page before realizing what Enoch was pointing at. A diagram labeled "Soldiers of Lilith lower rank mask". The drawing was quite impressive. Even in ink, it was clear that the mask was carved from some form of wood, designed to cover the wearer's eyes, while leaving their mouth exposed. The sides were carved into four simple horns, slightly curling around the face, and covering the knot of the string used to keep the accessory on. Despite what it symbolized, the mask was quite beautiful; almost elegant.

"Some demons wear masks to show their rank in a group or organization," Enoch explained. "The figure's mask was different in design, and I think it was made of metal, but it could be a similar situation."

Azazel nodded in return, gaze lifting from the book to look at Enoch. "You're right. I've heard the Soldiers of Lilith have been attacking cathedrals and Priests more often lately. Just small towns for the most part, but as a Pilgrim I was warned to keep an eye out during my travels."

Hearing this, Enoch returned the book to the shelf, using the movement to hide his face from Azazel. His tightened grip no doubt doomed several more pages to an unfortunate, adherent fate. "Right..." he replied. "Then, would you know anyone in that group?"

Much to Enoch's relief, Azazel shrugged and shook his head. "Not really, no. I try to avoid demons since they aren't exactly fans of people that work for the Church. Or angels, for that matter. Especially the demons in that group."

"True. Maybe you were going to end up befriending one?" Enoch suggested. "There's no way to know how far in the future the vision takes place after all. But I'm sure that with everything that's happened since, the vision probably isn't accurate anymore anyways." Regaining his composure, Enoch grabbed the two empty plates off the desk. He placed them on the counter, the sink still occupied by Azazel's drying jacket. Now that he was looking without panic and adrenaline clouding his vision, he realized the back was tailored to fit around the angel's wings. *I could've sworn Azazel's back was covered when he helped with the delivery,* he thought, letting out a sigh. The mysteries surrounding the man continued to pile up.

"Well, I've held up my end of the deal," Enoch said. "Now it's your turn. What's an angel doing in Terrael?"

"................"

When no response came, Enoch quickly turned around. Though he hadn't moved, Azazel's body was limp, his head hung low. Enoch felt a chill run down his spine. *Did he reopen his wounds? He seemed fine just a second ago! What—*

"Right!" Azazel suddenly jolted up with a disoriented look in his eyes. "My turn now? Right. Sorry. Ask away!"

The sudden shout had nearly sent Enoch's heart out his throat. Relief, disbelief and irritation flooded his mind, and he let out a long sigh. It seemed the man had just nodded off. "Actually, why don't you get some rest first."

The angel shook his head. "N-No! It's fine! That wouldn't be fair to you!"

Despite Azazel's arguing, Enoch walked over, moving the plate of cookies back onto the desk so that the angel could lay back down. "You can just tell me later instead. It's not like you can go anywhere right now anyways, right? There are too many people out. Not to mention your injuries." Moving over to the door, Enoch's hand drifted to his wrist. "I'll just go put in a request for a replacement bracelet, if they'll even let me get another. And I need to report the demon attack anyway." Enoch rubbed the back of his neck. "Of course, I'll have to figure out a way to report it that doesn't mention you being an angel."

Azazel stared at the Scribe, caught between embarrassment and gratitude. Unsure of which way to go, he simply lowered himself back onto the mattress, his cheeks turning red. "Right. Thanks. And sorry for the trouble."

"Well, you did save my life, so it's the least I can do. Plus, people learning that angels are hiding among us would probably turn into a whole thing, and I don't have the energy for that right now." Enoch grabbed his bag off the coat rack, heading over to the door. It felt strange to leave while someone was inside, but Azazel couldn't exactly cause much trouble without reopening his wounds. *It'll be fine, right?* He glanced over, realizing that the angel was already fast asleep. He had to admit, Azazel was nothing like the angels he'd read about in books.

For some strange reason though, he was most surprised to learn that angels ate cookies.

Chapter 16

COURCIEL, THE CAPITAL city of Terrael, stands in the middle of the world. It's said that if you look through the windows of the Grand Cathedral, you can see the entire human realm, from one side of the Ring Sea to the other. If that's true, then it would seem that no one happened to stop and enjoy the view that night. After all, if they had, they might have seen the young, injured demon fleeing the capital after dropping a Pilgrim to his death.

Mahway flew eastward, searching for some form of cover. The clusters of large rocks and hills scattered throughout the farmland had no shortage of places to hide. Exhausted and dizzy, Mahway collapsed to the ground. The surrounding rocks were oppressive and suffocating, but he was too tired to be picky.

The demon's breaths came out forced and heavy. His energy nearly spent, he feebly tried to remove the bracelet that had been his downfall. *Why?* he wondered, *why did the boy do that? I just wanted to help! Did he not see? Did I scare him?* It didn't matter anymore, he supposed. All that mattered was getting the bracelet off. He had to remove it. He had to! It was tight. Too tight. He felt trapped.

Trapped. Trapped. Trapped trapped trapped trapped tra–

The slivers of moonlight making it past the walls of stone around him suddenly disappeared. Mahway tensed, looking up to see the cause. Standing above him was a muscular, wingless demon woman. Her dark green skin contrasted the long, wavy, aquamarine hair that framed her face. Even pulled back into a ponytail, it reached down to her hips. She wore a tight, black and beige, sleeveless shirt, the collar covering her neck. The pants, on the other hand, puffed out somewhat before tucking into two calf-high boots. The only part of the outfit with any noticeable shine were the two metal bracers on her wrists.

The woman hopped down in front of him. Mahway tried to back away, barely making it even half a step before his muscles failed him. *I'm hurt. I'm in danger. What does she want from me?* Demon or not, this woman was a potential threat, just like all the others that had lurked in the darkness. His heart raced as he watched her slowly raise her hands. *Guardian. I need Guardian!* But... his friend was trapped within the horrible bracelet.

"Calm down, kid," the woman said softly. "We aren't here to hunt demons." She pointed to her two, short, white horns. They pointed straight up, the slightest curve at the end. At first glance, Mahway thought they were part of the wooden mask covering her face, before realizing that the mask itself only had six horns, not eight, the rest of it covered in decorative carvings. Now that she was closer, Mahway also noticed her thin, relaxed, snake-like tail curling upward behind her. "My name is Abyzou," she continued. "I can help you out if you'll let me."

Despite Abyzou's reassurances, Mahway still leaned away as she approached him. However, with his back up against a rock, he had nowhere to go. The woman crouched down, getting a closer look at him. "You look exhausted. Is it magic deficiency?" She noticed the wound on Mahway's side, still bleeding from where he'd removed Azazel's make-shift dagger. Her expression darkened. "Or blood loss."

With a slow and gentle movement akin to a mother comforting a frightened child, Abyzou reached down to the bracelet, pressing the button to remove it. The release clicked. The accessory opened up, falling to the ground. Mahway looked down in surprise before glancing back up to the mysterious woman. As he did, he noticed two silhou-ettes atop the rocks behind her. Though Mahway was quite used to seeing in dim light, he couldn't make out many details. Perhaps, he was in worse shape than he thought. Before he could try to get a better look, Abyzou stood up, looking west towards the distant city.

"Let's get you patched up, kid," she said. "Then we'll talk about how you got in and out of there alive.

Chapter 17

"I'M JUST SAYIN', if those masked demons people are whisperin' about even think about comin' into the city, they won't stand a chance against me!"

The Priest's deep, booming voice echoed throughout the cathedral halls. Enoch glanced over from the bench he was sitting on. Admittedly, he'd started nodding off somewhat while skimming through the notices on the bulletin board across from him. He wasn't sure how long it'd been since he'd started waiting outside the High Inquisitor's office, so he appreciated the wake-up call. That being said, the man it came from was someone he wasn't particularly fond of.

Asir, a hot-headed Priest stationed at the same cathedral as him and Cyrus. Though he never stopped by the library, Enoch did unfortunately run into him on occasion. The large, intimidating man never shut up. Enoch was certain the only reason he'd managed to pass the written portion of the Priest exam was through punching ink into the paper and getting lucky.

Enoch yawned, placing his watch back into his pocket after checking the time. He glanced over as the dark-haired man came into view, walking alongside a female Priest down the curved corridor surrounding the central hall of worship.

He'd also seen the woman around from time to time, as well as the crowds of Church workers following behind hoping to make a move. Thinking about it, he wasn't sure if he'd ever seen a single one succeed. It seemed that her most recent hopeful suitor was Asir. He was showing off for the woman, flexing a bicep the size of her head.

"With power like mine, I could squash those monsters like bugs!" Asir continued. The woman tossed her hair, continuing down the curved hall.

"I doubt they're intelligent enough to do a planned attack anyways," she added. "If the rumors really are true, they should just let us go and deal with them now."

The two of them walked out of view, leaving Enoch and the adjoined hall behind. The Scribe rolled his eyes, unaware of the now open door next to him.

"The Priests are as simpleminded as always it seems."

Hearing the familiar voice, Enoch snapped to attention, turning to the woman standing in the entrance of her office. Consultant High Inquisitor Cyrene Haven; known to the public as the Demon Executioner. She was a sharp woman, in both appearance and mind. A pointed nose, short spiked hair beneath her black fedora. Her cheekbones could slice through paper just as easily as the claw-like rings on her fingers. Though her status allowed her to modify her uniform, she'd done little to adjust the design. The long black and gold robes were fully fastened, not a string out of place. Small metal diamonds lined the edge of the red lapel. A pouch and gavel hanging from her belt contrasted the harsh angles of the rest of the outfit. She waved to a young Inquisitor as he left her office, before turning to Enoch.

"Good morning, Mr. Augnium," she said politely. "I thought you had today off. I don't believe I have any files for you right now." Enoch hastily got to his feet.

"Actually, I'm here for something else. I uh..." For reasons unknown to even him, Enoch trailed off. He knew he had to make this report. However, he could feel a strange, subtle force causing him to hesitate. This simple task suddenly felt far heavier than it should. He pushed the feeling aside. He was likely just intimidated by the Consultant Inquisitor's presence. Even after all his time working for her, the ferocity in her copper eyes still managed to frighten him at times. But this was no time to be afraid. If a demon was bold enough to enter the capital, then the Church needed to know. "I was attacked by a demon in the Hart District yesterday."

Haven raised an eyebrow, silent for a moment. It was the first time Enoch had ever seen her hesitate. She stepped back, gesturing to her office. "Come in."

The curtains of the single office window were drawn shut, the room lit by several candles and lamps instead. Organized bookshelves covered every wall, save for one or two small side tables. In the center of the room, Haven sat at a large wooden desk, piles of books and paperwork stacked neatly on top of it. The High Inquisitor held a paper in her hand, checking her notes as Enoch sat stiffly across from her. "The Pilgrim that chased after the demon. Did you see where he went?" she asked.

"No, ma'am. I lost track of both the Pilgrim and the demon while I was helping the woman."

"I see." Haven tapped her pen with her finger, the point of her metal ring causing a satisfying *click*. "And based on your description, the demon didn't seem to be part of any known military group. Or at the very least, wasn't in uniform." She placed her pen and paper back onto the desk. "I'll send Inquisitives to begin investigating the demon's whereabouts. I'm sure the outer city won't appreciate us meddling, but we can't afford to overlook this."

She folded her hands together, resting her elbows on her desk. Her expression softened somewhat, though Enoch might not have noticed if he hadn't known her for so long. "And what about you?" she asked. "Considering your history, I imagine a demon attack must have shaken you."

"At the time I was pretty panicked," Enoch replied. "But... I'm fine now."

Haven raised an eyebrow. The boy's gaze was glued to the floor as he spoke, and his tensed muscles were enough to tell her he was tightly gripping the fabric of his pant leg. "It seems you picked up Cyrus' inability to lie while in his care," she said, noticing the slightest glance from Enoch as he was found out. Haven waited for a response, but Enoch didn't seem intent on giving one. "I know you and I haven't spoken much aside from dropping off reports at the library, but Cyrus speaks of you often. I don't know how much help I can provide, but I'm here to talk if you need."

"I appreciate the offer, ma'am."

The room fell silent. With a sigh, Haven realized that poor deception skills weren't the only bad habit Enoch had learned from Cyrus. She grabbed a file off her desk. "For now, assuming you really are feeling alright, I believe this incident can be used as an opportunity."

Finally reacting, Enoch turned to see the file placed on the desk in front of him. It covered various reports of masked demons in the Courciel area, and their potential connection to the Soldiers of Lilith; every account carefully documented. The locations of the sightings. The identities and summarized histories of those that made the reports. Enoch couldn't help but wonder if it was something he wasn't supposed to see. After she'd given him some time to read, Haven folded her fingers together.

"The rumors of demons in the area are true," she said, the words feeling like a claw slowly tracing Enoch's spine. "We've had Inquisitives searching for them, but they've avoided detection for some time now. Which means they're likely better trained than the usual rebellious foot soldiers." Her gaze shifted to Enoch's bare wrist, the small scar from the needle still visible. "Despite working as a Scribe, you're listed as a Seer in the Church's registry. If the demon that attacked you is connected to the others, then it's possible that you could see their future actions, correct?"

Enoch rubbed the back of his neck. He'd had a feeling that the conversation would go this way. *Why couldn't I have been wrong for once?* he wondered. "I actually can't control what I see," he admitted. "So, I wouldn't be much help." He covered his wrist, expression darkening as he stared at the file again. "And I... I try not to use my power if I can help it. My visions don't end well for the people involved."

With a cool, neutral stare, Haven sat in silence for a moment. Then, she nodded, returning the file to its proper stack on the desk. "I see. I'm admittedly disappointed, but I'll accept your refusal." She moved slowly, deliberately, as she turned back to Enoch, her gaze locked with his. The subtle intensity petrified him in his seat. "But Enoch, an ability like yours could help a great deal of people. I understand your hesitation, but if you're truly as great as Cyrus claims, I hope you'll change your stance on it."

Breaking the daunting atmosphere, Haven turned away, beginning to write on a blank piece of paper. "Until then, give this to the receptionist at the House of Healing. It should help your request for a new bracelet to be accepted sooner." She signed the note with a flourish and handed it to Enoch. The Scribe nodded, sliding it safely into the journal in his bag to keep it safe.

"Thank you, High Inquisitor."

Haven's lips curled into the slightest of smiles. However, she quickly waved Enoch away despite this. "Now, if you have nothing else to say, I have work to do. Come by on your next shift to pick up this week's reports for filing." Enoch nodded, standing up quickly enough to make his head spin.

"Yes ma'am."

Chapter 18

THE CONCEPT OF routine is contradictory. On the one hand, falling into a routine is quite freeing. Your mind must simply repeat what it always does. The same tasks, the same route to and from work, the same exchanged pleasantries with the people you recognize but hardly know. With no thought involved, you're free to focus your attention on far more interesting things. On the other hand, routine can feel like trudging through a ditch, surrounded by the repetitive mundane, trapped in a fixed direction. The same tasks, the same route to and from work, the same exchanged pleasantries with the people you recognize but hardly know.

Regardless of the pleasure or pain one finds in routine, it's undeniable that it's quite easy to lose oneself in it. Due to this fact, Enoch had nearly forgotten the angel sitting comfortably in his bed, reading one of his textbooks. He jumped at the sudden, "Welcome home!" sent his way, the words accompanied by a smile bright enough to burn.

Enoch waved nervously back. "Oh, uh... yeah, hi."

"How did it go?" Azazel asked, setting aside the textbook he'd been using to pass the time. "Did they accept your request?"

"Well, it usually takes about a week for the request to be reviewed, but I should have a replacement in a few days thanks to High Inquisitor Haven." After hanging up his bag, Enoch moved to the table, leaning against it with a yawn. "As for the report, I told them that you followed the demon after the fight."

"Sounds good!" A small salute accompanied Azazel's words. "Seems like it all went pretty smoothly then!" Resting his hands on his lap, Azazel leaned against the aptly named headrest. In what had become somewhat of a routine, the two sat in an awkward silence until Enoch nervously rubbed the back of his neck.

"So, uh... are you feeling well enough to talk now?"

Azazel gave him a pained smile. "I'll admit, I was hoping you'd forgotten about that." The angel shrugged, adjusting himself into a more comfortable sitting position. "Alright, interrogate away. Just remember there's stuff I can't talk about."

Now that he had the opportunity, Enoch had no clue what he should ask. After all, he was speaking with an angel! The immortal beings created by the Archangels. The denizens of the divine realm. The warriors of Spira that had defended humanity against the demons in the First Surface War! No one had even seen an angel since the establishment of the Church decades ago, and yet one was now laying in his bed, covered in cookie crumbs. Enoch crossed his arms, deciding to start simple.

"Right. Well, I guess the most obvious question is what you're doing in Terrael?"

Azazel held up a finger triumphantly as he answered. "That one's simple! I'm here to help people!"

"Help them how?"

"However they need to be helped!"

Enoch's shoulders slumped at the empty clarification. *Either he's a master at keeping information close to his chest, or he's frustratingly oblivious,* he complained in his mind. *Maybe both?* Regaining his composure, Enoch tilted his head somewhat. "Is it just you then? Or are there a lot of angels walking around?"

"That's..." The brightness of Azazel's smile dimmed, the angel trying to decide what to do. After a moment of internal debate, he sighed. "Look kid, I know we made a deal, and I'm sure you have all kinds of questions about the secrets of the universe. But I'll be honest with you..." With a look of genuine remorse, he began to fidget with his heart-shaped earring. "I'm not supposed to let anyone know I'm here, and saying too much to a kid I barely know would cause a lot of problems for a lot of people. You do seem like a nice guy, and I'll admit it's kinda refreshing to talk to a human that knows my secret. But–"

"It's fine."

"R-Really?" Azazel turned in surprise, watching Enoch as the Scribe sat down at his desk. Enoch shrugged.

"Yeah. I'm curious, obviously, but I get it. I was honestly surprised you agreed in the first place, all things considered. But we all have things we don't want to talk about." With a soft smile, Enoch's hand moved to his wrist, still not used to the empty feeling. "And besides, it's probably best if I don't add the secrets of the universe to the list of things I have to worry about anyways."

Azazel couldn't help but stare. The soft smile on the boy's face felt familiar, and a dull pain filled the angel's chest. He turned away, hiding his face, unable to see Enoch crossing his arms.

"But I do have one question still," Enoch continued.

"If it's whether or not I like long walks on the beach, I do."

"Uh... no?" Enoch shook his head, more than a little confused by the response. Though he was starting to think that he should just expect strangeness from the man. "It's about your wings. If you could hide them again, you could go get proper treatment. So..." He glanced over to the wings comfortably folded behind Azazel's back. A few feathers had fallen off, sitting lazily on the bed. "How were you hiding them before?"

The brightness returned to Azazel's face. "Oh! That's another easy one!" He smiled ear to ear before gently placing a hand on his chest. "When you took my shirt, did you find a piece of old looking paper?"

Enoch pointed a thumb over his shoulder to the washroom door, where he'd left the aforementioned parchment. "I did, yeah. It was kinda torn and covered in blood though."

His answer caused the angel to grimace. "Yeah, I kinda figured that's why it stopped working." Recovering, Azazel held up a finger, reminiscent of a professor giving a lecture. "That paper is called an Illusion Paper. It's made by a friend of mine. I'll spare you the technical talk, but the short version is that it makes my wings invisible!"

Enoch's eyes went wide. "So, if you had another one of those then you could go to a House of Healing, right?" he asked excitedly. Hearing this, Azazel pouted, the teasing look in his eyes leaving the authenticity of it up for debate.

"Aw... Are you that eager to get rid of me?" he asked. Enoch's cheeks went red.

"Th-That's not it! I just, well..." With a sigh, Enoch's small spark of excitement failed to catch, sputtering out alongside the Scribe's confidence. "I'm not cut out for intense stuff like demon fights, or angels, or saving lives. So, you're better off getting treated by someone that knows what they're doing."

"Those just sound like excuses to me," Azazel argued, his brow furrowed. The interjection threw Enoch off.

"I... what?" he stuttered.

"Excuses, y'know? You don't wanna step out of your comfort zone, so you've convinced yourself you can't. But you've already proven that's a lie." Bewildered and mildly offended, Enoch raised an eyebrow. Oblivious to this, Azazel began to count on his fingers. "You were the one that stopped Mahway, right? And you must've been the one that got that woman to safety. Plus, you patched me up afterwards too. I'd say you're better at this stuff than you think."

Caught between feeling flattered and irritated at being outed, Enoch rubbed the back of his neck. "Yeah, but I could only do those things after you helped me first."

"But–"

"Look." Enoch raised a finger, cutting the Pilgrim's argument off. "Even if you did end up staying here instead of going to a House of Healing, there's still the risk of Noah or Namaah coming by. We need to hide your wings either way, so do you have any more of those Illusion Papers?"

Once again, Azazel pouted, this time feeling far more genuine. Nevertheless, he nodded in response. "Yeah, I should have one more back at the Ivory Inn."

"Alright then, I'll go get–" As Enoch stood up, he felt himself overcome by a sudden dizziness. He braced himself on the desk, knocking the empty plate of cookie crumbs onto the floor. Reflexively, Azazel reached out a hand despite not being able to reach Enoch from the bed.

"Woah! You okay?" he asked. Enoch waved off the concern as his mind steadied itself.

"Y-Yeah, just... I'm fine," he lied. Now that the angel took a closer look, Azazel could see the dark circles beneath Enoch's eyes; the slight sway in his stance despite supporting himself on the desk. The Scribe was fighting to keep his eyes open.

"Hey, Enoch, have you slept at all since the demon attack?

"Of course," Enoch snapped, unable to look Azazel's way as he spoke. He pulled out his pocket watch, checking the time. "If I leave now, I should be able to get the Illusion Paper and be back before curfew starts." The Scribe turned towards the washroom, hoping to grab the key to Azazel's room at the inn.

Pushing through the pain, Azazel leaned over, grabbing Enoch's hand. "Or you could wait until tomorrow and get some rest," he argued. As Enoch felt Azazel's hand, he stopped, letting out a sigh. Clearly, the angel wasn't going to drop it. With more force than probably necessary, he pulled his hand away.

"I slept, okay?"

"I don't think you did. If you need the bed, I could sleep in the bathtub or something."

"What are you–? No, that's not why I–" Enoch cut himself off, realizing what he was about to admit. Frustrated, he turned away with a dismissive wave of his hand. "Look, you have things you don't wanna talk about, and so do I. Let's just leave it at that."

Azazel tightened his lips. Perhaps he was pressing too much. He just couldn't understand why Enoch would be so stubborn about not sleeping. Did he not trust him? Or– He looked over in surprise. "Wait, this isn't because you don't have a bracelet, is it?" The brief hesitation in Enoch's steps was enough to show the angel had figured it out. The Scribe continued towards the washroom as Azazel's concern only deepened.

"Didn't you say your bracelet isn't coming in for a few days!?" he asked. "You can't just not sleep for that long!" Ignoring him, Enoch entered the washroom.

"I'll manage," he argued from around the corner.

"Enoch, that isn't healthy. It's just a vision, right? What are you afraid of?"

Enoch emerged from the washroom, key in one hand, the other pinching the bridge of his nose in frustration. Azazel's persistence was beginning to get on his nerves.

"Look, I–" He caught his tongue. He didn't have the time or energy for this. "Can you please just drop it? I don't wanna talk a–"

Knock Knock Knock

The argument ended before it could even really begin, interrupted by a sudden, soft knocking at the door. Enoch glanced over. *Did someone hear us?* His heart raced, the steady rhythm skipping a beat as a familiar, somewhat muffled voice called out from outside.

"Enoch? It's Cyrus, can I come in?"

Chapter 19

ENOCH HAD NEVER enjoyed unexpected visits. His apartment was his sanctuary, protected from everything he wished to avoid out in the world. A knock at the door was nothing short of a battering ram at the gate. However, with how his week had been going, he'd be a fool to think fate cared about what he did and didn't enjoy. Now, he stood paralyzed in the center of his home; eyes frozen on the door.

What is Cyrus doing here?

Enoch turned to Azazel. It was strange that the presence of a single person could turn a visit from a friend into a disastrous obstacle. The angel returned the gaze with a serious expression, waiting for the Scribe to act. Enoch would if he could, but he had no idea what to do! *Azazel can't be seen by the Church;* his mind reminded him. *But, even if Cyrus is a Priest, it should be fine, right? No. I know that isn't true. Cyrus has always been awful at keeping secrets.*

At the top of the stairs outside, Cyrus rubbed the back of his neck, growing more and more worried by the lack of response. "Enoch?" he called out. "You're there, right? I know you aren't the type to leave the window open while you're out."

Enoch had in fact left the window open, hoping it would help Azazel's jacket dry faster. The Scribe's face went pale as he remembered this. *Dammit! If I don't let him in now, that'll just make him suspicious, right? What should I–*

"Tell him you're getting dressed." Azazel's whispered words caught Enoch off guard, causing him to jump. He looked over in bewilderment.

"What?"

"Trust me. Just tell him that."

Despite having no idea where Azazel was going with this, Enoch nodded. "S-Sorry, just getting dressed!" he shouted, doing his best to hide the panicked shaking in his voice. Cyrus' tensed muscles relaxed.

"Yes, yes, of course. I'll give you a moment."

They'd managed to buy some time, but Enoch was still just as confused. "And now what?" he asked, turning back to the bed to find Azazel swinging his legs over the side. The angel winced as he started to stand.

"And now I hide in the washroom until he's gone," he answered. Enoch rushed over, bracing Azazel with his arm.

"You shouldn't be moving around though!" he argued. Azazel's lips curled into a wry, if somewhat pained, smile.

"I'll manage."

The Scribe tightened his lips as Azazel used his own words against him. With a frustrated sigh, he began helping Azazel over to the washroom. "Alright, fine," he muttered. "But don't blame me if you pass out on the washroom floor."

"Wouldn't be the first time."

Once Azazel was out of sight, Enoch rushed to the door. He opened it, seeing Cyrus wringing his cane like a nervous child. The tension visibly left the man's body at the sight of Enoch's forced smile.

"S-Sorry, I was just–" A sudden embrace knocked the rest of the air out of Enoch's lungs.

"Thank the Archangels, you're safe!" Cyrus sighed. The sudden force of the warm hug nearly toppled Enoch to the ground. His mind scrambled to remember what to do. For a moment, he went to hug Cyrus back, a nearly imperceivable twitch of the fingers before moving his hands away.

"What do you mean?" he asked. Cyrus reluctantly backed up. His hands continued to firmly grasp Enoch's shoulders, as if worried of what might happen should he let go.

"Cyrene– I mean, Inquisitor Haven told me you were attacked!" Cyrus explained. "I came over as soon as I heard! Are you hurt? How do you feel? What can I do to help?"

The onslaught of questions made Enoch dizzy. He awkwardly patted Cyrus' shoulder in an attempt to calm the man down. "I uh... I'm fine. Just a little scraped up."

The Priest nodded, finally letting go of Enoch's shoulders. Instead, he held his hand to his own chest, trying to reassure his frantic heart as he sighed. "Good, good. Haven said as much, but I had to check for myself." He smiled warmly. "I'm glad you're alright though."

His goal of checking on Enoch had been achieved, but Cyrus couldn't bring himself to leave. Not after everything that had happened in the past few days. His ignorance was a small blessing. If he'd known just how much had happened to Enoch outside of his knowledge, he likely would have fainted from worry right then and there. Despite being unaware, however, some part of the Priest's mind still seemed to sense that Enoch needed help. Cyrus clapped his hands together, a light in his eyes as inspiration struck. "Oh! How about some cocoa! Can't go wrong with a nice cup of cocoa."

It took all of Enoch's self-control to not glance at the closed washroom door behind him. "N-No!" he exclaimed, verbally slapping the smile off of Cyrus' face. Even Enoch couldn't help but wince at his overreaction. The older man shrunk away.

"Oh... Sorry. If I'd known you didn't like it, I would've made something else."

"No, that's not it, I..." Enoch felt a pain in his chest at the sight of Cyrus' undeserved guilt. "My apartment is a bit of a mess, is all. I haven't had time to clean."

The excuse seemed to soften the earlier blow, as Cyrus raised an eyebrow instead. He glanced past Enoch into the apartment. The guilt of letting Enoch run off in the cathedral before pushed him to act. He wasn't going to allow himself to abandon the boy again. "I'll help you tidy then," he said, gently pulling Enoch inside with him. "We can talk while we work!" Enoch opened his mouth to argue before realizing it was too late now that Cyrus was already inside. After a quick, involuntary glance to the washroom, he followed the Priest.

Cyrus scanned the room. Besides the unmade bed and the earlier knocked over cookie plate, the apartment was spotless. The older man couldn't help but chuckle. "This is your definition of messy now?" he asked, walking over to the fallen plate. "Your desk was always so cluttered as a kid. Seems your library job helped you with organization at least."

The man's movements slowed. Enoch couldn't see his face, but he didn't need to to know Cyrus' smile had faded as he lifted the plate off the floor. "Honestly though, what's really going on, Enoch?"

To move himself away from the washroom door, Enoch walked over to the table. "I'm fine, Cyrus, really," he re-assured. Cyrus placed the plate back onto Enoch's desk before facing the younger man.

"Enoch, you look exhausted, you were attacked by a demon, and you're clearly nervous about something. I know you aren't fine." To Enoch's surprise, he felt the air enter his lungs as he prepared to explain. The breath caught in his throat, his mind reminding him of Azazel's earlier words.

"I'm not supposed to let anyone know I'm here, and saying too much to a kid I barely know would cause a lot of problems for a lot of people."

He let out a sigh, choosing to close his mouth. He still didn't know the full consequences of Azazel being found out. Even with Cyrus, it would be best to keep the angel's secret for now. Frustrated, he grabbed his wrist out of habit. The movement was subtle, but Cyrus noticed it clear as day.

"I see..." he said with a frown. "You aren't sleeping again." It was too late to hide it, but Enoch still moved his hand behind his back. Cyrus's voice softened, the tone filling Enoch's mind with a painful nostalgia. "Enoch, we've been over this. You need to sleep."

"I'll be fine, seriously!" Enoch threw his hands up, starting to reach his breaking point. "Why are my sleeping habits suddenly so important to everyone?"

"Everyone?"

Enoch tensed, realizing his slip up. "Never-mind, I just... I don't wanna risk it, okay? You should know that better than anyone."

Now that he knew the cause of Enoch's stress, or rather, one of them, Cyrus took a step towards the boy. He'd held his tongue for so long, but Enoch was old enough for them to discuss this properly now. "Enoch, you know what happened wasn't your fault."

Unable to maintain eye-contact, Enoch turned away, crossing his arms. Had the comment come from anyone else, the Scribe would have replied with the reactive 'I know' that had become habit over the years. Perhaps it was the look on the man's face. Perhaps the lack of sleep was finally affecting his self-control. Whatever the reason, the quiet, painful truth slipped out instead.

"I knew it was coming, Cyrus."

"And you were a child." Despite his attempts to keep his voice calm, Cyrus' argument came out with vehemence. "Whether you knew or not, you couldn't have saved them." With his truth responded in kind, Enoch could feel frustration and denial bubbling up inside his chest.

"I know. But I could've at least been there!"

The intensity of the response caught Cyrus off guard. How long had the Scribe been bottling this up? Cyrus didn't have time to ask. He watched as Enoch gripped his sleeve, as if the arm held tight to his chest could hold back the emotions beginning to boil to the surface after years of being beaten down and ignored.

"I know better than anyone that I couldn't have saved them, Cyrus. For the last ten years people have told me that. I'm not a hero. I can't save people. I just... I wish I could've tried!" He sighed, pinching the bridge of his nose. "And I know I would've failed. I'm not dumb enough to think a ten-year-old kid with no magic could've stopped that many demons. But at least I could've died with my family instead of being miles away doing absolutely nothing while they suffered!"

As the fervency and volume of his words reached their peak, both Enoch and Cyrus's eyes went wide. Immediately, Enoch's posture receded, guilt replacing the pain and frustration that had come pouring out. "Wait, I didn't..." His voice trailed, muted by the heartbreak in Cyrus' eyes. He'd been caught up in the moment! He hadn't meant to say that! Like a dagger through the heart, he realized that wasn't entirely true. The realization only made Cyrus' expression more painful to see. The Priest gripped his cane in his hands like a scolded child.

"I didn't realize you felt that way," he said softly. The tension in the air was too thick to cut. Enoch's confession echoed in both their minds. Enoch desperately wished they could have simply sat and had cocoa instead, but that was a distant dream now. He'd made sure of that.

"Look, I just... I'm tired, Cyrus," he said, rubbing the back of his neck. He could feel a stinging sensation in his eyes, and turned away. He didn't want to hurt the man more than he already had. Nowadays, it seemed all he could do was worry and burden him; taking everything he'd done for granted. *Why?* he asked. *Why is Cyrus still trying so hard? Why hasn't he left yet? What does he still see in me?*

"I know you want to help me, but it's probably better if you just stop wasting your time."

Enoch had intended to cut the lifeboat free from his doomed, sinking ship. Cyrus deserved to be happy again. His words had the opposite effect, finally breaking the man. The Priest's heart sank. He stared at Enoch, oblivious to the tears in his own eyes. His hand moved on its own, lifting somewhat towards the young Scribe, a nearly imperceivable twitch of the fingers before moving his hands away. He had no idea how to help Enoch. He never had. He'd just never been able to admit it. He wanted to comfort the broken boy before him; the only person he had left, the child whose happiness came before everything in the world. But... had that happiness been a lie this whole time? Had he failed to give him even that? Still trying to process everything, Cyrus moved to the door. "Well... if that's what you want," he said, his voice hollow. He opened the door, hesitating just a moment. "I'm glad you weren't hurt, Enoch."

Cyrus closed the door behind him, leaving Enoch sitting alone. The Scribe held his head, arms resting on the table. Tears fell onto the wooden surface as he wished he could take back his words. But he couldn't. They were the truth.

Things would be better off if I'd just died back then.

Enoch was so distracted by his guilt that he forgot about the man waiting on the other side of the apartment wall, able to hear every word; every regret filled sob. Azazel sat on the washroom floor, leaning against the wall. A pain filled his chest, far deeper than the wounds Mahway had inflicted. He could tell Enoch's words had come from a guilt buried and ignored for years, but the angel couldn't help but feel responsible. His voice was soft, just like the muffled weeping filling the apartment.

"I'm sorry, kid."

Chapter 20

THE WEIGHT OF regret can shatter a person's very soul. A simple mistake made long ago, echoing in your mind. A decision haunting you with endless "what if's" till the end of your days. Words said in the heat of the moment that you'll never be able to take back. The past is set in stone, and the knowledge that we must live with what we've carved can be difficult for some to accept. The jagged, painful memories engraved by our regrets will remain etched for a cruel eternity.

Enoch added another regret to his ever-growing list before sliding the key to Azazel's room into his bag. He'd helped the angel back to the bed after Cyrus had left. Enoch's eyes were still red and swollen, and yet, the Pilgrim said nothing. In fact, the two hadn't exchanged a word since Enoch had let Cyrus inside. *I know he heard everything,* the Scribe thought, *he must think I'm some heartless jerk now... he wouldn't be wrong.* With a sigh, Enoch grabbed the doorknob.

"Hey, did you know angels don't age?"

Azazel's words cut him off. Turning his way, Enoch could see the angel in the corner of his vision. "That makes sense, I suppose," the Scribe replied, wondering why the man had decided to say that of all things. Azazel's expression gave no clues. Only a gentle sadness in his eyes as he looked towards the now closed window.

"We can be killed, of course. Though, even that's a gray area. But we never age. Gives you a weird perspective on life after a while." He forced a smile, turning to look at Enoch. "This is just between you and me, but I've been in the human realm for hundreds of years now, and I've had a lot of people I care about die on me in that time." The angel opened his hands, palms facing the ceiling. He stared down at them, focused on something far beyond their reach. "It caught me so off guard the first time that I could barely even comprehend it. That someone could just *end* like that... then it happened again, and again... Most were while I was off somewhere else. Some, it happened right in my arms." As if attempting to catch a lingering memory, he grasped at the air. Enoch remained by the door, listening without a word.

"Whether you're there or not, people are going to die. That's just how humans are. And sometimes, no matter what you do, you won't be able to save someone... even if you tell yourself you could've." Azazel's voice coated the bitter words in a soft, empathetic warmth. He paused, and Enoch could no longer fight his curiosity. Finally, he turned to face the angel, hoping to perhaps catch a glimpse of what the man was feeling. Despite the shaking in his voice, Azazel continued to smile.

"But Enoch..." he said, locking eyes with the Scribe as he said his name. "Losing those fights doesn't mean you should give up, or that you didn't do enough. If you can't save everyone, you just focus on saving the people you can.

Helping one person can have more of an impact than you realize."

The earlier tension in the air shifted to a pensive silence. After a moment, Azazel let out a soft chuckle, rubbing the back of his neck in embarrassment. "Sorry, got a little carried away there, didn't I? I'll let you get going now."

Just as Cyrus had, Enoch lingered in the door. "Right..." he said quietly, stepping outside. Once the door closed, the *click* of the lock signaling that it wouldn't open unexpectedly, the smile vanished from Azazel's face. With no one there to see, he allowed himself to feel the pain he'd been hiding behind his mask.

"Y'know... I think you two would've gotten along pretty well."

Far out of earshot of Azazel's private musings, Enoch once again passed through the archway leading to the Hart District. He'd made a point of sticking to the main roads, hoping to avoid any further complications or drama. Despite this, his thoughts still lingered on Azazel's words. *Carried away, huh?* he thought, *he knew exactly what he was doing.*

Enoch passed by the alley he'd nearly lost his life in. He'd only made the report a few hours before, but the area had already been blocked off for investigation. Haven was as prompt as always it seemed. Even from this far away, he could see the Inquisitives dragging his mangled bike out of the rubble. There was no getting it back now.

The events of the fight played through his mind, ending with Azazel's miraculous recovery from Mahway's final attack. He could still see the wings silhouetted against the amber, sunset skies. *It's easy for an angel to say saving people is easy, but I'm only human. Someone like me can't make a difference...*

...Right?

He let out a yawn, leaving the crowd lingering around the alley behind. He wasn't sure how far he'd walked. The crooked streets seemed far more slanted than before, the alleys and pathways blurring and repeating. The cobblestone felt more prominent, his dragging feet seeming to catch on every stone. Ironically, it was his own foot that nearly sent him falling to the ground. Catching himself, he steadied his swaying body on the nearby wall. His vision hadn't realized he'd stopped falling.

"That was close," he muttered. Now that he'd stopped walking, he noticed movement out of the corner of his eye; a shadow passing through a nearby alley. Panicked, he turned to look, finding nothing. Curiosity outweighed his better judgment, and he moved to the street corner, stopping at the edge where the outer city citizens could still see him. Those that could were no doubt questioning the sanity, health or sobriety of the disoriented Scribe, frightened by a simple alley.

Is it that demon again? he wondered, *or am I so tired I'm seeing things?* He rubbed his eyes, checking one last time. Still nothing. With a sigh, he continued down the street. *Maybe I really am that sleep deprived. Now that I think about it, I haven't slept for almost two days. Not since that stupid vision.* As if waiting for him to realize this, his surroundings blurred and swayed, his heavy eyelids dragging him down. *I guess Cyrus and Azazel had a point... Trying to tough it out... was a pretty dumb idea...*

Reaching his limit, Enoch felt the world shift beneath him. He could barely feel the impact of the ground as he collapsed. All he could see was the vaguely person-shaped blur rushing towards him, their voice too muffled to hear as he finally lost consciousness.

Both sleep and ignorance blessed Enoch with a brief peace of mind. Had Enoch known that his dazed dismissal of the shadow had allowed a demon to sneak into the capital, he'd have yet another painful regret to add to his slate. Though his decision to leave the alley behind would add to Enoch's guilt, Furcus, the elderly, male demon pressed against the alley wall around the corner, felt nothing but relief.

After waiting just a moment longer, the slender demon dusted off the back of his long, dark red tailcoat. Narrow, vertical gray stripes covered the garment, just slightly darker than his white hair and long pointed beard. Furcus was grateful that he'd managed to hide in time, his dark gray skin conveniently helping him blend with the nearby stone. Once he was certain no one was coming, his grip on the decorative silver trident in his hands relaxed somewhat. It seemed he hadn't been spotted after all.

He continued swiftly down the alley; his dress shoes surprisingly silent against the cobblestone. At the speed he was moving, his long, thin, white ponytail glided gracefully behind him. His somewhat torn, pointed tail matched the movement. His horns were understandably quite stiff in comparison, sprouting straight up out of the man's head. As he continued, the demon's gaze remained forward, purple eyes peering out from behind his wooden foot-soldier mask.

With dexterous movement perfected through years of training and experience, Furcus snuck through the city. Through the shaded, outer city alleys. Beneath the bridges of the Holy Wall as the guards changed their shift. Climbing above the rooftops to avoid a group of patrolling Priests as he approached his target. His body buzzed with an eager, vindictive energy as he thought about how vulnerable the Priests looked below, but he quickly shook the thoughts away. Lady Abyzou had instructed him to avoid conflict. They didn't want the Inquisitor to know they were coming, after all.

Ignoring his impulses, he turned back to the cathedral. Even with the stone wall and busy streets around the building, the demon could see both the front and back entrances of the cathedral from his rooftop vantage point. Now all he had to do was hide, wait and observe, enjoying the feeling of the fresh air against his skin.

Inside the cathedral, Haven took a sip of a somewhat cold cup of cocoa, oblivious to the watchful eyes outside her curtain. She looked over a document titled "Hart District Attack" in her hand. She hardly needed to review the content, having written the report herself, but the information had taken hold of her mind. Expression as serious as always, she once again glanced through the description Enoch had given of Mahway. Lowering the cup of cocoa, she stared intently.

"Feathered wings, huh?"

Perhaps it was time to pay the Researcher a visit...

Chapter 21

IF STORIES ARE to be believed, personal change must be preceded by grand actions. Without some life-changing event, a person will remain stagnant, trapped by their own mindsets and beliefs. However, while these events and moments may act as catalysts, this shift of perspective is often the result of something far more subtle. Small moments adding up until change is all but inevitable.

Moments like an army commander bandaging the wound of a young, winged demon, found hiding from the capital in the safety of shadows. Or a Priest and High Inquisitor in a candlelit office, sharing their troubles over hot cocoa, offering advice as dear friends do. Or even a familiar woman helping a young Scribe she saw collapse on the street, resting his head on her lap as she waits for a doctor to arrive.

Sometimes, all someone needs to change is a few encouraging words; a step in the right direction, followed by another, and another. Then, when you're faced with life-changing events, you'll find that the moment is less a catalyst, and more a mirror, showing the change that has already taken place.

The pain Enoch was feeling from his sudden collapse was equally subtle. A dull throbbing in the arm that had taken the brunt of the fall. He opened his eyes, immediately assaulted by the bright light of the sun. *Didn't I close the window?* he wondered. Groggily, he lifted a hand to shield his eyes. Far more swiftly, his memory of what happened returned to him. He sat up; eyes wide. The woman whose lap he'd thought was a pillow leaned back in surprise. "Oh! You're awake!" she exclaimed, watching Enoch take in his surroundings.

"Yeah, I..." The Scribe had barely heard her words, focused instead on the curious bystanders looking his way. Eventually, his gaze did find its way to the redheaded woman, double-taking as he realized who it was. It seemed that the person that helped him was none other than the woman from the alley attack, far less frightened and sick than the last time he'd seen her. "Oh... it's you!" he said, somewhat slack jawed at the coincidence. "Hello again, uh..."

"Josephine."

"Josephine," Enoch repeated. He realized she was kneeling on the sidewalk. Actually, for some reason he was too. "We're... on the ground?" he wondered aloud. Color flushed through his face as he put two and two together. "I passed out, didn't I?"

"You did, yeah."

Despite trying his best to save what little dignity he had left, Enoch swayed somewhat as he struggled to his feet. Josephine rushed to her own, hoping to steady him. "Careful!" she exclaimed. "You may have hit your head when you fell!" Enoch's raised palm cut her off as he managed to regain his balance.

"I'm fine," he reassured. He tried to rub away the dull ache in his arm, the pain growing now that he was properly waking up. "The only thing that's bruised is my pride. And maybe my arm."

With a nod, Josephine stepped back. Even the curious bystanders dispersed now that Enoch was on his feet again. Making sure to stay at just the right distance to respect Enoch's personal space, but still close enough to come to his aid if needed, Josephine respectfully folded her hands together. "Even if you say you're fine, I sent someone to get a doctor, they should be here soon. I'll wait with you until then."

"I should be okay." Enoch reassured. *I don't need a doctor to tell me what happened. I passed out because I'm a stubborn idiot. Simple as that.* He sighed. "There's no need to go through all that trouble. I just... didn't sleep well."

"I see..." Josephine gripped her arm, a sadness overtaking her expression. "Honestly, I didn't sleep well either. How could anyone sleep after getting attacked by such a terrifying demon?" Her words sent memories of the fight running through Enoch's mind, finally settling on the moment she had pushed him to safety at the cost of her own.

"R-Right," Enoch replied. "Um... thank you, by the way. For saving me before." Apparently, his words were amusing somehow, as Josephine let out a soft chuckle.

"Isn't that my line?" she asked, catching Enoch off guard. He looked over in confusion.

"I mean, I would've been crushed by the debris if you hadn't pushed me away," he argued. "Besides, Az–" He caught his tongue. It was probably best not to use the angel's real name without his permission. "Uh... Gregory is the one you should be thanking, not me. It was my fault you got attacked in the first place."

"The Pilgrim's name was Gregory, then?" Josephine replied with a smile, followed by a nonchalant shrug. "He did help a lot as well, but he wasn't the one that carried me away from danger and back to my family. You helped save my life too, and I don't even know your name."

Between her praise and the genuine warmth of her smile, Enoch couldn't help but blush. He rubbed the back of his neck, turning somewhat to hide his face. "Oh, uh... it's Enoch."

The woman smiled in return, placing a gentle hand over her heart. "Well, thank you Enoch. My daughter still has a mother thanks to you and Gregory."

"Your... daughter?" Perhaps Enoch's mind was still half asleep, as it took him a few seconds to understand. However, after a moment he managed to recall the young girl that had been with Josephine's husband. As he thought about this, he realized Josephine was beginning to rummage through her bag.

"Actually, I was hoping to run into you again, Enoch," she continued. "Fate must be on our side." After a few seconds of searching, she pulled out a folded piece of paper, holding it out to the young Scribe. "My daughter made this for you."

Enoch took the paper, carefully unfolding it. As he did, it felt as if his heart stopped for a moment. The feeling was unfamiliar. He'd had his heart freeze in fear, or race in panic, but this... it was as if a warm hand had reached out to embrace it. The paper was a painting, the colorful art-style leaving much up for interpretation, as is often the case with the art of children. Despite this, he could still make out the artist's intent. Based on the hair, he could tell that it was him in the middle of the page, heroically lifting a beam to save Josephine sitting next to him. To the side, Josephine's family cheered him on with cartoonishly bright smiles.

In the moment, all Enoch had thought about was getting himself and Josephine to safety. He'd never considered how that would affect things after the fact. But... it seemed he actually had accomplished something in that alley. *I guess I did help save her, didn't I?* he realized. *Me of all people.* As this realization stole his voice, all he could do was stare silently at the paper in his hand.

"It was her way of saying thank you," Josephine explained. "You don't need to keep it if you don't want to, but she'll be happy to know you got it."

"Josephine, I brought the doctor!" The arrival of an elderly woman, as well as the young doctor she had left to get, caught their attention. The older woman waved as she approached, stopping as she noticed Enoch tucking the painting into his journal. "Oh, looks like the kid woke up!"

"Yeah. Sorry for causing a scene. I just pushed myself a little too hard," Enoch replied, once again feeling the burning sting of embarrassment. *Just how many people have I inconvenienced with this?* he thought. He slid his journal back into his bag, attempting to sneak away as nonchalantly as he could. "I just need to pick up some stuff from the Ivory Inn and then I'll be heading home to rest. I'm fine, really."

The doctor's surprisingly strong grip stopped Enoch in his tracks. "I'll be the judge of that," he said sternly. "I came all this way, so let me do my job before you run off."

"Y-Yes sir."

With no other choice, Enoch sat through the various tests and questions of the doctor. The man's medical know-how put Enoch's to shame. Perhaps he'd been a Healer before ending up in the outer city? Enoch was admittedly curious, but also felt it would be rude to pry. After all, many citizens living on the outer side of the Holy Wall didn't get there by choice.

"So..." the doctor said after a bit. "How's the other guy?"

"The other guy?" Enoch repeated. "You mean Gregory?"

"That's the angel's name then, is it?"

Once again, Enoch's heart stopped. This time, he recognized the chilling fear behind it. "A-Angel?" he asked with terrible acting. "I don't– What do you mean? There hasn't been an angel in Terrael since–"

"No need to lie," the doctor interrupted. "Folks out here aren't as strict about curfew. More than a few of us saw him fall." As if reliving the moment, the doctor looked towards the sky. "Thought I was hallucinating when I saw the wings appear right at the end."

Making up for the seconds it had stopped, Enoch's heart raced. If multiple people had seen it, he could hardly tell the man it had actually been a hallucination or a trick of the eyes. He searched his brain for some kind of excuse, but found no such escape. Before he could even try to bargain or beg for silence, the doctor placed a hand on his shoulder, no doubt noticing Enoch's panic.

"Calm down, we aren't planning on ratting him out," he reassured. "He saved Josephine, after all. Least we can do is keep his secret as thanks. He should be a bit more careful though. Not everyone out here would be as considerate."

Enoch hadn't realized how tense his body was until it finally relaxed. "I see," he sighed, letting out a relieved chuckle. "Wish I'd known about this the night of. Would've been helpful to have a proper doctor there to save us a trip." The amusement in his smile faded into gentle pride. "But he turned out okay in the end. I have a bit of medical training myself, so I patched him up. He's just resting now."

"Medical training, huh?" the doctor repeated, subduing his curiosity just as Enoch had. "I suppose it's pretty lucky that you're the one that found him then."

"Yeah, I suppose so," Enoch replied, the words feeling almost freeing in a way. This moment of realization found itself interrupted by Josephine's hand waving in front of his face.

"Well, I should probably get going," she said once she had his attention. "My family will get worried if I'm out too long." She rested a hand on her hip, the other pointed sharply at Enoch. "Let's hope you aren't lying on the street again next time we run into each other."

"Right, I'll try my best," Enoch promised with flushed cheeks. His fingers traced the seam of his bag as he remembered Josephine's gift from before. "Oh, and uh... tell your daughter thank you, for the painting."

His gratitude brought a beaming smile to Josephine's face. "Of course!" she exclaimed before giving one final wave goodbye. As she and the others left Enoch to himself, satisfied that the small amount of rest would spare him another painful collapse, Enoch realized that he was smiling as well; the warm embrace enveloping his heart once more.

Chapter 22

I F HE FOCUSED, he could see it. The golden bracelet that had covered Enoch's wrist had long since disappeared with Mahway's escape, but he couldn't help but imagine its shine as he stared at his empty arm.

Enoch had made it back to the apartment, dropping Azazel's heavy suitcase to the floor with a hefty thud. Unsurprisingly, given the man's injuries, even the accidental noise failed to wake the sleeping angel. *He makes it look so easy,* Enoch thought. He tidied things up, returning the open textbook on the angel's lap to its place on the shelf. "Property of Enoch Augnium" still marked the front page, a lingering scar of what could have been.

Perhaps things would go differently now.

The thought tickled the back of Enoch's mind as he left the desk behind, collapsing into the chair by the door. His earlier nap had granted him a short respite from exhaustion, but he knew that he'd need proper rest to avoid collapsing again. And so, he found himself entranced by an empty wrist, weighing pros and cons in his mind.

"Just gotta take the risk..." he whispered. "It's only a vision. You'll be fine."

His deep breaths and heavy eyelids gave some weight to the argument; fear and hesitation overcome by fatigue. The chair was hardly a comfortable replacement for the bed, but it might as well have been a pile of pillows for the Scribe's weary body. But the same nagging worry still poked and prodded his mind. A persistent "what if?" over and over again. However, a surprising memory shielded his consciousness. A paper covered in paint. Proof that should the worst come to pass, he had the potential to succeed in spite of it. Like a lullaby, the thought of the painting lulled him into security.

"I'll be fine," he said softly.

And for once, the universe decided to listen.

Enoch awoke in the blink of an eye. Or rather, that's what it felt like. In reality, he'd finally managed to get a proper rest, his body stiff and sore from his seated position. Drool dripped down his chin as he groggily opened his eyes. Azazel noticed the movement, smiling at the young Scribe.

"Good morning! Sleep well?" he asked. Enoch wiped away the drool, smiling in relief.

"Surprisingly, yeah." he replied. "Not a single vision!"

Hearing this, Azazel raised his hand in a half-shrug, having gotten used to moving around the pain of his injuries. He gave Enoch a smug smile.

"See, I told you! Nothing to worry about!" The angel watched as Enoch stretched. He could feel and hear the cracking bones from the other side of the room. Enoch raised an eyebrow once he finished.

"Is that how you put it?" he asked. "If I remember correctly, you just said I was making excuses, and then said something about sleeping in the bathtub."

"Well, I thought it at least," Azazel replied. He watched as Enoch turned his attention to the angel's suitcase, still sitting on the floor. The Scribe glanced over.

"Can I open it?" he asked. Azazel nodded.

"Yeah, I was gonna say. Looks like you brought back more than just an Illusion Paper."

"Well, your wounds will take at *least* a week or two to heal..." With a *click*, Enoch opened the suitcase, revealing the angel's personal belongings inside. Clothing, make-up, books, a small mirror and various other items explained the heavy weight that had added to the soreness of Enoch's muscles. However, it was the small netted pocket sewn to the inside that caught the Scribe's attention, as well as the familiar looking paper within it. Carefully, just as he handled the delicate papers in the library, Enoch slipped it out. "...I figured you'd probably appreciate having your stuff while you're staying here."

The words brought a smile to Azazel's face. "Oh! You aren't gonna kick me out anymore?" he asked as Enoch carried the paper over to him. The Scribe's cheeks flushed at the comment.

"I'm not. And uh... sorry about that. If there's complications with the healing, I should be able to help... probably." He handed the Illusion Paper to Azazel, embarrassment stealing away any attempt to make eye-contact. "And besides, even with your wings hidden, it'd be safer to heal up here with someone that knows your secret."

"Hey! Look who found some self-confidence on his little solo adventure!" Azazel exclaimed. Taking the paper with a smile, Azazel swung his arms out with far more excitement than the situation called for. But at this point, Enoch expected this kind of overenthusiasm, managing to dodge the movement. "Congrats kid!"

"What're you–?" Red enough to burn, Enoch turned away. *Why does he have to be so energetic all the time?* he wondered, having no clue how to handle it. "How does that thing make your wings invisible anyways?" he muttered.

Azazel stifled a chuckle. It was too easy to get a reaction from him. Deciding to show a little mercy, he clapped his hands together. "It's quite exciting actually!" he answered. "Each paper is imbued with my friend's magic. When you say the trigger word, it summons whatever illusion is written on it. In this case, the paper describes the wings not existing. Or uh, appearing not to, at least. He even made sure to write about the holes in my clothes disappearing." Slowly, Azazel emphasized his words by extending his wings somewhat. "The wings are still there of course, and I do have people bump into them from time to time. But even if they're touching them, they don't feel a thing! I still do though, and that gives me a chance to back away before they notice."

Having recovered from Azazel's kindness, Enoch took a seat at his desk, listening intently. "So, the other one stopped working because the paper was damaged?" he asked. The angel lightly tapped the bandages covering his chest.

"Yup. I had it in my shirt pocket when Mahway did this. So that's the likely culprit." Azazel scratched the back of his head. "A similar thing happened when I jumped in a lake a while back and washed away the ink. Almost drowned trying to swim far enough away for people to not see me. I should really start carrying it in a little box again, but that was always such a hassle." The angel's embarrassment was short-lived, and he turned his attention back to the paper, gripping it tightly. "But that's enough explaining, it's time to actually use this thing!"

The angel closed his eyes, extending his arm to the side. Reflexively, his wings opened as well, the tips of the feathers brushing against the wall as they stretched as far as the space allowed. Enoch sat at the edge of his seat, watching in curiosity. Locked away in the library or his apartment most of the time, he rarely saw magic abilities in action despite working for the Church. What would this look like? He waited with bated breath as Azazel closed his eyes. And then–

"Action!"

The moment the trigger word left the angel's lips, his wings vanished in a puff of smoke. It was so sudden that Enoch tensed in surprise. *It's like they were never there!* he thought. The Scribe reached out, grasping in the air out of disbelief. "You're right, I can't feel a thing!"

"Probably because I pulled them back in," Azazel replied with a mischievous grin. "Here, I'll move them out again."

With more annoyance than curiosity now, Enoch reached out once more. This time, his hand stopped, blocked by the air. "Oh! I think I found it," he said. Despite knowing he was touching the wing, Enoch couldn't feel a thing. Not the softness of the feathers. Not the warmth one would expect from touching a living thing. The only sign there was something there at all was the resistance keeping his hand from moving. As Enoch found himself fascinated by the situation, Azazel squirmed somewhat, barely holding back a laugh and a wince.

"I'm glad you found it, but I'm kinda ticklish there, so if you're all done..."

"Oh! Sorry!"

Enoch moved his hand back, allowing Azazel to relax. The angel tucked the paper into his pants pocket, trying to get comfortable on the mattress again. "So, now that you're more rested, and my wings are hidden, what's the plan?"

The simple question dug its fingers into the fresh wounds on Enoch's heart. The plan was an unpleasant one. He retreated into himself with guilt filled eyes. "Well, if you don't need me here, I was planning on apologizing to Cyrus," he admitted. Though, he wasn't sure words alone would be enough to make things right. Azazel's expression softened.

"That's the guy from yesterday, right? Sounded like he was a good friend of yours."

"Cyrus is..." Enoch's voice trailed. Honestly, he had no clue where to begin. "Well, he's a lot of things. It's a long story."

"It's not like I'm short on time," Azazel replied, finally finding the perfect comfortable spot on the bed. He leaned back, turning an empathetic stare Enoch's way. "You don't have to tell me if you don't want to. But if I knew more about what you guys were talking about yesterday then maybe I could help."

Hesitation and uncertainty held Enoch's tongue. His and Cyrus' story was hardly one of happiness, and despite having rested, he wondered if he had the strength to share it. For a moment, he considered simply dropping the subject. Azazel had said silence was an option after all. But... Enoch could feel a force pulling him forward. A lifeline, no wider than a thread. Maybe... just maybe, Azazel really could help him. If anyone could, an angel seemed the best candidate.

Or perhaps the faint thread would simply snap from the emotional weight. Perhaps doing this would be a mistake.

There was the chance Azazel would treat him differently if he knew. Everyone else had.

The force pulled again. A voice. *His* voice in the back of his mind. That quiet, newfound confidence slowly growing in volume.

Maybe he'll be different.

The small hope felt foreign, but somehow right. With a deep breath, Enoch grasped the fragile lifeline, allowing it to lead him to the best place to begin.

"Cyrus is, or *was,* my teacher. That's how it was when I first met him at least. Back in our hometown..."

Chapter 23

THE FLOWERS OF Peycile bloom in blood, tears and rain. The colorful town sat at the edge of a winding river, the scent of spring permeating through the streets. Though it was a farming town, it was best known for the flowers lining every window, pathway and building. Red, yellow, green, blue, violet, every color in between, the people of Peycile took pride in the peaceful beauty of their home. It was a shame that Enoch's memory of it was far less tranquil.

"He was one of the kindest, most patient people I'd ever met." Enoch began, thinking back to his and Cyrus' first meeting. Enoch, only six years old, hid behind his mother in the almost empty classroom. In front of him, Cyrus knelt down with the reassuring smile Enoch had distanced himself from over the years.

"Why don't you pick the book we read today?" he'd asked, knowing the boy's fondness for pen on paper. With just one offer, he managed to get through to him. A single offer. A single book. A moment showing that Cyrus saw and understood him. Over the years, Enoch worked to make Cyrus proud. He valued the man's opinion as much as his parents'. Striving for good grades, taking care of his younger sister to help his family, Enoch did what he could to be the kind, successful person they claimed he could be.

"He always had such high hopes for me," Enoch continued. "And honestly, when he told me I'd achieve great things, I actually believed it. But then..." Rather than his wrist, Enoch's fingers wandered to his pocket, tracing the chain of his pocket watch. "Well, you heard everything we said yesterday, so you already know I lost my family."

Azazel slowly nodded, listening carefully to every word. He could see the vulnerability in Enoch's eyes as he shared his scars. "Yeah, I heard," he admitted, though they'd both already known this. "You said it was demons, right?" Enoch winced at the question. He felt as if he could choke on the words lingering in his throat. The truth that had thrown his entire life, if not the very world, into disarray.

"They... They died in the Peycile Massacre."

For once, Azazel was speechless. An icy knife shot through his spine, and he needed a second to recover. Even after doing so, all he could manage to say was "Enoch, I'm so sorry".

The flowers of Peycile bloom in blood, tears and rain. This saying was quite common in the months following the incident, popularized by an article in the Daily Courciel paper. In a single night, ten years before Enoch shared this tale with Azazel, the recently formed Soldiers of Lilith slaughtered the entire farming village of Peycile. Their motivations were often debated, even years after. Had they wished to make a name for themselves? Had they been targeting the town's Bishop, rumored to be in a relationship with the Almighty Voice, leader of the Church. Or had it simply been a mindless slaughter perpetrated by monsters, targeting a town of innocents? No matter the reason, the bloodstained result was all too clear.

The number of survivors could be counted on a single hand. The Peycile Massacre signaled the start of a new war. Once again, humans and demons would fight for control of the surface.

"Wait! Hold on!" Azazel said, eyes wide in horror and realization. "So yesterday, when you said you knew it was coming–"

"Yeah." Enoch cut him off, his expression overcome with guilt and sadness. "The massacre was one of the first visions I ever had. At the time though, I just thought it was a nightmare."

The angel struggled to find the words to reply, unsure of what to do. Certainly, anything he could say to the boy would have already been said by someone else over the years. However, there was no need to respond as Enoch simply continued his story.

"I wasn't there when it happened. Cyrus and I were in the capital at the time. He said my talents were wasted in a small-town school, so with my parents' permission, he and I went to the Capital to see if I'd be interested in the schools there."

"Your parents didn't go with you?" Azazel asked, immediately regretting it. *Of course they didn't,* he realized. He winced, but Enoch seemed unphased by the inquiry.

"No. They couldn't," the Scribe replied. "They had their hands full with work. Plus, they had to take care of Lydia, my little sister, so a long trip was out of the question. Cyrus was practically part of the family though, so they trusted him to take care of me." Enoch's lips curled into a pained smile. He reached into his pocket, taking out his pocket watch. A single, engraved daffodil decorated the metal.

"The trip was actually pretty fun at first. It was my first time in a big city, so Cyrus took me sightseeing after we saw the schools. He even bought me this watch as a souvenir the last day we were there. It was the most beautiful thing I'd ever seen, and I remember being so happy when he gave it to me." The strength of Enoch's grip on the watch turned his knuckles white as he mourned the memory. The considerate gift from a friend had been butchered along with his home, now nothing but a painful reminder. And yet, he couldn't bring himself to get rid of it. Enoch's voice began to shake.

"Everything was going great until we got ready to go home. When we reached Central Station, the Peycile platform was closed off. There were Priests, Pilgrims and Healers everywhere, all rushing to get on the train we were supposed to be taking. They needed all the help they could get back in town, after all." As he described it, the memory became all the more vivid in Enoch's mind. The bumps and bruises from navigating the crowd. The sound of rain against the station skylights mixing with the rhythm of rushing footsteps. The smell of coal and wet metal. The feeling of Cyrus' hand holding his. The Priest's explanation that shocked his mentor enough to let go.

"When we found out what happened, I refused to believe it. So, while Cyrus was distracted, I snuck onto the train and hid for the entire trip. I convinced myself it was just some big lie, and was determined to prove it." In a futile attempt to calm his emotions, Enoch slowly spun the watch in his hand, just as he had while crouched beneath the seats of the train. "He was lying. He had to be. That's what I told myself over and over again." The spinning stopped, tears stinging Enoch's eyes. "I learned the hard way that he was telling the truth."

As they had many times before, the memories of the evening flashed through Enoch's mind, as vivid as the day itself. The crimson puddles in the streets, now filled with corpses that were once his friends. His frantic footsteps slipping in the mud as he rushed to his home. All around him, the Church workers there to help called out, trying to stop him. He continued to run. He ran and ran until he finally reached his home. He ran until he reached the wooden door scratched and torn beyond recognition. He refused to stop until he stood in the entryway, lungs screaming for air; nose filled with the sickening combination of blood and flowers. Someone was screaming. But his mother, his father, his sister... what remained of them simply laid there unmoving.

His throat hurt.

Enoch took a breath, grounding himself as the memories began to overtake him. He ran his finger over the engraving on his watch. It wasn't as effective as the bracelet, but the rough texture worked for now. After surviving the events of the last couple days, the memories felt less dangerous. Less suffocating. Having calmed himself somewhat, he continued.

"At some point I wandered back outside. I don't know how long I sat there crying in the mud before Cyrus showed up. I didn't even hear him get close, I just realized he was holding me. Even though he'd lost his own family; his own friends... he went to me first. I held onto him, terrified that he'd disappear too. He was the only one I had left." Enoch choked on the words, stopping to wipe away the tears in his eyes. With a deep breath, he managed to regain his composure somewhat.

"We moved to the Capital with the few other people that had managed to survive. Just four of us in all. Thanks to Cyrus offering to act as my guardian, I managed to avoid ending up in an orphanage. And Inquisitor Haven made sure all our identities were kept private, despite certain members of the Church wanting to use the incident to their advantage." The Scribe's gaze wandered over to the textbooks on his desk, his mind focused on something far more distant. "I completely shut down for a while after that, but Cyrus took care of me the whole time, even getting me my job at the cathedral. Honestly, he's done more for me than I deserve."

Placing the pocket watch onto the desk, Enoch turned to Azazel. "I still have mixed feelings about not being there that day, or whether or not my vision could've changed anything. But I shouldn't have said all that yesterday. He didn't deserve it. He... he didn't deserve how I've treated him over the years either. I just– it hurt to get close, y'know?"

Hearing himself say it out loud, Enoch winced. He'd gotten carried away. "That's uh... that's way more than you asked for. Sorry." Trying his best to release the tension that had been building in his body, Enoch let out one final sigh. "So yeah, that's what Cyrus is to me, and what we were talking about yesterday. It was probably a lot heavier than you were expecting, so sorry about that too." The lingering tension came out as a light chuckle that felt quite out of place. "Y'know, now that I think about it, I don't think I've ever told anyone that. I guess we've both shared secrets now."

Despite forcing a smile, the pain Azazel was feeling from Enoch's confession was clear in his eyes. "It's not quite the secrets of the universe, but I'm glad you felt comfortable enough to tell me," the angel replied. "Your secret's safe with me, Enoch." It hurt somewhat to lean over far enough, but Azazel placed a reassuring hand on Enoch's shoulder anyways. "And if it's any consolation, I'm sure Cyrus will forgive you."

The guilt Enoch was feeling weighed down his smile, a frown taking its place. He nodded, placing his watch back in his pocket. "Yeah..." he replied, knowing Azazel was right.

Regardless of whether or not he deserved it, Cyrus would forgive him.

He always did.

Chapter 24

"LOOKS LIKE RAIN."

The marbled blue and gray sky hastened Enoch's pace. The clouds were still scattered, but he knew better than to push his luck. Not that he needed to push himself very long, having already reached the streets surrounding the Penemue Cathedral. The aroma of freshly brewed coffee from the nearby cafes infused itself with the cathedral gardens, a relaxing and rejuvenating fragrance dancing through the air. However, as Enoch approached the closest gate, a combination of new scents cut in.

Metal, grease and steam.

The source of the smell came to a halt at the side of the road, just in front of the cathedral's front gate. The sight of the automobile unsurprisingly caught the attention of those nearby. A group of children gathered, marveling at the metal beast. Even Enoch found his gaze drawn. It wasn't uncommon to see automobiles parked outside of Church-run buildings, especially in Courciel, but it had been some time since he'd seen one in person. Now, he found himself so distracted that he nearly failed to notice Inquisitor Haven passing through the front gate. Had it not been for the rumbling of her suitcase's wheels, he likely would have missed her entirely.

"Oh! Inquisitor Haven!" he called out, reminded of his goal. "Do you have a second?" He rushed over to his superior. Hearing his voice, Haven stopped, turning a cold stare his way.

"Oh, Mr. Augnium. Good morning," she said with a passive aggressive monotony. "Cyrus isn't here right now. He's on patrol." Without wasting a second, Haven lifted her suitcase towards him. Enoch's short-lived confusion at the action shifted to surprise as two brawny arms took the luggage. Haven's chauffeur now stood directly beside him. How someone so large had moved so stealthily was a mystery for another day. For now, Enoch turned back to the High Inquisitor.

"How did you—"

"He and I met for cocoa yesterday," Haven explained. "He seemed distraught when you were brought up, despite claiming he was fine. I assume something happened between you two?"

Something was certainly putting it lightly. Guilt pricked at the back of Enoch's neck. He tried his best to rub away the discomfort. "Uh... yeah. I was hoping to apologize to him."

"Well, it would be difficult to track him down on patrol, but I believe you're both scheduled to work tomorrow morning. So, that seems the most appropriate time to talk." Maintaining her swift pace, Haven opened the door of the automobile, placing her striped briefcase in the back seat.

"Probably, yeah," Enoch agreed, the words nearly muffled by the loud slam of the automobile trunk. "Um... are you going on a trip, Inquisitor?"

"I have business out of town for a few days. High Inquisitive Foster will be handling my responsibilities in my absence, so you'll be collecting the paperwork from her until I return."

"A High Inquisitive?" Enoch repeated, "Don't they usually handle criminal investigations?"

"There were no Consultant Inquisitors available on such short notice. But I can assure you that she is fully qualified despite her Inquisitor branch," Haven replied. "So, you'd do well to treat her with just as much respect as you would myself."

"O-Of course, High Inquisitor," Enoch reassured, fighting the urge to salute. "W-Well, Uriel's blessings for your travels then."

"Thank you."

Socially inept as he was, even Enoch could tell the Inquisitor was unhappy. He doubted it was simply the stress of readying for travel. The Scribe's shoulders hunched. As Haven finished her business in the back seat, her height dwarfed the now even shorter Scribe. "By the way," Enoch said meekly. "I'm sorry I couldn't be more help with the uh... situation, we were discussing before."

Much to Enoch's relief, the High Inquisitor's expression softened somewhat at the apology. Only somewhat. She dismissed his words with a wave of her hand.

"It would be inefficient to use a power you can't control for the investigation. Apologies are unnecessary," she replied. In a movement somehow both graceful and stiff, she stepped into the automobile, turning to face Enoch once she was seated. "However, if Cyrus is still distraught due to your actions when I return, you'd best prepare more than a simple apology." The subtle softness of her expression all but vanished, leaving an icy glare reminiscent of a bird of prey. "He is one of the few people I consider a friend, and as such, I am quite invested in his well-being. Keep that in mind, Mr. Augnium."

Caught in her cold, unbreaking gaze, Enoch feared for his life yet again. Suddenly, Mahway's attack felt far less terrifying.

"Y-Yes ma'am," he stuttered, hiding his fear behind a smile. Haven nodded in return and closed the door. The sudden SLAM broke the tension, and Enoch stepped back in relief. He watched as the automobile drove away, letting out a sigh once she was truly gone.

He hadn't achieved what he'd set out to do, but if Cyrus was on patrol, he had no choice but to wait. He glanced over the cathedral. Tomorrow, he'd find Cyrus within those familiar stone walls and make things right.

Chapter 25

HE HADN'T LEFT.

When Enoch returned to the apartment, Azazel greeted him with the same enthusiastic, "Welcome home!" as before, sitting right where Enoch had left him. It could have been because of his injuries, of course. The angel couldn't walk out the front door without a fair amount of pain and effort. But somehow, Enoch felt that wasn't the reason.

Azazel seemed genuinely happy to see him. The smile on his face as Enoch handed him dinner seemed real. The conversations they had about Enoch's books and belongings didn't feel forced. The fear softly chipping at the back of Enoch's mind began to fade. Azazel had no intention of treating him differently now, it seemed. He wasn't going to run away or use him after learning the truth. Though Enoch should have felt relieved at that, a subtler grating took the place of his old anxiety, the headache returning.

He hadn't left, but would that make it all the more painful when he did?

Two crumb covered plates sat neatly on the counter. The paper grocery bags beside them had been carefully folded, the contents now sorted into various cupboards and shelves. Enoch closed the washroom door behind him after changing into his nightwear. The outfit caught Azazel's eye.

"Y'know, there's still room in the bed if you don't want to sleep in the chair," he offered with a teasing smile. The effort to get a flustered reaction went over the Scribe's head.

"The chair is fine. I've slept in worse."

"Suit yourself," Azazel replied with a pout. He watched as Enoch got comfortable across the room. Though the chair seemed to not give him any trouble, his bare wrist was not as kind. Enoch rubbed it, tracing the paler patch of skin with his fingers, lost in thought.

"Worried?" the angel asked. Enoch quickly released his wrist like a kid caught in the cookie jar.

"I–" He took a breath to argue, but now that Azazel knew everything, he supposed there was no need. Enoch sighed. "I know I didn't have a vision yesterday, but yeah. I'm still nervous." Uncertainty clouded the Scribe's face as he looked down, staring at the open hands resting on his lap. "When a Seer sees the future, that's the fate that'll happen if they don't change what leads to it. So, if I see something bad... If... If I see someone die, and I do nothing to stop that future from happening..." The words trailed off. Even hypothetically, he couldn't bring himself to say it aloud. He didn't want to jinx himself. "Who wouldn't be afraid of that kind of responsibility?"

Enoch paused, realizing what he was saying. Even with Cyrus, he'd never been great at being open with how he truly felt about things. The people in his life had enough to worry about without him adding his own burdens to theirs. But Azazel... something about that man just seemed to break down people's defenses. Perhaps it was the look of genuine compassion in his eyes. A feeling that the Pilgrim truly wanted to help. Or maybe it was simply the knowledge that once the angel's wounds healed, he'd likely never see him again. Then, any secrets shared would be too far away for consequence.

He wouldn't say it out loud, but that hurt to think about.

"It's definitely not an easy situation to be in," Azazel replied, interrupting the Scribe's thoughts. He crossed his arms, searching for the right words. The answer, oddly enough, was apparently sitting on the shelf above Enoch's desk, based on the angel's nod in its direction. "Have you read all the textbooks here?" he asked.

Admittedly, Enoch was happy for the change of subject. Based on his previous conversations with the man, however, he couldn't help but feel a tad suspicious. So far, the Pilgrim's seemingly out of the blue comments ended up disguising some form of advice or life lesson. That being said, it would probably happen whether he wanted it to or not. "It's been a while, but yeah, I have," he played along.

"Great!" Azazel pointed to the shelf, an excited and somewhat prideful smile on his face. "It actually turns out that I'm in one of them! 'History of the Three Realms', right there." His voice took on an almost mocking tone, subtle enough that Enoch couldn't quite tell if it was intentional. "And the Archangels sent nine messengers to teach us the ways of the heavens," he recited. "It is from their divine knowledge that humanity prospered..."

"The angel Azazel taught men to mine and shape the earth beneath them;" Enoch continued the quote, eyes wide at the familiar words. "...To make swords, knives, shields, breastplates... You're *that* Azazel?"

"The one and only!" A pout cut the Pilgrim's pride short. "Y'know I also taught you guys how to create makeup and jewelry, but people always seem to forget that part."

Azazel's complaints fell on deaf ears. Enoch held his chin as the implications added up. *I knew he had to be old. I mean, he said he'd been in Terrael for hundreds of years. But I thought the story of the nine Watchers dated back to the Age of Enlightenment! The thought that the guy sitting in front of me is that same Azazel... well, it's hard to wrap my mind around.* The Scribe's head shot up as Enoch physically pulled himself from his mental calculations. "Wait, I thought all the angels mentioned in that book left when the Church was founded?"

"Kinda," Azazel said, teetering his hand ambiguously. "It was more like a vacation for a bit." His answer did nothing to lessen Enoch's confusion. The angel smiled. His gaze drifted to the window, accompanied by a reminiscent smile. Thinking back to his past, his muscles tensed. "Like I said, I'm here to help people. It's the reason we came down here in the first place, and the reason I stayed. I saw humanity in its earliest years. I saw you all struggling to survive, to live; learning every lesson the hard way. I couldn't bear to watch it when I knew I could help."

Azazel pulled his gaze back to Enoch, noticing the Scribe listening far more intently than he had up to that point. The mix of wonder and curiosity was actually somewhat cute, and the angel let out a soft chuckle. "I may not have had a vision, but I could see the path humanity would take without guidance. So, me and the others stepped in. And that one decision changed the course of history. To be honest, I still don't know if it was the right decision, but I do know I'd do it again in a heartbeat."

Enoch's wonder faded somewhat as he began to see where Azazel was going with this, just as expected. Nevertheless, he continued to watch and listen as the angel made his point. "So yeah," Azazel said, "maybe you'll see something you don't like in your visions. Maybe you'll end up having to make tough decisions because of it. But you have the power to save lives, Enoch; to change fate itself." The Pilgrim leaned back in the bed, careful to avoid straining his injuries. He managed to dodge the pain, and yet, his smile still faded. "I can think of quite a few people that really could've used an ability like that."

In the seconds after, the room fell silent. Azazel lost his train of thought, detouring to distant memories. After a moment he came back to the present, looking Enoch's way as he got back on track. "We didn't shy away from what we had to do, and look how it turned out. Could you imagine how different things would be if we'd thought it was too much responsibility?"

"That's... a fair point," Enoch replied, trying to process everything he'd been told. Though Azazel's identity as one of the first angels to contact humanity certainly added some weight to the man's words, it also made it quite hard to properly focus on them. Try as he might, Enoch found himself far out of his element with it all. With a sigh, he expelled the thoughts from his mind. "I guess I don't really have a choice anyways. Trying to not sleep didn't exactly work after all. As for the rest of the angel stuff you just told me, that's for morning Enoch to process."

Azazel chuckled, relieved by Enoch's casual response. "You shared your secrets, only fair I share a few in return. At this point I think it's pretty clear I can trust you."

The same warm embrace he'd felt with Josephine enveloped Enoch's heart once more at the angel's words. Trust. It was a nice feeling. Enoch nodded. "Yeah, your secret's safe with me."

Having said enough already, Azazel simply smiled in return. With a nod, he leaned back on the pillow. "Good night, Enoch. Sleep well."

"Oh, uh…" Enoch had been getting comfortable on the chair, but looked over in surprise once more. "Yeah… you too Azazel." Perhaps it was some form of angelic magic, as Azazel's words washed away Enoch's worried thoughts.

Good night. Sleep well.

With this simple lullaby repeating in his mind, Enoch drifted to sleep.

Chapter 26

LIKE THE FIRST strummed note of a minstrel's lute, the thread shook at Enoch's touch. The silent prologue to the coming cacophony, resting at the bottom of a dark abyss.

Cool light from the thread filled the Scribe's body. It flowed through him, painting lines and symbols beneath his skin before collecting in his eyes. As they snapped open, the light revealed the Scribe's surroundings. A curved stone hall stretched out on either side of him. The two ends faded into darkness a short distance away, beyond the reach of his sight. Beside him stood a large, decorated wooden door. It was a door he'd passed almost every day for the last few years; the hall of worship in Penemue's Cathedral. Somehow, he had ended up at work.

A figure began to emerge from the darkness. As Enoch turned to look, he recognized the back of the blue-toned Priest uniform jacket. His brow furrowed. Why would the person walk backwards down the hall? No, that wasn't quite right. The movement was too uneven to be a walk. They were leaning? Struggling? Enoch took a few steps in the figure's direction, his light moving with him to reveal more of the scene. As he did, his heart would've skipped a beat, were it beating at the time.

The struggling figure was none other than Cyrus, currently fighting for his life. The man held up his cane, a meager defense against the other Priest currently using it to force Cyrus backwards. Enoch recognized the attacker as Ormond. The gentleman often came by the library for books on geography, and would complain if Enoch was even a second late to unlock the door in the morning. He was undoubtedly confrontational, but hardly violent. Or so Enoch had thought. Now, the older man's eyes were bloodshot and filled with a primal rage. He pushed against Cyrus' cane with enough force to slide Enoch's mentor back along the smooth cathedral carpet.

Enoch rushed over, hoping to pull away the hands reaching for Cyrus' throat. Much to his dismay, his own hands passed through the two men. Enoch stumbled at the lack of resistance. As he did, his gaze landed on Ormond's neck, as well as the peculiar punctures on it. Bite marks. Blood still dripped from the wounds. Had he been bitten by some fanged beast? Before Enoch could wonder any further, Cyrus finally managed to push Ormond away.

Cyrus' mouth moved, the silent plea failing to reach Enoch and Ormond's ears. From the man's frantic gestures, however, Enoch assumed it was an attempt to get through to the aggressive coworker. It must have failed, because Ormond lunged once more. Cyrus dodged to the side. His hands began to glow green. Just as it had during the presentation, the light spread through the man's cane. Mid-dodge, Cyrus swung the now loose cane wide, the aid swinging around Ormond's torso and arms. The glow vanished as Cyrus pulled the cane tight. He attempted to hold his opponent in place. Ormond struggled against the solid wood restraint, but it proved too strong for the older man. In one final desperate attempt to win, he pushed backward, knocking Cyrus through the door to the hall of worship.

Rushing forward, Enoch followed his mentor. The swinging wooden doors might as well have been a light fog with how easily the Scribe passed through them. Inside, the grand hall was mostly bathed in shadow, too large for the range of Enoch's vision. He could see the floor near the entrance, a knocked over candlestick or two, the back of the closest pews. Those were hardly important right then though. All that mattered was if Cyrus was okay.

The Priest picked himself up off the stone floor. Once he had recovered, he froze at the sight of Enoch at the door, fear in his eyes. The feeling of guilt that rushed through the young Scribe felt like a punch to the gut. However, he quickly realized he was not the Priest's concern. A shadow passed by; a figure that had been hidden behind the door. Enoch was decently tall, and yet this figure still stood a head taller. Before Cyrus could get away, the silhouette grabbed him, biting into his neck. The man silently cried out in pain, clutching at the wound as the newcomer dropped him to the ground. Enoch rushed toward him, but...

Time slowed. As the figure turned to face Enoch, all he could see was their six-horned mask. The decorative carvings in the wood were the same ones carved into his memory. An empty, soulless void stared back where their eyes should be. His legs refused to move even a step closer, shaking instead as the muscular silhouette passed him by, walking towards the door. The shadows surrounding Enoch's vision seemed to close in around him.

That mask...

The Soldiers of Lilith...

It was happening again.

As the figure left the worship hall, Enoch's warped sense of time returned to normal. Cyrus still held his neck, the older man collapsed on the floor in pain. Enoch called out to him without a sound, his legs finally overcoming their earlier weakness. With every step, the ground began to melt away, dragging Enoch into the darkness below. He couldn't get closer! He couldn't reach him! He grasped out towards Cyrus. The surrounding void engulfed the man as Enoch fell too far to see him. Still, Enoch called out without a voice. Only the abyss remained, and it had no interest in his silent cries of desperation.

"Cyrus!"

Drenched in sweat, Enoch nearly fell out of his chair as he reached out into the apartment. His vocal cords strained to wake as well as he shouted out to a man too far to hear.

Chapter 27

THE WOODEN MASK swung in the morning breeze as it hung from the young demon's neck. Her lavender skin stood out against the cool, gray cathedral balcony she stood on. Thankfully, the early hour left few people awake to see this. This was a stealth mission, after all.

The girl shifted her weight from foot to foot. The cold of the stone couldn't make it through her dance slippers, but she still felt a chill. Was it impatience? Excitement? Nerves? Perhaps all of the above? Or maybe fresh air was simply cooler than the humid heat of her underground home. Her black tank top, specially designed to fit around her magenta, bat-like wings, did little to keep her warm. She could feel the cold all the way from her curled-back horns to the tip of her pointed tail. The bandages wrapped around her arms, hands and calves kept some of the warmth in at least, along with her somewhat poofy pants, reminiscent of the ones worn by her superior officer Abyzou.

Maybe I should've brought a coat, she realized. *Something fancy, like the one that demon boy was wearing!* She scanned the horizon from the cathedral balcony, golden eyes searching for the cluster of rocks they'd left him in. This far in the city, she couldn't quite make it out. The cathedral was certainly taller than the surrounding buildings, but there was still too much in the way. Granted, it was probably a good thing that she couldn't see him. It meant the humans couldn't either. For now.

"You sure it's okay to leave him on his own like that, Aby?" she asked, turning to Abyzou. She instead found a dark green hand leading her dangling mask back onto her face. The thread slid easily past the young girl's short, magenta hair.

"Agrat please, at least keep it on for the mission," Abyzou said. Agrat reluctantly adjusted the string to fit above her pointed ears, holding it in place. As she did, she watched Abyzou scan their surroundings as well. "As for Mahway, he was in no state to come with us. We'll head right back to get him once we're done though. So, he won't be alone for long."

"But what if he ends up disappearing too?" Agrat asked, gaze still searching the horizon despite Abyzou's reassurances. Her superior smiled softly at the girl's concern.

"He'll be fine," Abyzou replied. "Even if he does get captured like the others, we'll know where they're being sent soon enough." That's what she hoped, at least. Her thoughts contradicted the confidence of her words. She knew fully well how risky their mission was, but they were running out of options. If their target didn't know the truth behind her missing men, then... No. She couldn't think like that. This had to succeed.

She had to save them, no matter the price.

Abyzou turned to Furcus, the slender demon staring up at the cathedral's central dome. He stroked his beard, scowling at the various stained-glass windows depicting the First Surface War. Angels and humans banding together.

Demons banished below ground, trapped in a prison of the Archangels' making. Their "home" seemed much brighter when depicted in glass.

"You're sure this is the right cathedral, Furcus?" Abyzou asked, pulling the elderly man from his musings. Furcus turned to face her, leaning forward in a formal bow.

"Of course, my lady. I saw the Inquisitor spend quite some time in this building during my scouting mission. I believe it's safe to assume this is her place of work."

Finding the answer to her liking, Abyzou nodded, moving closer to the balcony entrance. Agrat snuck over to Furcus, overdramatically mimicking the man's bow. A slight spread of her wings added a flourish to the movement.

"Of course, my lady!" she parroted, trying her best to mimic the demon's deeper rasp. Her hands moved behind her head as she stood back up. The nonchalant pose added to her cheeky tone as she smiled at her elder, oblivious to the figure inside passing by the foggy cathedral window. "Y'knooow, you could just call her Aby like the rest of us," she said. Furcus shrugged.

"I believe I'm a tad too old to use the same cool nick-names as you younger demons," he replied. The young girl's smile grew as she reached up, playfully tapping the man's mask above his nose.

"Aww, c'mon Fur Coat, you're still plenty young!"

"At heart, perhaps."

A rattling at the door cut the conversation short. Abyzou pressed herself against the wall next to the exit. "Get ready. Our first distraction is coming." In an instant, Furcus and Agrat prepared themselves, moving out of view. A dark green aura covered their leader's body. Scales appeared on her skin. Silently, the three of them watched the balcony door open, a Priest walking outside with a groggy step. He pulled a pipe out from his jacket.

"Where did I put those matches?" he asked, searching the various pockets of the uniform. The door swung shut behind him, the sound masking the soft steps of Abyzou approaching her prey.

"The air feels so fresh this morning. You sure you want to ruin it?" she said, causing the man to jump. Caught off guard, the Priest swung around, fear replacing his shock at the sight of the three demons on the Church's doorstep. His body glowed blue. Whatever words he took a breath to say would remain a mystery as Abyzou sank her fangs into his neck. The blue glow vanished, and the man doubled over as Abyzou pulled away.

"Could you get the door, Agrat?" she asked, wiping her mouth. With a nod, Agrat skipped to the entrance.

"Got it!"

The Priest's head hung limp as Furcus lifted him up, dragging him across the balcony. "On your feet," he ordered with a growl. "It's time to get to work." He tossed the man through the open door, and Agrat quickly closed it behind him. Inside, the Priest slid across the carpet, body trembling as he managed to lift himself onto his hands and knees.

His neck burned. His skin felt tighter. His eyes stung. A subtle green glow filled his veins, his body shaking. As his reality shifted around him, the man's gaze darted about before landing on his hands. Fear and panic slowly overtook him, his eyes now glazed and bloodshot. Once the green glow faded, merging with his body and mind, he grasped at his head, nails digging into his scalp. Everything hurt. Everything burned. It got worse and worse and worse and then—

It vanished.

The man stared in absolute terror at the empty hall before him. The sight of it caused a pressure to build in his chest, growing and growing before erupting from his lungs.

"AAAAAAAAAAAAAAAAHHHHHHHHHHHHH!"

Chapter 28

"**H**UH!? WHAT'S HAPPENING?"

Enoch's sudden outburst woke Azazel with a jolt. Coincidentally, a jolt is also exactly how the resulting pain felt shooting through his body. The words came out of the half-conscious angel's lips in a mumble. Holding a hand to his aching chest, Azazel watched as Enoch scrambled to his feet, grabbing his bag off the coat rack next to him.

"Hey, what happened?" Azazel asked, more concerned after Enoch ignored the first inquiry. Actually, the angel couldn't tell if he'd heard it at all. The Scribe was in a trance as he slid on his shoes, muttering words too quiet for Azazel to hear. "Did you have another–"

SLAM!

The door slammed shut. Azazel stared in silence, now fully awake, very confused and completely concerned. There was no doubt in his mind that Enoch had had a vision of some sort, but... that reaction was a little extreme, wasn't it?

What's got you so freaked out, tough guy?

Outside, the clouds that had begun to gather the day before now covered the sky entirely. Enoch ran down the stairs so quickly, he was practically falling. *It's already morning?* he realized. *How long was I asleep?* Skidding around the corner, he ran to the nearby alley to grab his bike. *There's no time to waste. The Soldiers of Lilith are going to attack Penemue's Cathedral! But when? Today? Tomorrow? A month? A year? Until I know for sure, I've gotta warn them as soon as possible!* The boy's frantic state earned no shortage of worried and frightened glances from the people nearby. The sudden frustrated groan he let out as he remembered his bike was gone did little to ease their concern. After a moment of hesitation, he took off, sprinting down the street towards the cathedral.

On his bike, the trip took about half an hour. On foot, he had no idea. But in his panicked mind, running was his only option. *High Inquisitor Haven said that Cyrus would be working in the morning. He's there right now! He could be in danger!* All Enoch could do was run, begging the Archangels to let his worry be for nothing. To tell him the attack would happen another day.

Begging them to keep Cyrus safe.

Every heavy breath pushed Enoch's lungs further past their limit. His face dripped with sweat, twisted in pain as he tried to maintain his pace. As he ran, he went through what he knew in his mind. *The demon in the vision was wearing a mask. Could they be with the Soldiers of Lilith seen near the city? I mean, Mahway managed to sneak in undetected, so it's possible they could as well.* Enoch braced himself on a street lamp as he took a corner a little too quickly, nearly toppling to the pavement. Instead, he pushed off the smooth metal surface, ignoring aches and cramps as his body demanded he stop. But Enoch wouldn't dream of doing such a thing. *Now that I think about it, maybe Mahway was a scout of some sort! If a demon that strong is targeting the cathedral... If I'm too late, then—*

Memories of Cyrus flooded his mind. A comforting hand on his back helping him through a panic attack. A warm hug outside his door accompanied by words of relief.

Why didn't I hug him back?

He remembered the two of them long ago, boarding a train, smiling and waving to their friends and family, certain they'd meet again soon. As he ran, the rain began to fall, poisoning the memory. The rain had fallen that day as well. When Cyrus had sat with him for hours and hours, surrounded by the sickening scent of flowers and blood. His chest had hurt then too, and now...

Cyrus.

He's going to be attacked.

It's going to happen again.

It's happening again. It–

Pain burned Enoch's palms as he lost his footing at the edge of the canal bridge. His dragging feet caught the edge of the structure. He fell to his hands and knees. Dripping sweat joined the raindrops beginning to paint the cobblestone. The air stung his lungs as he struggled to catch his breath.

"I can't..."

The words came out strained and quiet. Enoch didn't notice. Instead, his mind was far in the past, back to when he and Cyrus first met; when he nervously hid behind his mother, staring at the smiling, kneeling man in front of him.

"Hello, your name is Enoch, right? Your mother tells me you're quite the reader!" Cyrus held up a handful of books for Enoch to see. *"Well, I'm having a little trouble choosing which book to read to the class."* Curiosity replaced the fear in young Enoch's eyes as he leaned out further. Cyrus smiled brightly.

"Do you think you could help me, Enoch?"

In the present, at the edge of the canal, Enoch clenched his fist, ignoring the pain; ignoring the sweat and rain dripping into his eyes. Emotion bubbled up within; a buzzing energy that caused his body to shake. Adrenaline, terror, determination; it felt as if it could shatter him. Years of insisting he was fine; of numbing and repressing his feelings; of pushing everything aside because it hurt to feel... all of it came to the surface, bursting out as a scream that could pierce the borders of Spira itself.

"I can't lose you too!!"

Filled with newfound determination, Enoch got to his feet, continuing towards the cathedral. Even if the attack wasn't happening that day, he couldn't afford to wait. He couldn't risk it. He had to be there. This time, he would be there. He had to know Cyrus was okay. He had to warn him.

He had to save him.

It took a moment for Enoch to fully stop running, even after reaching the streets surrounding Penemue's Cathedral. Every breath struggled to fill his exhausted lungs, and left as a painful sounding wheeze. As he approached the main gate of the cathedral's surrounding wall, Enoch heard the murmurs of a crowd through the ringing in his ears. Shortly after, he saw the group crowding the entrance.

Steeling himself, he pushed his way through, bag hugged close in a weak attempt at comfort. He noticed a wooden barricade set up, blocking the courtyard. No doubt that was the cause of the gathering crowd. On top of the pain assaulting his lungs, he felt a tightness in his chest.

Has the attack already started?

Once Enoch reached the front of the group, a Priest grabbed his shoulder, holding him back. "No civilians past this point kid," she said. Enoch lifted his Church-issued bag, showing the Priest the symbol on the flap. Any properly trained member of the Church would be able to tell it was the real deal.

"I work in the cathedral. In the library," he explained, hoping this would be enough to help him get inside.

"Well, your shift is canceled today," the Priest snapped back, crushing his hopes. "The cathedral is closed due to a high concentration of magical energy."

There was no doubt in Enoch's mind now. The events of his vision really were unfolding right at that moment. But the Priest's words didn't quite sit right. *She said the reason is magical energy?* he thought. *Are they covering up the fact that demons are involved? Or do they not know the cause yet?* Either way, he needed to get inside as soon as possible.

"I'm not here to work. My friend, he... he's stuck in there. I need to help him!" Enoch's pleas simply caused the Priest to cross her arms.

"The Church is already working to resolve the situation. I'm sorry, but you'll just have to wait. Friend or not, you're a civilian, you'd just get in the way."

The Scribe took a breath to argue, until the Priest's words sunk in. *She's right. What am I doing?* he realized. *Am I planning to just barge in there and fight the demon myself?* He glanced at the cathedral once more. He'd come to warn them of the attack. If it had already started, then what could he possibly do? Something like this would be far bigger than lifting a beam off of someone, or treating an injury. This was a demon.

And he was only human.

His posture lowered as he reluctantly accepted the situation. Now that the adrenaline was beginning to wear off, logic was prevailing. His emotions once again found themselves cast aside, almost out of habit. *The Church is already handling things. Cyrus will be okay, right?* "Right. Of course. Sorry, ma'am..."

The rain began to properly fall as Enoch followed the base of the cathedral's outer wall. He gripped his bag tightly, a defeated look in his eyes. *He's in there. He's right there, and I can't do a damn thing! Why did I think this time would be different?* As he chastised himself, a sound broke through his thoughts. A woman, raising her voice nearby.

"What do you mean nothing?" Glancing over, Enoch found the source of the commotion. In the outdoor eating area of a café across the street, Priests and Inquisitors hurried about. The fenced off area had been turned into a makeshift base of operations. The canopy above kept them out of the rain, protecting the various papers, maps and files scattered about the tables. In the center of it all, past the Priests keeping guard, stood a woman carrying herself with an air of authority. The red and gold bands hanging from the Church symbol pin on her chest marked her as a High Inquisitive.

She was a burly woman with dark, frizzy hair pulled into a bun. A few curly gray streaks dotted the strands here and there, matching the silver pen tucked behind her ear. Scars of varied size and age marked her smooth, dark brown skin, most of the wounds faded over the years. Her most notable trait, however, was that she had no right arm. The design of her High Inquisitive robes had been adjusted to accommodate this. The remaining arm currently leaned on one of the paper-covered café tables, clenched tightly as the woman stared at a young Inquisitor in front of her.

"S-Sorry, High Inquisitive Foster, uh… ma'am, the messages have completely stopped," the Inquisitor explained. Their posture was rigid enough to make bystanders' backs hurt. Inquisitive Foster let out a sigh, a hint of pain in her eyes that vanished with a blink.

"She had a high tolerance, so I doubt it was the residual energy," she replied. "She must've been affected by the ability somehow, or killed by one of the infected." Frustrated by this development, the High Inquisitive turned her attention to the table. She scanned the map of the cathedral, and the employee profiles laid out across it. Surely, the solution to this situation could be found hidden within them. Finding it, however, had just gotten much harder. "Her message ability was our best way of figuring out what in the Three Realms is going on in there!" she complained.

"It's the Soldiers of Lilith!"

The sudden, new and unfamiliar voice caught the attention of every Priest and Inquisitor in the makeshift base. They turned to look, finding Enoch a short distance outside the fence. One of the Priests on guard grabbed him before he could enter. No doubt the man had hoped to do so before Enoch could speak, but the Scribe still managed to get close enough. Enoch stared at Foster. He didn't fight against the Priest's grip, but his determination to assist could be seen in his eyes. Intrigued, but also highly suspicious, Foster straightened her posture.

"Who are you? And how could you possibly know that?" She moved closer to the young man now restrained by her subordinate.

"I'm Enoch Augnium, ma'am; a Scribe that works in this cathedral. And I know because I saw the attacker's mask." Foster raised an eyebrow, hand resting on her hip.

"My men didn't see anyone escape the cathedral, and I was told all the exits were sealed from the inside. How did you see this mask?"

"I'm a Seer. I saw it in a vision." Enoch hesitated, just for a moment as he thought back to what he'd seen; to Cyrus falling victim to the demon's attack. "Someone very important to me is trapped inside there. I... I saw a demon bite him. The Priest that attacked him also had a bite mark on their neck, so I think the ability is probably a Beast Manipulator type transmitted through the demon's teeth."

Beast Manipulators, as stated by Enoch, are individuals capable of transferring their magic into other living creatures, so long as certain requirements are met. They're split into two categories. Hijackers, who control the actions or behaviors of their target; and Influencers, who will affect the creature in some way without gaining any control over them. If an ending condition is met, or the target moves beyond the range of the user's ability, the effect will end.

The dangerous thing with Manipulators, more so than the fear of losing one's control or capabilities through an ability, is that the very act of their foreign magic entering the target's body can be fatal to those with a low enough tolerance. Though powerful, Manipulators must exercise caution in the use of their abilities, lest they end up with blood on their hands.

After hearing Enoch's explanation, Foster grew quiet, reading the boy's expression; searching for any signs of deception. After a moment, she waved her hand, signaling the Priest to release him. "Who else have you told this to?" she asked as Enoch rubbed his arms.

"No one, ma'am. I came here as soon as I had the vision."

"Explains the outfit."

Enoch glanced down, face going red as he realized he was still wearing his night clothes. He'd been in such a hurry he'd forgotten to grab even a jacket to cover up. His loose white shirt clung to his chest, soaking wet from his run through the rain. Ignoring Enoch's embarrassment, Foster waved for him to follow her.

"Before she went silent, a Pilgrim was sending us intel on what was going on inside. She mentioned neck wounds on the infected too. I figured this attack was organized by the Anti-Church Movement, but…" She led Enoch to the table she was standing at before. "To think the S-O-L would attack this far into the capital. They're getting bold. And of course it had to happen on the day Haven ran off. Last thing I wanted to do today was clean up messes on her behalf." The High Inquisitive rested her hand on the table as she turned to face Enoch.

"But we can't just ignore the problem in front of us, can we? Tell me everything you saw, Mr. Augnium. Every single detail."

Chapter 29

RUNNING WAS FUTILE, but it was all the Priest could do. Normally, the floor of the hall of worship was a spectacle to see. Colored light from the stained glass above would shine across the circular chamber below; across the pews, the polished floor, the altar of the Archangels, the pillars holding up the balcony that surrounded them all. Every surface would shine with a brilliant luminescent rainbow.

Now those same lights bathed a far more gruesome scene. An iridescent, thick fog covered the ground. Priests, Pilgrims, Inquisitors, they all laid scattered across the pews and floor. Some, though unconscious, still clung to life; others added to the growing red puddle spreading across the floor. Suddenly, one of the pews shattered, crushed under the sheer force and speed of the body thrown into it. He'd tried to run, realizing that he was no match for the man they'd come to stop.

The Priest's body went limp, blood dripping from the gashes caused by broken wood. A burst of purple magical energy erupted from his body, a small, brief explosion reaching a few meters away before thinning into a fog, adding to the haze carpeting the floor, and leaving the body a lifeless husk. The cause of death, as well as the source of the bruises on the man's neck, stood laughing at the altar. Adir. The dark haired, muscular Priest laughed uncontrollably, his eyes foggy and bloodshot. They'd come to stop him, but no opponent could win against his strength! No one could escape the crushing grasp of his blood-soaked hands! Truly, he was the strongest man in the cathedral! No, in all of Courciel!

Up above the massacre, Agrat walked along the balcony railing like a tightrope. She'd watched the fights beneath them, Adir picking off the others one by one. Their distraction had worked exactly as planned, even if Abyzou had to infect more humans than expected.

The big muscly one probably could've handled it all if we'd gotten to him sooner, she mused. Agrat frowned, disappointed that every single person had resorted to violence. *Maybe humans really are as bad as Furcus says.*

She turned away from the gruesome scene, watching Abyzou stare out the nearby window. "Everything okay, Aby?"

The green-skinned demon shook her head. From her vantage point, she could see the commotion below. Priests, Inquisitors, bystanders, all scurrying about in the rain, trying to find a way to safely resolve the situation. "I didn't expect so many so soon. This is going to complicate things."

"I was sure I locked all the doors though!" Agrat replied. "How did they find out already?"

Creeeeeeak. Behind them, a door slowly opened. Abyzou and Agrat both prepared for a fight, relaxing as Furcus entered the chamber. The red handkerchief in the elderly demon's hand casually wiped away the blood on his trident.

"One of the humans had the ability to send her thoughts to others," he explained. "She was sending information outside, which allowed them to organize faster than expected. I was hoping to use that to our advantage, but unfortunately, she refused to cooperate."

"Seems to be a common theme with humans," Abyzou said. Furcus nodded.

"Indeed."

Furcus and Agrat's posture grew more alert as Abyzou left the window, the two waiting for their orders. Their commander was silent for a moment as she considered their situation. "The leak of information may work in our favor," she finally said. "If they know how many have died, they'll be less likely to send in their men." The muscular demon scanned the bodies on the lower floor with a disappointed sigh, most of them half covered by the fog of magical energy. "Unfortunately, there's still no sign of the Inquisitor, so she likely didn't come in today. But bad luck aside, there may still be records. Keep looking for now."

As his commander came close, Furcus opened the door for her with a slight bow. In an impressive show of balance, Agrat perched on the balcony railing again. "Same plan if things go south?" she asked.

Abyzou nodded. "Yes. Make sure you don't get caught, Agrat. And save your magic just in case."

"Oki doki Aby!" Agrat replied with a small salute. Having received her orders, she spread her wings, gliding down to one of the lower-level doors.

"And off she goes," Furcus said with a sigh, left behind by both his companions. He began heading to one of the distant balcony doors, his voice dripping with sarcasm. "Oh no, don't mind me. I'll meet you down there. I'm sure the cold, silent stairs will be pleasant company for this old demon." The door closed behind him, leaving nothing but

Adir behind, the man's bloodthirsty laughter still echoing throughout the hall.

Chapter 30

THE PATTERNING OF the rain mixed with the tapping of Inquisitive Foster's fingers on the table. She had listened silently as Enoch described his vision. Now the young Scribe stared intently, searching her expression for any sign that the information had helped; searching for the small glimmer of hope that he so badly needed.

"I'll admit, I was hoping for more," Foster finally replied. "But at the very least, now we know the ability is caused by a bite, and that we're dealing with demons, not humans." The High Inquisitive turned back to her notes, looking through the files and maps spread across the table. Enoch waited for her to continue. Surely, she could form some kind of plan now, right? Her silence caused anxiety to build within his chest. His gaze darted to the side, glancing at the cathedral.

"Now that you know the method, you can send in Priests to save the people left, right? They're safe as long as they don't get bit."

"Things aren't that simple, kid." Foster's words pulled the Scribe's attention back to the table. Confused, he watched as the High Inquisitive tapped the map, finger resting on the circular hall of worship in the center of the building.

"The demon's bite makes people manic and aggressive," she explained. "Our source told us that because of this, some of the infected started using their abilities to kill each other, caught up in some kind of personalized hallucination. Most of them died in the hall of worship to some Priest that can strengthen his body." The woman turned to Enoch, adjusting her arm to lean on the table. "The corpses of a bunch of high-capacity magic users are all grouped together in there. Which means..."

The anxiety in Enoch's chest slowly morphed into dread as he realized where she was going with this. "Their final bursts..." he replied softly.

"Exactly. You catch on quick, kid." Foster looked to the cathedral. Though she couldn't see inside, she could easily imagine the bloody massacre within the stone walls; the all too familiar iridescent haze that lingered after a fight to the death between magic users. "Our bodies aren't built for extended exposure to foreign magic. A magic user could probably last quite a while if it was only one or two bursts, but the total was at least ten before our info got cut off. My men are strong, but if they got caught up in a fight with a Priest or a demon in that much residual magic, they wouldn't last long enough to win."

Foster's words received a few grateful nods from the Priests and Inquisitors nearby. She tapped the hall of worship on the map once more. "We still don't know the attackers' motives, but I'm sure they know we're out here waiting for them now. If I had the magical tolerance of a demon, I'd be using that cloud of magic as a shield against us." As she listed their obstacles aloud, Foster pinched the bridge of her nose, closing her eyes in annoyance. "On top of that, as long as the Priests are out of control, we have to worry about their abilities too. They clearly have no problem using lethal force. It's going to be a legal nightmare when they go back to normal."

Reluctantly, Foster lowered her hand. The momentary relief from her growing headache ended. Turning back to her papers, her voice took on a dismissive tone. "So no, I can't send in my men. Until the magic inside dissipates, it'd be too risky. The demons are staying inside for now, so all we can do is wait."

"We can't afford to wait!" Enoch shouted. "If we don't do something then Cyrus is going to end up dead!" He understood the logic behind the woman's hesitation, but now wasn't the time for caution!

Hearing Enoch raise his voice, Foster raised an eyebrow. Her eyes slowly moved to the Scribe, sending a glare his way. "Cyrus...? Right, he was the one you saw in your vision. I'm guessing he's a friend?" She gestured to the Priests around her. Many were now on guard after Enoch's outburst. "Well, all of them have friends and family too. I'm not going to send them in there unprepared just to watch them all die."

"But what about the people inside? You're fine letting them die instead?" Enoch asked, slamming his hand on the table. The pain of the impact wasn't enough to smack some sense into him. He knew he was arguing with a high-ranking member of the Church, but his frustration got the better of him. At this point, he couldn't help but wonder if it was directed towards Foster or himself. Was he mad at her inaction, or his own helplessness?

A forceful finger jabbed at his chest. Foster leaned towards him. "Look kid, I appreciate the new info, but if you can't behave, I need you to remove yourself from my work area before I remove you by force." The intensity in her unblinking eyes was enough to catch Enoch off guard. Though his feet refused to move, he leaned away somewhat, retreating from her dominant demeanor.

Doing his best to subdue his anger, Enoch took a deep breath. Once he'd calmed himself, he nodded. "I can control myself. Sorry," he apologized. Foster's hand returned to the table. As things de-escalated, Enoch tried his best to direct his frustration to his hand instead of his voice. His nails dug into his palm. "But please, if you don't want to risk the lives of your men, then send me in instead. I can't stop the demons, but I know my way around, and I have a high magical tolerance. I should be able to last long enough to save him."

The growing feeling of helplessness began to reach its limit. Enoch could barely hold back the tears beginning to sting his eyes. For a moment, Foster seemed to be the one caught off guard. Hearing the Scribe's request, she hesitated before looking over to a Priest behind Enoch. She pointed to her hip as Enoch continued, his emotions blinding him to the exchange. "I can't lose him too. Please, just let me go save him before it's too late."

Click Click! Cold metal closed around Enoch's wrists. He glanced down in shock and confusion as the Priest locked the handcuffs in place. "H-Hey! Hold on! I'm just—"

"Just trying to get yourself killed," Foster interrupted. "I can't have you running in there and causing trouble, kid. We'll take them off after everything's been sorted out." The High Inquisitive let out a sigh. Her quick, fierce demeanor softened for just a moment. "I get it. It's your coworkers in there. Your friends too. I wanna save them as much as you, trust me. But going in right now will just add to the body count and make things worse. If you rush in there, you're as good as dead."

Once again, she gestured to the Priest, nodding her head to the side. The man gently grabbed Enoch's shoulder as his commander continued. "Just stick with Matthew there for now and leave this to the professionals. As soon as we can get in there safely, we'll do our best to stop the demon and save who's left. Please cooperate, kid. Don't make things harder than they need to be."

The words he needed escaped him. Enoch desperately wanted to argue, but his hands were literally tied. Reluctantly, he nodded, shoulders hunched in defeat as he allowed himself to be escorted away from his one shot at saving Cyrus.

Chapter 31

THOUGH SIMILAR TO his bracelet in both shape and weight, the silver metal on Enoch's wrists brought him no comfort. The cold, metallic surface that had once filled him with a sense of security, now drowned him in overwhelming helplessness. A harsh and horrible emotion. A recipe of so many painful feelings. The sinking weight of guilt. The suffocating depths of sadness. A desire to act battered down by the inability to do so. Helplessness is a constant battle between good intentions and harsh reality.

Once again, he would simply sit on the sidelines as the people he loved suffered.

He couldn't save anyone.

Enoch walked along the cathedral's outer wall, following Matthew, the Priest assigned to keep an eye on him. The shackles on his wrists rattled and chimed with each guilt-filled step. He dug his nails into his palm, trying and failing to distract himself with the pain. *Has Cyrus already been attacked?* he wondered. *Has the demon already reached him?* All he could do was hope that the events of his vision would happen towards the end of the demon's attack. Maybe then, Cyrus would have a chance.

No. That wouldn't happen, would it? Cyrus and I aren't lucky enough for that.

If he waited for Foster and her men to handle things, then Cyrus would get hurt. The growing body count adding to the cloud of residual magic meant anyone that survived physical attack would likely succumb to magical overflow instead. If he could get inside, then maybe he could sneak some of them out before that happened, but...

"If you rush in there, you're as good as dead."

Foster's words snuffed out his hope. Enoch let out a sigh. *She's right. I can't take on a cathedral full of insane Priests. Not to mention the demon. I'd be dead before I could even reach the hall of worship.* Despite his desire to help, he couldn't save them. He was useless. Trapped. Helpless. He couldn't save them. He couldn't save them. He couldn't–

"If you can't save everyone, you just focus on saving the people you can." Like a ray of sunlight breaking through the rain clouds, Azazel's words echoed through Enoch's mind, stubbornly arguing against the boy's despair. For a moment, Enoch looked up in surprise. Just for a moment. Then, the frown slowly crept back onto his face. "Easy for you to say," he muttered under his breath, receiving a confused glance from Matthew. The Priest shrugged it off as Enoch grew silent once more.

Even if he did try to save them, he was handcuffed, stuck on the wrong side of the wall, and was currently being monitored by a Priest ordered to keep him out of the cathedral he'd need to get inside of. Tears mixed with the rain on his face as he grew irritated at his own incompetence. *I really thought things would be different this time, but I guess I really can't change fate.*

That is, unless fate decided to have a change of heart.

CRASH!!!! The sound of breaking glass rang out from the cathedral, followed by a dull THUD and sickening *CRUNCH*. Enoch and Matthew glanced over in surprise; their vision blocked by the wall.

"What in the Realms...?" the Priest said. A soft hum filled the air on the other side of the wall, slowly growing louder and louder. Suddenly, Matthew grabbed Enoch, using his own body to shield the Scribe as the wall beside them shattered outward. He moved both of them to the side. The dust began to settle. Once it had, the Priest glanced around the newly formed gap in the wall.

In the courtyard, a panicked Inquisitor crawled through the grass beneath a broken second story window. The source of the humming, and the new hole in the wall, seemed to be his outstretched arm, currently glowing red with magical energy. The man's eyes were bloodshot, darting about as he struggled to stand; to escape some unseen threat. Unfortunately, the unnatural and painful bend of his leg was preventing this from happening.

"No! Get away from me! I'll... I'll kill you!" The Inquisitor threatened the empty air.

"Crap, he's still trying to move!?" Matthew exclaimed, noticing the man's injury. He looked between Enoch and the Inquisitor, body tense with indecision. As the Inquisitor's hand began to hum again, Matthew let go of Enoch. "Stay over there! I'm going to go restrain him!" he shouted, grabbing a pair of magic-suppressing cuffs from his belt. He ran towards the injured man. The infected Inquisitor thrashed about as Matthew grabbed his arms, pinning him to the ground. It took all his strength to keep himself from being pushed away.

Enoch watched in disbelief, still processing everything that had just happened. Down the street, he could hear the voices of other Priests rushing over from the closest gate.

"It came from over here!"

"Look! The window! Did someone jump?"

Enoch looked from the street, to the hole in the wall, to the cathedral that was now enticingly close. Any second now, more Priests would arrive to investigate. Hesitantly, he stepped on the crumbled stone bricks. Once again, Foster's words rang through his mind. "*If you rush in there, you're as good as dead.*"

I know that! his mind argued. *I'm not a hero. I know I'm out of my league. But... this time I'm going to try! I have to!* He took another step through the wall, fingers lingering on the broken stone bricks. *If our positions were swapped, I know Cyrus would risk everything to save me.* Enoch closed his eyes, swallowing his fear. He couldn't keep making excuses. If Foster wasn't going to save Cyrus, then Enoch was all he had left. Before reason could slow his steps, Enoch rushed into the courtyard. *I'm going to save him!*

Matthew watched as Enoch ran by, the Priest still occupied with holding the infected Inquisitor down. "What are you doing, kid?" he shouted in disbelief. "You're gonna get yourself killed!" Enoch refused to listen, focusing on nothing but his goal. He practically skidded around the corner, shoes scraping the rain-soaked grass out of the ground as he hurried to the cathedral's back entrance. The doorknob turned easily, but the door itself refused to budge no matter how hard he pulled. Realizing the demon must have blocked it somehow, he looked around for another way in. The voices of the Priests grew louder, coming from just around the corner. "He went that way! Go stop him before he gets inside!"

His heart raced. Enoch's gaze landed on the nearby windows. He had no other choice. Rushing to the familiar glass, he could see the library inside, his desk sitting safely where he'd left it, oblivious to the chaos occurring in its home. That is, until it was suddenly showered in glass. Enoch swung the large rock from the garden a second time, making sure the opening was large enough for him to fit through.

"Just hold on a little longer Cyrus. I'm on my way!" A few sharp shards remained in place as the Priests appeared from behind the cathedral wall. Enoch climbed inside anyway, his shirt snagging and tearing somewhat on the glass. He pulled free, sliding over his desk and rushing over to the closest bookshelf. The footsteps of the Priests finally reached the window. He glanced at the door. *Could I make it there before they get in and grab me?* Before he could find an answer to that, a familiar voice called out from the courtyard.

"Leave him." Foster rounded the corner, her hand on her hip. Though one would expect her to be angry, her eyes were instead filled with a subtle pain as she spoke. "He made his choice. We can't risk going in with a large group yet. I'm not risking your lives for a kid with a death wish." She pointed over to the two Priests at the window. "You two, help Matthew with the injured Inquisitor. The rest of you, continue to monitor the cathedral. His recklessness may cause the demons to take action."

The High Inquisitive swiftly turned away. A moment of hesitation interrupted her next step as she looked back to the cathedral. The stalemate they'd found themselves in had been forcefully ended. Anything could happen now.

But perhaps that was a blessing in disguise. If the demon hadn't heard the breaking glass, then maybe the kid really could save a few of the survivors.

She shook her head. She'd seen his file among the lists of employees. He had no magic ability. No way to defend himself. More than likely, she'd have to prepare one more death certificate.

"Stupid kid," she muttered. "Archangels, grant him luck."

Chapter 32

ENOCH HAD WORKED in the Penemue Cathedral library for four years. He'd spent hours organizing the shelves, transcribing text, helping Church workers find the resources they needed. He'd memorized the location of every book; knew every groove in every desk and table. It was practically a home away from home. But as he hid behind the bookcase by the window, the room felt cold and unfamiliar.

The pounding of his heart drummed throughout his entire body. Even after the Priests' footsteps moved too far to hear, Enoch waited. He'd spent four years in that room, what was a few seconds more? Once he was sure they'd given up the chase, he relaxed. "Good. They aren't trying to stop me," he whispered, a subtle fear replacing his relief as he realized that also meant he was on his own for this. Pushing aside his worry, he scanned the room. Despite the stressful atmosphere, everything seemed to be in order.

That makes sense, he supposed, *the demon probably isn't here to check out a book.* He approached the door, listening for any noise on the other side. *Based on my vision, I know Cyrus will end up outside the hall of worship, so that's my best bet for finding him. I'll just have to avoid the large amount of magic built up there if I can.*

For once, Enoch felt grateful for the fact he was born a Seer. After all, they were known for their high tolerance to magical energy. This hardly made up for the guilt the visions had forced upon him as payment, but it was a start. At the very least it would buy him some time. *If I pass out from overflow before I find Cyrus, I'm as good as dead. I have to be careful.*

As if to emphasize this point, Enoch suddenly heard soft footsteps outside. They were so quiet he'd nearly missed them over the sound of the rain through the broken window. The doorknob began to turn. Panicked, Enoch crouched down, ducking underneath a table covered in books he'd usually be sorting. Just as he pulled his legs out of sight, Furcus entered the room.

"Agrat? Are you in here?" the elderly demon asked. Enoch held his breath, as well as the chains of his handcuffs, trying his best to keep silent. Furcus' tail flicked in front of him, narrowly missing the Scribe's face. A chill ran down Enoch's spine, far colder than the draft coming in from the shattered window. *What is the demon doing in the library of all places!?*

"You'd think this would be the first place she'd search," Furcus said, scanning the room; stopping as he noticed the shattered glass covering the desk. He let out a thoughtful hum, moving further inside. The floorboards creaked beneath the demon's feet as he walked over to Enoch's desk. Rain was beginning to stain the smooth wooden surface, and he gently moved a book out of the puddle on the floor. A puddle far out of the storm's reach. Furcus held his breath, listening carefully to the room around him. Had the door gotten stuck before closing?

The sound of the library door creaking opening once more filled the hall. Furcus leaned out of the room, glancing both ways, a subtle glow surrounding his hand. Finding nothing but an empty corridor, he returned to the library. Just a few feet away, Enoch continued to press himself against the stone wall with as much force as he could muster, just narrowly managing to hide behind the pillar built into the bricks. After a minute that felt more like an eternity, he finally relaxed.

That was way too close, he thought, glancing at the library door. *But that's weird. The demon was looking for someone. Does that mean there's more than one in here?* He swallowed the fear crawling up his throat at the thought. *I have to find Cyrus as soon as possible.*

Far more carefully than before, he began to head towards the circular central hall, keeping close to the pillars lining the wall, just in case. A slow, dripping sound echoed throughout the cathedral. It got louder as Enoch continued forward; the movement interrupted as he suddenly slipped in a wet spot on the floor. Thankfully, he managed to catch himself, as well as the scream that nearly escaped his lips at the sight of what he'd nearly fallen in.

Blood. A thick puddle of it covered the width of the hall. His eyes followed the path of red, tracing it back to a woman leaning against the wall. Blood dripped from the Pilgrim emblem hanging around her neck, the golden sheen painted crimson. For some reason, the woman seemed familiar, but he couldn't quite place where he'd seen her before.

"Hey, are you okay?" Enoch asked, not realizing the woman had said the same thing to him only a few days prior. He pushed his fear aside as he rushed over to her. "I have medical training, I can–" He cut himself off. Her eyes were still open, but now that he was closer, he noticed the three, evenly spaced stab wounds in her chest. She was beyond saving.

In an instant, Enoch's mind returned to Peycile. The bloodied bodies in the street, staining the puddles red. His chest began to hurt. The pounding of his heart outpaced the rhythmic dripping. The beat was deafening. Could the demons hear it!? As his panic began to grow, Enoch clenched his fist, nails digging into his palm.

"No, no, no. I'm okay. I'm okay." He closed his eyes, trying to stifle his fear and panic. "You can't freeze up. C'mon, calm down. You're okay."

He wanted to ground himself, but at that moment, his surroundings only worsened his mental state. *Calm down! C'mon!* He begged his mind to listen to him. He couldn't afford to panic right now. Amidst the torrent of painful, jarring memories, he tried to remember what would calm him down in the past. *My bracelet?* Gone. *Cocoa?* Clearly not an option.

Cyrus.

Enoch tried his best to focus on his mentor. His friend. Pushing aside the memories of Peycile, he brought himself to his room in Cyrus' home. He hugged his arms to his chest, remembering how Cyrus would hold him close, speaking in a calming tone.

"Shh, shh, it's alright. I'm here. You're okay Enoch. Deep breaths."

In the cathedral, Enoch forced his breathing to slow. "You're okay..." he told himself. "It's alright... You can save them this time, but you need to calm down first." A deep breath in. A deep breath out. "C'mon Enoch, you got his. Just relax. For Cyrus."

With one final exhale, he opened his eyes. Though he'd managed to ease the pain in his chest, his hands still shook. Even the overwhelming beating of his heart seemed to have quieted down, replaced by a new sound further down the hall. The sound of someone struggling. Without wasting a second, Enoch rushed over to a nearby pillar, happy to move away from the puddle of blood. Peering around the curve of the hall, he found the source of the commotion.

Down the hall, Ormond struggled to escape the curved, wooden cane holding his arms in place. The Priest thrashed about the hall, crashing into walls as he tried to break free. The sight felt like a bolt of lightning through Enoch's body. If Ormond was there, then...

Throwing stealth and caution to the wind, Enoch sprinted to the door of the hall of worship. Ormond lunged as he got close. Enoch quickly dodged to the side, and the older Priest fell to the floor, unable to get back up with his arms restrained. Enoch didn't waste a second as he threw his entire weight against the worship hall door, stumbling into the large chamber.

The first thing Enoch noticed was the smell. He froze, covering his nose and mouth with his hands. Compared to the subtle, sickly scent of blood in the hall, the stench here was nauseating. The air clung to his lungs, coated in a fog of magical energy. Enoch had known there would be a number of bodies here, but this... If he'd eaten breakfast, he certainly would have lost it at the gruesome sight before him. The pews, the floor, the wall; blood covered all of them like paint tossed haphazardly onto canvas. Metal candle stands still lined the aisles, a few managing to remain lit, others extinguished when knocked to the floor. The lingering firelight flickered across the bodies draped over the pews. Bloody footprints led away from the altar, but Enoch couldn't see a single person still standing.

"There's so many..." he said, voice muffled by his fingers. Despite his attempts to quell it, he could feel panic building within him once more. He hugged his chest again, trying to picture Cyrus' voice in his mind, only to hear it in the chamber itself. Behind the back pews, Cyrus groaned as he began to lift himself off the floor.

"Cyrus!" The relief at seeing Cyrus alive overpowered the Scribe's panic. He rushed to his mentor's side, kneeling down to help the man up. "Are you okay? I... I saw you get..." Enoch's voice trailed at the sight of the fresh bite marks on Cyrus' neck. He was too late. His already churning stomach tightened.

"Cyrus, It's Enoch. I'm here to help you," he reassured. *Inquisitor Foster said the demon's bite caused hallucinations. If I can help him tell what's real and what isn't, that should keep him from going crazy like the others, right?*

Cyrus lifted himself up, kneeling on one leg. The man's breathing was heavy, his short brown hair clinging to his face. "Enoch...?" he mumbled.

"Yeah! I'm here Cyrus!" Enoch replied, visibly relieved that the Priest had heard him.

"Enoch... is here?" The Scribe's hope began to fade as quickly as it had surfaced, the smile vanishing from his face. He held Cyrus' arm as the man slowly stood. "No... he, he wouldn't be here," the Priest said, voice clouded in confusion and uncertainty.

"Cyrus?" A chilling fear flowed through every vein in Enoch's body as Cyrus turned to face him. He took a step back. Cyrus' eyes... The caring eyes, usually warm as hot cocoa, stared back at him with a hatred as scalding as boiling water.

"How dare you try to trick me, you monster," Cyrus growled. "After everything your kind took from him; from us!" The Priest lunged toward Enoch, hands reaching for his throat. Caught off guard, Enoch couldn't dodge in time. The man's fingers gripped his neck as the two fell to the ground, the fog swirling and shifting from the movement. "You have no right to speak his name! He's all I have left thanks to you, and I'll ensure you never harm him again!"

Every attempt to take a breath was met with a struggled pain. But the sight of Cyrus above him, eyes filled with bloodthirsty hatred, hurt more. Enoch stared up at him in horror, trying to break free. Unfortunately, he couldn't get the chain of his cuffs past Cyrus to pull his hands away. All he could do was cling to the lingering air in his lungs, hoping it would last long enough for him to come up with a plan.

For a moment, he wondered if the lack of oxygen was causing him to hallucinate as well. He could swear that a figure was on the balcony above them. A demon, watching the fight below as his vision began to blur. Unbeknownst to him, his and Cyrus' confrontation did in fact have an audience.

"Hmm... He wasn't here before," Agrat said. Her tail curled around the balcony railing beneath her; a curious gleam in her eyes. "Interesting..."

Chapter 33

I *HAVE TO protect Enoch.*

When Cyrus wrapped his hands around the demon's neck, that one goal ran through his mind, over and over again. The Priest didn't enjoy violence. The very thought of injuring or harming other people made his stomach churn. But he'd lost enough loved ones already, and he wasn't about to let this demon take another.

I have to protect Enoch.

A tighter grip. A stronger force. *Once the demon loses consciousness, I can restrain him... No. That isn't enough.* The unexplainable rage boiling through his veins urged him further. *The demon can't be allowed to live. What if it got away? What if innocents died as a result? One life to save many.* That was the justification in Cyrus' mind as he forced himself past the point of comfort.

The demon, or rather, Enoch through the lens of Cyrus' hallucination, stared up at his mentor and attacker in terror.

"C-Cyrus, it's... I can't–" The words just barely managed to escape. He couldn't breathe, no matter how hard he begged his lungs to work. He tried to push Cyrus off of him, but the larger man was stronger; heavier, and Enoch's muscles were beginning to fail him. Though it pained him to do it, Enoch had no choice. Gathering his remaining strength, he forced his knee into Cyrus' gut. The Priest let out a gasp of pain, loosening his grip. Though brief, the moment was enough for the Scribe to force his mentor off of him.

Enoch scrambled to his feet, backing away. His hand moved to his neck, the lingering pain proving this was real, no matter how much he wished it was just a bad dream. "I'm sorry... I didn't want to do that," the Scribe said between gasps. He watched as Cyrus recovered, the man swaying somewhat as he got back on his feet. The unnatural, aggressive stance contrasted his mentor's usual reserved demeanor; a kind-hearted puppy now a vicious wolf. It was too late. Despite Enoch's best efforts, the demon's ability had already taken control.

With the demon's magic flowing through Cyrus' body, Enoch knew he had to lead him away from the hall of worship, lest the toxic haze push him past the brink. There was only so much foreign magic the man could handle before it would claim his life in a painful burst. Beads of sweat ran down Cyrus' forehead as he glared at Enoch. The glazed, bloodshot eyes were not the eyes of his teacher and friend. His rising body temperature signaled the looming threat of magical overflow.

The clock was ticking.

"Where is Enoch? What did you do with him!?" Cyrus growled. Enoch slowly raised his hands, taking a step back towards the door; towards the safety of the hallway beyond the fog's reach.

"Cyrus, I'm right here. It's me!" he said, "Let me take you somewhere safe and we can figure this out. Please!"

Cyrus answered his pleas with a bloodthirsty charge. "I won't let you take him too, demon!" he shouted. This time, Enoch dodged to the side, hearing a metallic scrape on stone beside him as Cyrus grabbed one of the toppled candle-stands. The Priest gripped it tightly in both hands, ready to kill. Fear took control of Enoch's body. He backed away, right into one of the nearby pews. Once more, he raised his hands.

"Whatever you're seeing isn't real, Cyrus! You need to fight it!" Cyrus lifted the candle-stand. The mist swirled and shifted around him as he charged Enoch. Splinters fell from the pew onto Enoch's head from the stand's impact. He'd managed to crouch in time, but he could still feel the force of the attack reverberating through the pew behind him. The stand bounced back. Cyrus recovered, swinging from the side instead.

Crouched on the floor, Enoch knew he had no way to dodge. He held up his arms, hoping to at least protect his head. The chains of his shackles rattled as his forearms took the brunt of the attack. The force knocked him to the side with a cry of pain and a stomach-churning CRACK! His arms burned. The force radiated throughout his entire body. It was difficult to tell if the swirling mists were from his own head spinning, or Cyrus lifting the stand for another swing. Not willing to wait and find out, he tried to crawl beneath the pew for cover. Each time he pulled himself forward, the pain in his arms brought tears to his eyes, but he had no choice but to push through.

"Cyrus, this isn't you!" he pleaded through gritted teeth. "The Cyrus I know is the most peaceful guy I've ever met!" The sound of metal clattering on stone echoed throughout the hall. Two strong hands grabbed hold of Enoch's legs, dragging him out of his cover. Enoch struggled, trying once again to kick Cyrus away, but the Priest pinned him to the ground with his knee. Unable to move, Enoch stared into Cyrus' eyes, desperate tears flowing from his own.

"You... you made cocoa for me when I was scared!"

The candle stand scraped against the stone.

"You took care of me after we lost everything!"

Cyrus gripped his weapon with both hands, lifting it above his head. Enoch felt the world slow around him. In that moment, it wasn't death that Enoch feared; he was living on borrowed time anyways. No. What he feared most was leaving Cyrus behind. He feared the guilt that Cyrus would undoubtedly carry once the demon's magic faded. That the Scribe would never get to apologize for the hurtful words said in his apartment. That he'd never be able to thank Cyrus for being there.

That he wouldn't have the chance to be there for him in return.

The hall faded away into the mist, leaving only him and Cyrus. His teacher. His mentor. His friend. His... Enoch closed his eyes, bracing for the impact, desperation cracking his voice between sobs.

"You're the only family I have left, Cyrus! Please... Please stop!"

A pause. A breath. Hearing Enoch's cries, Cyrus' muscles tensed for a brief moment. Tears began to flow down his cheeks as he swung the stand. The resulting clatter rang through Enoch's ears, echoing through his skull and the hall around them. The Scribe opened his eyes, seeing the metal candle-stand rolling on the ground next to him. Hope grew within him to replace the fading ringing in his ears. He'd gotten through to him! "Cyrus?" he said, turning to his mentor just as the man's weight suddenly vanished.

The sight that met him snuffed out his hope like a fallen candle.

Cyrus' legs dangled above him. Adir held the man aloft by his throat, looming over them both as he smiled like a madman. The muscular Priest's hands glowed with an eerie mix of green and yellow. Now, it was Cyrus' turn to gasp for air. As he watched the older man struggle, Adir raised an eyebrow.

"Huh, thought I got everyone in here already. Where were you hidin', old man?"

"No!" Not wasting a second, Enoch pushed himself to his feet. He lifted his arms high, having to jump to reach above Adir's towering form. The chain of his shackles caught on the man's neck. Adrenaline blinded Enoch to the crumbling sensation in his fractured arms as he pulled back with as much force as he could muster. "Let him go!"

One inch. Enoch's full strength only managed to pull the man one inch lower. Distracted by this new attacker, Adir tossed Cyrus away into the closest pew. The older man rag-dolled to the ground after impacting, eyes now closed. Enoch didn't even get a chance to look his way before feeling the ground fall away beneath his feet. Wait, no... that wasn't right. He was going up!? The shackles' chain pulled tight in Adir's grip as he lifted them off his neck, bringing Enoch with them.

"You... I know you." Adir held Enoch in front of him like a hunter appraising their game. "So, even the puny Scribe thinks he's stronger than me? Huh?" Enoch swung his legs, trying to escape, but the Priest's grip was too strong. Even with a single arm fully extended, he held Enoch with ease. His other hand reached out, squeezing Enoch's already broken arm. This time, the adrenaline failed to numb the pain. Enoch's face twisted in distress as Adir watched with an insulted glare. The glow on his hands covered his face in a haunting hue. "You think I'm weak enough for someone like you to beat me? You have the guts to insult me like that!? I don't even need my ability to kill you!"

The glow around Adir's hands vanished. The world turned upside down as Enoch's eyes adjusted to the sudden dimness. Mist flew past his face. His hair and clothing drifted, following the movement of Adir's arm as he swung Enoch over his head by the chain of his cuffs. It was hard to tell if it was the ground or more of Enoch's body that cracked. The impact forced the air out of his lungs. Enoch felt nauseous. The violently swirling mists seemed almost still when viewed through his swaying vision. Had it not been for the immense pain he was feeling, he likely would have passed out then and there.

A heavy boot on his chest helped Enoch regain a fraction of his sense of direction. Through shaky eyes, he could see Adir lifting his hands above him, the yellow-green glow returning. "I'll show you just how strong I am. You're gonna regret not runnin' when you had the chance!" he growled.

Despite his brain still rattling in his skull, Enoch looked for a way to escape. If he couldn't make it out of this, then Cyrus would be next! All he could manage to move was his head, but that was still enough to notice the candle-stand beside him. Based on the surrounding carnage, he doubted the metal would be enough to block the attack, but it was the only chance he had. He just had to–

SNAP!

The grotesque sound of snapping flesh and bone froze Enoch in place. Suddenly, it was easier to breathe as the force pushing down on his chest vanished once again. Adir's body fell into his field of vision. The sight of his neck, twisted and mangled like a rung-out cloth, caused Enoch to gag.

Against every better instinct, Enoch turned to look at his savior. The light of the stained-glass above mixed with the mist, silhouetting her body, wings and horns. Once the demon leaned in closer, however, he could see the horrify-ingly familiar mask dangling from her neck. Agrat placed her hands on her hips, speaking with a cheerful, singsong voice.

"Hello!"

Chapter 34

A CHAOTIC AND thorough storm named Abyzou blew through High Inquisitor Haven's office.

"Applications... Notes... Investigation reports..." The masked demon rummaged through a broken desk drawer. The contents of the others, still wide open, now laid scattered across the floor. Pressed for time as she was, there was no point in maintaining order. It didn't help that the Inquisitor seemed to write many of her notes in the celestial script. Abyzou's ability to read the foreign alphabet was passing at best, and now she was wasting precious time translating useless memo after useless memo.

One of the files stood out from the others. The inevitable dust that manages to make it into even sealed drawers had yet to reach this page. She lifted it up, skimming the neatly written words. A winged demon. An attack in the city. A Pilgrim giving chase.

"Mahway..." she said softly. "You'll be dealing with him too I see." Far more gently than she'd been handling the papers before, she slid the file into her pocket and resumed her search. "Come on. It has to be here somewhere..."

SLAM!

The desk shook from the force of the closing drawer, frustration escaping from behind the woman's mask now that her friends weren't there to see. "Damn it," she whispered, leaning on the polished wood with a sigh and tightened fists. "Where are you taking them?"

Chapter 35

A STRANGER IS someone you don't know, or that you're unfamiliar with. But if you've spent your entire life hearing stories about someone you've never actually met; if that person feels as familiar to you as a friend you've known for years, can they still be called a stranger? After Peycile, Enoch had researched the Soldiers of Lilith. He'd followed the news of their growing influence. He studied any stories of their customs and members he could find. Though information on them was scarce on the surface, he did the best with what he had. He never quite knew why though. Was he studying an enemy? Was it to help him feel safe? To prepare if they returned? Or was the reason simply a desire to find exactly that? A reason.

The obsession had faded over the years as he'd tried to bury his past, but Enoch still considered himself knowledgeable on the demonic freedom fighters. Or, he *had* at least. While the demon standing over him was hardly a stranger in the unfamiliar sense, she was still undoubtedly strange as she stared down with a sweet smile.

"Sorry for butting in like that! Hope that guy wasn't a friend of yours," Agrat said casually. So casually in fact, that Enoch's confusion outweighed the fear that would've otherwise tied his tongue.

"No... he wasn't."

"Oh! Good! That would've been awkward." As Agrat smiled in relief, Enoch's gaze darted over to Cyrus. A momentary glance at the mention of friends. *Is he still alive?* The older Priest laid unmoving where Adir had tossed him aside. Through the mist and distance between them, Enoch couldn't quite tell if he was breathing or not.

"That guy *is* your friend though, right?" Agrat asked, leaning into Enoch's line of sight. Enoch jumped at the sudden threat in his personal space.

How long has she been watching? he wondered. *Anyone that heard me during that fight would know that we're friends. Closer even. If I lie, will she kill me like she killed Adir?* He tried to glean some sort of clue from her gaze. Unfortunately, though he was quite adept at reading, the truth behind her expression was indecipherable. Hesitantly, he nodded his head, hoping he hadn't just sentenced Cyrus to the same twisted fate as Adir.

Now that Agrat was closer, the mask hanging from her neck lightly swayed above Enoch. A simple, light, wooden accessory outweighed by the bloodied symbolism it carried. There was no doubting it now. Her and the demon in the library truly were part of the Soldiers of Lilith. But then...

"That Priest, you–" Enoch glanced over to Adir, instantly regretting it as his stomach twisted as much as the man's neck once more. "Why did you save me?"

There was no hesitation in Agrat's voice or movement as she squatted down next to Enoch. With a smile, she gestured over her shoulder to Cyrus, now behind her. "You were risking your life to save your friend! I figured that meant you aren't one of the bad humans Furcus is always talking about." The hand pointing over her shoulder suddenly came Enoch's way. *A surprise attack!?* He flinched, closing his eyes; anticipating the sickening crunch of his own neck.

With his twisted stomach tightening into a knot, Enoch opened his eyes, seeing Agrat's outstretched hand a short distance away. Agrat rolled her eyes, though the expression seemed more amused than annoyed. A familiarity typically reserved for the playful antics of an old friend. "Oh c'mon. I'm not gonna rip your arm off or something," she replied. "Well, unless you cause trouble."

Reluctantly, Enoch took hold of the clawed hand. Though it didn't hurt him, the strength of her grip explained the ease at which she'd spun Adir's neck like pastry dough. As Agrat lifted him to his feet, Enoch's body cracked and protested. Sharp and aching pains nearly sent him back to the floor once Agrat let go. *Something is definitely broken,* he realized. A shifting, grinding sensation within his body blurred his vision. *Actually, a lot of things are broken.*

More unsettling than the state of his body, however. Was the cheerful and helpful demon looking back at him with a curious stare. Despite having killed a man seconds before, not to mention causing the chaos in the cathedral that had claimed so many others as well, she was acting so friendly. As if she'd run into an old pal on the street. *Is it an act? Is she trying to get me to lower my guard so she can bite me too?* He leaned back somewhat as Agrat casually grabbed the chain of his shackles.

"So... what's up with these?" she asked. "You a criminal or something?"

"N-No. I just... ran into some trouble on the way here."

"I see... I see... Furcus was right! You humans sure do like cuffing things!" Letting go of the shackles, Agrat began to stroll over to the door. "Well, if you and your friend lay low, you should be able to survive until we're done. So, see ya!"

Enoch watched in disbelief as the demon simply walked away. *Is she serious? She's going to let me live?* He hesitated, waiting for the inevitable moment she would suddenly turn and attack. But no such moment came. As the distance between them grew, he decided to risk moving. He rushed over to Cyrus' side, checking for a pulse.

He's still alive!!

The heartbeat brought only a fleeting relief, however. Though its existence proved Cyrus was still with him, the rapid speed meant he wouldn't be for much longer. Enoch recognized the symptoms. Increased heart-rate, a high fever; confusion and dizzied vision would explain some of the man's earlier unbalanced movements as well. Between the demonic magic infecting his body, and the residual magic around them, it wouldn't be long before Cyrus' magical overflow reached the point of no return. If Enoch couldn't get him out of there soon, the colored lines would appear and Cyrus' life would end in a painful magic combustion.

But maybe... He glanced over to Agrat. The demon held her chin, looking around the room like a lost child, muttering to herself about directions. The plan forming in Enoch's mind made him sick to his stomach, but regardless of his hesitance, it would be his best shot at saving Cyrus. Doubt continued to hold him in place, until Agrat shrugged, turning to the door. Fueled by the same panic clouding his better judgment, Enoch called out across the room.

"Why did you attack the cathedral?" he asked, stopping Agrat in her tracks. The demon turned to face him, resting a hand on her hip.

"Oh, sorry, I'm not allowed to tell you that," she replied. Having dismissed his inquiry, she opened the door to head out.

"W-Wait!" Enoch cried out again, reaching out to her. "I'm asking because..." his voice trailed. Once he said this there was no going back. "...Because I want to help."

Though Enoch's offers of assistance were genuine far more often than not, this time the words burned his tongue. The winged demon closed the door, looking his way with her interest piqued. "You want to help?" she asked. "Why?"

"My friend has a low magic tolerance," Enoch answered, gesturing to Cyrus with a slight wave of his hand. "If I don't get him out of here soon, he'll die. I can't risk just sitting around and waiting for you to finish. But..." The Scribe let out a sigh, disgusted by his own words. The offer he was about to make felt like betraying his family. Working with the very demons that had taken them away. He wondered if they would be willing to forgive him. "If I help you with what you're here for, you'll leave sooner. Since I know I couldn't stop you even without the handcuffs, and I doubt you'd let me just leave, it's my best option if I want to save him."

With the slight echo of Enoch's offer fading into the upper balcony, Agrat silently held her chin. Once again, Enoch found himself unable to read the expression. Agrat raised a finger, as if she were catching the thought that had just formed in her mind. "Oh right!" she exclaimed. "Humans have sucky magic resistance, right? I always thought that was just a rumor!" Embarrassment painted her cheeks a darker pink. "To tell ya the truth, this is my first mission on the surface! I'm still learning how you guys work."

Enoch wasn't quite sure how to react to that, nor did he have time to as Agrat simply shrugged. "Y'know, sure, why not?" she said. "Like you said, it's not like you could stop us anyhoo. We're here to find some lady named Haven. She's got some info that Aby needs. Apparently, she's here every day, but we can't seem to find her."

They're here for Haven? That makes a lot of sense actually, Enoch supposed. High Inquisitor Haven had been behind the capture of many demons, and oversaw many investigations involving the denizens of the demon realm, Diapogeum. It seemed those same responsibilities had now spared her from the demons' wrath.

"Y-Yeah, she's not here right now," he explained, having been there for the High Inquisitor's departure from the city. Agrat sighed.

"Really!? Guess she must've left when Furcus came to get us." The winged demon shrugged with a disappointed frown. "We'll just have to look for the files after all. That'll take forever though."

Though Enoch hardly wanted the demons to succeed at their goal, their problems were now his own. He knew first-hand how long it could take to find a file. Cyrus and the other survivors didn't have that kind of time. He turned to Agrat, his determined stare masking the guilt seeping through every vein in his body. "I can help. I'm the cathedral Scribe, so I know the files here better than anyone. If you help me move my friend somewhere safer, I'll get you whatever file you need."

The demon's posture perked up at Enoch's reply. "You're the file guy? Perfect!" she said with a smile. "Guess we're lucky I didn't let your head get crushed!"

Enoch's determination and hidden guilt swiftly found themselves replaced with a sickening, crushing discomfort. Her cheery demeanor had nearly chased the reality of his situation from his mind. This was still a demon. A demon capable of killing him in an instant if she felt the desire to. A demon who had murdered a man in front of him only minutes before.

And he now had to help her.

He tried to hide his fear, forcing his words through a painted smile. "Y-Yeah, really lucky."

Chapter 36

T HE SCENE PLAYING out before Enoch was almost cute. He watched as Agrat lightly set Cyrus down in the cathedral hallway, safe from the lingering magic miasma in the hall of worship. She patted his head with a warm-hearted smile and gentle hands. An interaction that would have brought a smile to Enoch's face, if those same hands hadn't spun a man's neck 360 degrees minutes before.

Agrat stood up, giving Enoch a thumbs up and a small heart attack. "Oki doki, now that your friend is safer, let's get going!" she said cheerfully. "I wanna make sure I help my own friends too!" With a skip in her step, she made her way down the hall.

Enoch gave Cyrus one final glance; a reminder of why he was taking this risk, and perhaps a request for forgiveness when he inevitably didn't return. After all, there was no doubt in his mind that he'd be disposed of after helping the demon's. It would be too big a risk to let him live now that he knew what they were after. Agrat may have saved him and Cyrus, but she was still a member of the Soldiers of Lilith. As he followed her, his thoughts wandered back to the massacre in the hall of worship, his grip tightening in frustration. *Her and her partner were willing to let all those people die just to get some information? No matter how cheerfully she acts, she's still a killer. The Soldiers of Lilith haven't changed at all.*

Enoch's next step didn't land. Instead, he found himself pulled backward, a gloved hand covering his mouth and yanking him towards its owner. The startled yell in the Scribe's throat was silenced by three evenly spaced points digging sharply into his back. The force was light, but deliberate; a warning in the form of a polished trident. The weapon's wielder leaned forward, speaking in a low, menacing growl. "If you take one more step towards her, I will skewer you as slowly and as painfully as I'm able. Close your eyes if you understand."

Enoch didn't need to be told twice. He closed his eyes, recognizing the voice of the demon he'd avoided in the library. No doubt this was the "Furcus" that Agrat had mentioned several times. Seeing Enoch do as he was told, the demon nodded.

"Smart choice," Furcus said. The trident points dug a little deeper, tearing through the fabric of Enoch's shirt. The Scribe could hear his heartbeat echoing in his ears, his mouth going dry beneath the leather glove. *Has this guy been tailing me since the library? I didn't even hear him get close!* The soft, jovial tapping of Agrat's feet quieted with each passing skip, leaving him alone with her far more murderous friend.

Could I talk my way out of this? Enoch wondered. *Or fight him off? Maybe I could run if I move fast enough!? No. Even if they're unlocked, the doors didn't work when I tried to get in before. If the demons tampered with them, I'd be trapped in a dead end. Not to mention the fact that this guy would probably skewer me before I could take a single step.*

As Enoch jumped from plan to hopeless plan in his head, Furcus' attention was instead drawn to the Scribe's wrists, noticing the shackles shaking along with the boy's hands. "You're clearly not a Priest, and it makes no sense for a criminal to break *into* a cathedral," he said. "Why did you sneak in here?" He removed his hand from Enoch's mouth, moving it down to firmly grip his throat. "And remember, it's in your best interest to answer truthfully."

"Furcus! What are you doing?" The sudden voice caused Enoch to jump, a movement he quickly regretted as the trident points pierced the skin somewhat. Agrat stomped over to the two of them, hands on her hips. The intimidation lost some effect as Furcus' tall, lean form stood a good foot taller. "He's helping us, Furcus. You don't need to threaten him."

"Helping?" Furcus' gaze darted from Agrat to Enoch. Despite the mask covering his expression, his disbelief was made plainly evident by the sarcasm dripping from his words. "It was my understanding that your Church had laws against aiding demons. Did they have a miraculous change of heart?" As sarcasm shifted to quiet rage, the older demon's grip tightened around Enoch's throat. "Agrat dear, you can't trust what they say. There's a chance this boy was simply lying to save his life. Or to get you to lower your guard so he could attack."

"But he didn't attack," Agrat argued with a small pout. "And he put himself in more danger by offering to help. He's a Scribe here, so he can help us get the files we're looking for!"

Though it felt an eternity longer for Enoch, Furcus grew silent for a moment, thinking things over. With an irritated flick of his tail, he turned back to Enoch.

"Open your eyes," Furcus ordered. Enoch did as he was told, now seeing the older demon nodding to his shackles. "Tell me boy, if you work in the library, why are you handcuffed?"

Somehow, Enoch's body managed to tense further than it already had. It was clear that Furcus didn't trust him, so if he got caught in a lie he was as good as dead. Though that was likely just a matter of when, not if. Choosing his words carefully, he answered with a trembling voice.

"I do work in the library here. I saw the cathedral was being attacked and tried to get inside to help my coworkers." He nodded to the nearby window, the rain blurring the distant crowds at the edge of the courtyard. "I was stopped by the Priests outside, and they cuffed me for trying to interfere. But I managed to get inside while they were distracted."

Furcus glanced at the window as Enoch finished. Had he not heard the commotion of the boy's entry himself, he wouldn't have trusted a single word. But so far, he seemed to be telling the truth. "So, you thought you'd play hero then? Save the day by taking down the evil demons?" he asked with an almost mocking tone. Enoch shook his head.

"N-No sir," Enoch replied. "I know I'm not strong enough to fight a demon. To be honest I wasn't really thinking at all. I just... I didn't want anyone else to die."

Furcus' grip loosened an almost unnoticeable amount. After a painfully long silence, he sighed. "I don't trust you," he growled, pushing Enoch forward with the trident as he began to walk. "But I do trust this, and my own speed using it. If you work in the library, then you're going to help us find what we're looking for. Then we'll let Lady Abyzou decide your fate."

Enoch had no choice but to follow Furcus' lead. His stomach knotted at the mention of Lady Abyzou. Just how many demons had managed to sneak inside? As they passed by Agrat, the young demon now smiling once again, Furcus glanced down at her. "And you, young lady. We will need to have a discussion on the trustworthiness of humans once this mission is over."

The smile vanished once again. Agrat's shoulders slumped as she followed the two of them down the hall.

"Fiiine."

Chapter 37

THE TICKING OF Enoch's pocket watch counted down to his inevitable doom. Seated in a library chair with Furcus and his trident standing too close for comfort, Enoch could feel the demon's hateful glare. Furcus' tail swished impatiently. The trident spun slowly in his fingers as the older demon grew restless. If Agrat didn't come back soon, Enoch wondered if he'd be stabbed simply out of impatience. Thankfully, that hypothetical would remain exactly that as the library door swung open, revealing Agrat on the other side. The lavender skinned demon smiled; her hands folded behind her head. "I'm *baaack!*" she sang "And I brought Aby!"

Abyzou filled the empty space in the door, entering the room as Agrat stepped to the side. Her stern, commanding demeanor sent a chill down Enoch's spine, far worse than the cold of Furcus' icy gaze. Forcing himself to continue looking, he noticed her mask was different from the others. Until then, he'd thought Agrat had been the demon in his vision. Now that he saw Abyzou, there was no doubt that she was the one who'd infected Cyrus and the others. Abyzou's eyes locked with Enoch's. "So, you're the Scribe I was told about?" she asked.

"I am, ma'am."

"You're younger than I expected." Abyzou made her way over to the records room, pointing to the locked door. "But still old enough to be responsible for some pretty important documents. If you really are this cathedral's Scribe, then you're in charge of what's in here, right?"

Enoch nodded, and Abyzou gestured for him to approach. A mix of pain and fear froze Enoch in place, until a shove from Furcus knocked him to his senses. The Scribe winced, the movement reminding him of how bad a shape he was in. Once he'd regained his balance, Abyzou grabbed his bag, sliding it over his head.

"I'm assuming the key's in here?" she asked. Enoch nodded again. He watched as Abyzou dumped out the contents of his bag. Pens, medical supplies, old forgotten packaging for purchased baked goods; it was all scattered across the floor. His journal landed on top of the pile, flipping open with a flutter and *thud.*

Rather than going straight for the keys, Abyzou instead reached for a folded paper that had slid out of the journal. The crudely written signature of Josephine's daughter was plainly visible on the outer side, and the muscular demon found herself curious. She picked it up, looking at the painted scene of Enoch's heroics in silence for a beat before glancing to the painting's star with a thoughtful hum. Carefully, she folded the painting once more before tucking it back into the safety of the journal, now grabbing the keys that had landed beneath it.

"Which one is it?" she asked.

"The silver one," Enoch answered. "Next to the one you're holding right now." As Abyzou unlocked the records room door, Enoch prayed to the Archangels to keep Josephine's family safe. He didn't know why Abyzou had chosen to look at the painting, but the last thing he wanted was for them to be dragged into this. Enough innocent people had suffered at the hands of these demons already. This hope for protection was swiftly cut off as his own safety came into jeopardy once more. Abyzou grabbed hold of Enoch's shackles, stepping through the door.

"I've got it from here Furcus," she reassured as the older demon stepped forward in concern. Furcus seemed hesitant, but stepped back nonetheless.

"Of course..." he replied, watching as Enoch and Abyzou descended into the room below.

Their shadows danced across the filing cabinets as Abyzou lit the oil lamp, turning to face Enoch a short distance away. "Alright. Where are Inquisitor Haven's files?"

The words lingered on the back of Enoch's tongue. *Can I really just give the demons what they're looking for? If they were willing to risk this much to get it, the file they want has to be important, right? But if I don't help, or if I try to buy time for the Priests outside to act, then...* He sighed, trying to breathe out the doubt and guilt. Cyrus was worth the risk.

"Inquisitor Haven's files should be in the top drawer there," he said, gesturing to the far corner of the room. "You'll need to use the smaller gold key to get into it."

Following Enoch's directions, Abyzou opened the drawer without issue, quickly flipping through the files inside. "You didn't lie. I guess you really are the hero type," she said. Enoch certainly didn't feel that way. He tried to ignore the possible worst-case consequences of his actions.

This is for Cyrus.

"Finally!" Abyzou's exclamation filled the room. The light of the oil lamp lit up the file for just a moment before she tucked it into her pocket. Enoch glanced over, trying his best to figure out which file she'd taken. Far as he was, he could only make out the word "Confidential". In fact, he couldn't even remember placing that file in there in the first place.

"Congrats, you just saved a lot of lives, mister hero," Abyzou said, using her body to block the cabinet as she grabbed several more files. When she turned back to the stairway, Enoch repeated his motivation in his mind.

This is for Cyrus. This is for Cyrus. All of this is to keep him alive. To save him. "Wait," he said, standing between her and the exit. Abyzou stopped, raising an eyebrow as she looked down at him.

"You aren't going to be able to beat me kid," she warned.

"N-No, that's–" The idea of fighting her caused Enoch to stumble his words somewhat, but he quickly recovered. "You've gotten the file. So, please, release the Priests you're controlling."

Though her mask hid her expression, Abyzou still felt her body tense, caught off guard by Enoch's words. He knew the venom ability was hers? "You really think you're in a position to make demands?" she asked. "If I release the ability, the infected Priests will stop us from escaping."

"Then use me as a hostage so they can't!" Enoch offered. To his surprise, Abyzou responded with an amused smirk.

"What an odd offer for a member of the Church to make," she said, crossing her arms.

"I... I went against the orders of a High Inquisitor to get in here, so I'll likely be arrested anyway. My friend was also infected by your ability. If I wait for it to wear off on its own, he'll probably die from magical overflow." Tears began to flow down Enoch's face as he finally made eye-contact, practically begging at this point. "I want to save them this time, so please, end your ability! I'll do whatever you want!"

Abyzou had to admit, the kid was either heroic, stupid or planning something. Either way, he was starting to grow on her. After a moment of silence, she continued to the stairs, gently patting his shoulder as she passed. "Alright, mister hero, I'll end my ability once we've safely gotten away. Now c'mon."

Relief and guilt melded together into a swirling mess in Enoch's gut as he followed Abyzou to his certain demise. There was no time to wonder if this was the right decision. All he could do was hope that it was enough, and that he'd be lucky enough for the Priests outside to show no mercy. If it meant saving Cyrus as well as stopping the demons, he'd gladly give up his life. Until that morning, it hadn't amounted to anything anyways. He couldn't help but wonder, though. What weight would his death even carry, if he hadn't truly lived in the first place?

Upstairs, Enoch could see Furcus' shadow looming in the doorframe, waiting with bated breath for his superior to return. Behind him, Agrat sat cross-legged on the table, flipping through a book. "Find it?" she asked as Abyzou came into view.

"I did. Let's head to the roof."

Before Enoch could follow, Furcus held out his trident, stopping him in his tracks for the second time that day. "And what of the human? Shall I cut our loose end?" he asked with far more eagerness than Enoch liked. Abyzou stopped, the library door half open.

"The Scribe's offered to be a hostage," she explained.

"He what!?" Furcus' gaze darted between Abyzou and Enoch, searching for an explanation.

"He's coming with us, Furcus," Abyzou replied. Her tone left no room for argument, though Furcus' momentary silence betrayed his desire to. Begrudgingly, he grabbed Enoch's arm tight enough to feel the broken bone within shift. Enoch stifled a yelp.

"...Of course, my lady," Furcus replied through gritted teeth, dragging Enoch to the hall with Agrat in tow; hoping, just as Enoch had, that if things went south, the Priests would show no mercy to their hostage.

Chapter 38

"THE ROOF IS clear for now. Let's do this quickly, Agrat." Abyzou waved the others out onto the large balcony, the stone now painted dark with rain. The few times Enoch had visited it before, the benches had been filled with Church workers enjoying some company on their breaks. Back then, he'd found the crowd intimidating. Now, he wondered how many of them would never get to enjoy the view again.

Agrat rushed ahead of the others. When Enoch went to follow, Abyzou gently held out her arm to stop him. She didn't notice Enoch's confused glance. The muscular demon's attention was held by her young accomplice.

"Okaaay! Let's do this!" Agrat said softly, hyping herself up. Like a distant sunrise, a golden glow covered her body, mixing with the lavender shade of her skin. Her hair began to rise, as if she had dived into the rain. The grace and balance of her dance was so far removed from the jovial personality Enoch had seen before that it would have been unsettling if it weren't so beautiful.

"Messengers of haunting destruction, join me in my dance..." Agrat said, twirling and pirouetting around the rain-kissed balcony. The rain itself seemed to vanish as it reached the growing golden light. "Higher and higher, carry me above the howling winds..." Agrat's hand slowly raised, her magic moving to surround it until the light was nearly blinding. "I summon thee, Spiritual Chariot!"

In a flash, the magical light burst from Agrat's hand, forming a golden chariot on the roof behind her. Eighteen, winged, wolf-like creatures stood harnessed to the front of it, awaiting the young demon's commands.

The sudden light was a literal beacon, catching the attention of Foster down below. The High Inquisitive looked up from her makeshift base just in time to see the chariot appear.

"A summoning ability? They're going to make a break for it!" Her earlier hesitation vanishing, Foster turned to her men. "Range attackers, get ready to open fire on the chariot! Lethal force is permitted, but we want them alive for questioning if possible!"

Foster's men wasted no time getting into position. The High Inquisitive's glare could evaporate the rain itself as she stared at the balcony, speaking under her breath. "I'm not going to let you waltz out of here after the massacre you caused," she swore.

Ignoring the growing commotion below, Agrat opened the door to the chariot with a smile. "Ta-daaa!" she sang. Abyzou patted the young demon's head as she boarded.

"Good job, Agrat," she said, earning a flattered blush in return. Furcus followed behind Abyzou with Enoch in tow.

"I don't believe I've seen you do that particular dance before," the older demon said. He sat next to Abyzou as Agrat closed the door behind them, using her wings to hop into the driver's seat.

"I figured I'd add some flare for my first surface mission! Was it too much?" she asked.

"It was beautiful," Furcus replied. "But perhaps it's best to save the flare for when we aren't making a hasty escape." His young companion's eyes went wide in realization as she took hold of the reins.

"Oh, true! Didn't think about that!"

Having no desire or way to join the conversation, Enoch simply stood where he'd been pushed to, unsure of what to do. Noticing this, Furcus held out his trident, pointing to the outer edge of the chariot.

"You stand there, where the Priests can see you," he ordered. Enoch glanced over the edge, seeing the distant courtyard below. For a moment, he considered jumping. The demons would lose their hostage, and maybe he could manage to survive with just a few more broken bones than he already had. Unfortunately, his plan was as short-lived as he expected himself to be, since Abyzou hadn't ended her ability yet.

"But, won't you lose your hostage if I fall?" he asked.

"You're lucky I'm not pushing you over myself," Furcus replied. Enoch shut his mouth. He'd just have to hold on as tight as he could and hope that would be enough. Once he had, Agrat smiled excitedly.

"Okay guys, hold on tight! These roof tiles are gonna be bumpy!" With a thundering THWACK, she whipped the reins. The winged wolves began running along the flat top of the long cathedral roof. Just as Agrat warned, the chariot shook and rattled with each tile. Enoch could feel his teeth chattering, every shake reminding him of the crumbled remains of what used to be his intact bones.

Once the chariot left the cover of the cathedral's spires and buttresses, Foster raised her hand on the street to signal her men. "Ready..." she began, unable to finish as the Priest next to her pointed toward the escaping demons.

"Inquisitive Foster! Isn't that the Seer boy from before?" he asked. Foster looked back in surprise, followed by irritation.

"Damn it! Stupid kid," she muttered. She clenched her fist. Her men were still awaiting her orders. There was no time to overthink this. "He knew the risks going in there," she said with a darkened expression. "Stopping the demons' escape takes priority!" Holding out her hand again, she pointed to the chariot now approaching the edge of the cathedral. "OPEN FIRE!"

Various magic attacks began to fly through the air as Foster lowered her arm. Despite her attempts to hide it, the pain was still clear in her face. "Sorry kid," she said softly.

"WOOHOOOOOOOOO!!!!" Agrat yelled, far more enthusiastic than the High Inquisitive's tone below. Abyzou and Furcus simply sat in silence, contrasting the sheer terror on Enoch's face as the roof suddenly vanished beneath them. Though he doubted the demons' escape plan involved plummeting to their death, he still braced himself for impact. The winged wolves were unphased, however. Small golden ripples appeared beneath their paws with each stride, the creatures running on the air itself. But the magic of the moment was short lived, as the magic of the attacking Priests reached the chariot.

In a burst of embers and heat, a ball of fire slammed against the chariot's side. The resulting lurch from Agrat steering away sent Enoch tumbling backwards, his eyes still adjusting after the sudden bright light. Abyzou's gaze darted from Enoch to the other incoming attacks.

"So much for our hostage," she said with a tone that suggested she'd expected this. "Might as well stay down there and out of the way, hero."

Furcus swung his trident wide, now standing, balanced on both the edge of the chariot and his seat. He swiped at a swarm of small, white birds. Each one erupted into a small explosion on contact, and the older demon shielded his face with his arm. "You could also stand and enjoy the view. I promise it's safe."

"Absolutely none of this is safe, Furcus!" Agrat argued, pulling the reins far to the side again to dodge an incoming beam shooting out from the cathedral.

Down below, Foster sprinted away from said cathedral to the main road. A handful of her men followed close behind. "Do we have anyone that can follow them?" she asked. The closest Inquisitor shook her head.

"The only Priest in this district with a flight ability was in the cathedral."

"Damn it!" Foster clenched her fist as she ran. *I was prepared for an air escape using natural wings, but this chariot is too fast!* she realized. *Why didn't I plan for something like this?*

The group skidded to a stop at the main road. Upon Foster's arrival, an Inquisitor opened the door of a prepared car. As the High Inquisitive climbed inside, she turned to one of her men. "Tell groups A and B to head to nearby cathedrals and see if they can find anyone that can follow or track the chariot. Group C, focus on rescuing the survivors in this cathedral."

"Yes ma'am!" the Priest said with a two-hand salute, crossing her wrists to form wings with her fingers. They turned back to the others, ready to relay the directions as Foster slammed the door shut.

"Follow that chariot!" she ordered. The driver nodded, speeding off down the road to follow the flying chariot now a fair distance ahead of them.

Furcus scanned the city, oblivious to their tail. Or perhaps he simply paid it no mind since there was no way it could possibly catch up now. With a nod, he sat back down. "It seems we've escaped the range of their attacks for now."

"We should still stay on guard," Abyzou warned, placing a hand on her friend's shoulder. "We aren't out of the city yet, and flying up high will only do so much to avoid potential ambushes." The words earned a nod of agreement from Furcus, and a curious glance from Agrat.

"Does this mean we won't have time to pick up Mahway?" the young demon asked. Hearing the name, Enoch looked up in surprise. It seemed his earlier attacker was linked to the Soldiers of Lilith after all.

Without turning her head, Abyzou glanced over the side of the Chariot towards the rock clusters they'd left the young demon in. Hesitation delayed her response. "It'd be too dangerous to land that close to the city now," she said reluctantly. "He's a smart kid though, I'm sure he'll be fine. How much further until we reach the countryside?"

Thwack! Agrat whipped the reins again, picking up speed. "At this rate, under a minute!" she replied.

"Good." Abyzou leaned back in her seat with an approving nod. Enoch was far less comfortable on the floor, even more so as Furcus' trident turned his way.

"And what about him? We can't exactly bring him back to the rift," Furcus asked. The older demon was simply pointing, but Enoch had no doubt that his muscles were tensed, ready to close the gap as soon as the word was given. The two of them turned to Abyzou, waiting to see what exactly that word would be. The suspense built as Abyzou simply stared back in silence, weighing her options in her mind.

"Let's wait until we're a safe distance from the city to decide his fate. The Priests at the cathedral may have seen him as expendable, but that doesn't mean all of them will."

In an exchange that was slowly becoming a pattern, Furcus sighed, reluctantly pulling his weapon away from Enoch. The points still lingered a little too closely for Enoch's liking though. Like a pouting child, Furcus's shoulders slumped as he leaned on the side of the chariot. "I feel you're overestimating the humans' compassion, my lady," he said, gaze slowly crawling back to Enoch with an air of pure hatred. "But if that is your decision, I'll respect it. Let's just hope our escape will come swiftly. He's only of use to us within the city, after all."

And as those words left Furcus' mouth, the border of Courciel passed beneath them. For the first time in years, Enoch left the capital. The safety of his home; the mentor he had risked everything to save. The angel that was likely still laying confused in his bed. He left it all behind, giving one final glance over the chariot's edge. Even in the rain, the city was truly beautiful from above.

It wasn't that bad for a final memory, all things considered.

Chapter 39

I T'S A SHAME that our lives seldom follow the pleasant plots of our dreams, while our nightmares often become our waking reality.

For example, Enoch had spent many days daydreaming by his window, watching the birds flying weightlessly above. They could go anywhere. Do anything. They weren't confined to the walls of Courciel. A bird could leave their nest behind and find true freedom.

Enoch would imagine sprouting wings, leaving everything to live a life free of the numbing depression drowning him. But eventually fear and uncertainty would drag him back down, and the escape would end. He'd be back on the surface, in the mundane safety of his apartment; his freedom nothing but a dream. He wasn't an angel. He was just Enoch.

Now, just like in his dreams, he found himself amongst the clouds, watching a bird fly below the floating chariot that would soon be his coffin. He'd escaped, but still found himself trapped. The bird flew ahead, landing by Agrat at the front. The young demon sent it a smile. As if returning the gesture, the bird chirped politely before taking off once again, leaving the group behind.

Enoch wished he could do the same. Instead, the Scribe glanced through the small gap between the chariot door and its side, knees hugged to his chest. The capital was nothing more than a lump on the horizon now. Despite his body being several miles away, his mind remained in Courciel; in the cathedral. *We've been flying for a while now. I wonder if the Priests finished rescuing everyone; if all of this was worth it...* With no way to find an answer to that, he turned to look at Furcus.

The older demon was searching the horizon for threats. Though Enoch was glad that he'd finally turned his trident elsewhere, he had a feeling that blessing was fleeting at best. The Soldiers of Lilith weren't the type to show mercy. These breaths of cool morning air were likely the last he'd ever get to take.

Realizing today would be his last day of living, Enoch thought back to the days that had led up to it. Now that he really considered it, he realized that not much would change once he was gone. Noah and Nammah would find a new tenant. The cathedral would find a new Scribe once they'd finished repairing the damages from the attack. Eventually, Azazel would realize he wasn't coming back and leave to go wherever angels go. It'd be like he was never even there.

I never really was fully there, was I?

He'd survived Peycile, but he'd done nothing with his life! At least, not until his attempted heroics in the cathedral. Even if he hadn't truly lived before his inevitable death, at least he got to help others get another chance. *At least I got to make a difference right before the end. Just one time.* That's what he told himself. The cruel truth if that weren't the case would be too bitter a final taste.

The lingering fear came out in a sigh as heavy as Enoch's shackles. The nail in his coffin. Even if he survived through some miracle, he'd be arrested for defying High Inquisitive Foster's orders. Not to mention helping the demons achieve their goal. His life was over either way. At least this ending would be quick.

But still, though his grievances seemed to be piling up now, he didn't regret the actions he'd taken that morning. His methods could be questioned, but the lives of the people in the cathedral, the life of his friend and mentor were more important than the law or his own safety. He did what he had to do to save them, and hopefully, he *had* saved them.

"Well, I believe we have safely outrun our pursuers," Furcus said with a stretch. He stood up, leaning on his trident to maintain his balance. "So, it's about time we decide what we're doing with our hostage. Don't you agree?"

A pit formed in Enoch's already knotted stomach. It seemed the time had come. As he stared back at Furcus, Agrat turned around to face them, reins still in hand. "We can just drop him off somewhere and leave, right? I mean, he did help us," she suggested. Furcus shook his head.

"I'm afraid that's too risky my dear. He could have an ability capable of tracking us, and he knows too much about our actions in the cathedral."

"I don't have a magic ability," Enoch argued. Despite the pain it caused him, he held up his shackles. "And even if I did, I couldn't use it while wearing these."

"That doesn't change the fact that you know too much," Furcus replied. "We can't risk the Church getting ahead of us on this."

"He isn't the only one that saw us," Abyzou interjected. Enoch and Furcus turned to watch as she leaned back in her seat. The muscular demon tapped her pocket where she'd safely tucked the stolen files away. "And even if he can somehow tell them the exact files we stole, our window of opportunity will stay the same. The truth of the matter is that this boy hasn't harmed any of us. Killing him now would be breaking my rules."

In an instant, confusion replaced Enoch's fear. The demon's last words... they didn't quite sit right. Furcus seemed to feel the same way, though his reasons undoubtedly differed. He gestured to Enoch once more.

"He's young, but he's no child, my lady. I feel the rule hardly applies here."

Slowly, Abyzou stood up. Though she was shorter than Furcus, the man seemed smaller in comparison as she stared right into his eyes, her voice laced with a threatening undertone. "It's not the age that matters, Furcus. It's the guilt. We don't kill innocents."

At that moment, something snapped in Enoch's mind. A single sentence pushing him past the brink. Though every logical, rational, sensical part of his brain tried desperately to silence him, the emotions that had been building within him, leaking out in small bursts, smothered by his desire to survive, finally emerged victorious. His eyes widened. His fist clenched. His body felt like a pot boiling over. Abyzou had seemed reasonable enough so far, but she'd had the audacity to say those words? After everything the Soldiers of Lilith had done!? "What do you mean, you don't kill innocents?" he asked, anger and accusation dripping from the words.

Both Furcus and Abyzou looked down in surprise at the Scribe that had finally borne his fangs. "Excuse me?" Abyzou said as Enoch slowly picked himself up, steadying himself on the chariot's edge.

"The Soldiers of Lilith have killed tons of innocent people. But you're going to pretend that you have some sort of moral high ground now? Do you have any idea how many people have been hurt by your group?" Once he was sure he wouldn't fall, he took a step towards the two demons. He no longer cared about what they planned to do with him. He couldn't face his family if he let her words go unchallenged. "There were people in that cathedral that had never even seen a demon before! But you didn't mind letting them kill each other to get your hands on a single file!"

Furcus shoved Enoch away before he could take another step, leaning him back against the railing. The forest far below them flowed past like a never-ending river of green.

"You're in no position to judge, boy," Furcus said, practically spitting out the words. Agrat glanced back in concern.

"Furcus!"

"Just keep flying, Agrat." With one hand tightly holding the fabric of Enoch's shirt, Furcus lifted his trident with the other, seconds from tossing him over. Enoch grabbed the older demon's arm. His heart pounded in fear and anger. Though Furcus could kill him then and there, like Enoch with Abyzou, he couldn't let the Scribe's words go unchallenged.

"The Church has killed countless demons; and even humans, yet those supposedly innocent people decided to join it nonetheless. But, if you insist on disagreeing with Lady Abyzou's position on this, I'd be happy to grant your death wish."

"Calm down. Both of you," Abyzou ordered. At first, neither listened, too caught up in the moment. But a gentle hand on Furcus' shoulder finally pulled him to his senses. After a few more seconds of hesitation, he reluctantly and forcefully dropped Enoch into the chariot. As he did, Abyzou pinched the bridge of her nose, looking very much like a mother tired of dealing with her bickering children.

"I can't say we don't have blood on our hands, but I did what was necessary to achieve our goal," she said. Agrat, somewhat more relaxed now that the fight had been broken up, nodded in agreement.

"Plus, we attacked early in the morning so there'd be less civilians there!" she added.

"The morality of our actions aside, we aren't discussing the events at the cathedral. We're discussing what to do with you," Abyzou continued. "Up until that little outburst, you did nothing but cooperate. So, I'm not going to kill you. But we can't waste time landing, and we definitely can't bring you back with us." As she spoke, the muscular demon scanned the horizon. Her eyes lit up for a moment, and she placed a hand on Agrat's shoulder, pointing to the distance with the other. "Agrat, steer about ten degrees right."

"Oh, uh... Yeah. Can do Aby."

Somewhat confused, Agrat tugged gently on the reins. Once their heading had been adjusted, Abyzou turned back to the others. They watched as the commander moved to the side of the chariot, next to Enoch, glancing over the side to the surface below. "So, I'm going to compromise. If your luck continues, I'm sure you could make it back home in a day or two."

The wind caused the chariot door to quickly swing open as Abyzou unlatched it. The magically created metal slammed against itself with a *clang*! "If he wasn't caught up in another fight, your friend is likely still alive thanks to you, Mr. Hero," Abyzou said, having kept her side of their bargain shortly after they left the capital. "If you wanna live long enough to see him again, I suggest you hold your breath." The commander turned to Furcus, inviting him to act with a wave of her hand.

It took less than a second for Enoch to realize where he was standing, and what Abyzou considered a compromise. "Wait! Hold o–"

Furcus' outstretched foot cut Enoch off. He kicked the Scribe back with a smile. Enoch grasped desperately at his surroundings, trying to grab something; anything! Nothing but air met his fingers. Fear in his eyes, he watched as the chariot grew smaller and smaller above him. Wind roared in his ears; stinged his eyes; disoriented him as he struggled to see what was beneath him. It was approaching fast. *The forest? No, it's... blue? A lake!* Realizing this just in time, he adjusted himself for the landing, closed his eyes, and took a breath.

SPLASH!!!

Like the rain after booming thunder, Enoch's surroundings fell silent for just a moment as the water embraced him. Sinking through the rippling, dark water, he drifted downward. Lower and lower into the abyss. The light breaking through the surface cut through the surrounding shadow. Enoch fell backwards between the beams, eyes closed in his dream-like state, the light reflecting off his dark, wafting hair and clothing.

Slowly, Enoch began to right himself, his eyes flitting open as he felt the bottom of the lake beneath his foot.

Gently, he pushed off the muddy lakebed, swimming back up to the surface.

Water drenched the soil as Enoch crawled up the shore, coughing up the liquid burning his lungs. The Scribe collapsed onto his back. Staring up at the few clouds drifting above, he shielded his eyes from the sun. Exhaustion paralyzed his body, yet relief still buzzed throughout it. He let out a chuckle.

"I'm alive! I... I actually survived!" he said, throat still hoarse from coughing. Unable to hold them up any longer, his arms fell. The chains of his shackles clattered against the wet fabric of his clothing. Fatigue began to overtake him, the adrenaline, fear and anger that had driven him forward finally fading. He could barely move his body. His arms were numb. In fact, despite the pain he'd been feeling since his fight with Cyrus, he only now realized how badly they were broken.

Laying on the shore, completely covered in water, soil and bruises, Enoch slowly drifted into a deep sleep.

"Everything hurts," he mumbled to himself. "But I'm alive... Cyrus, you better be... alive too..."

The moonlight shimmered on the water's surface as Enoch continued to rest. The sound of shifting plant life and thudding hooves broke the silence. A large deer approached the sleeping Scribe. The deer's dark blue and black fur contrasted Enoch's pale skin as she nudged Enoch's face with her nose. She let out a huff, turning to face her approaching rider.

The woman stepped quietly, her cloak drifting somewhat in the light breeze. She pulled her wolf-skin collar closer to her, hiding her slightly tanned skin. The rider placed a hand on the deer's saddle, looking down at her discovery. The boy had dark curly hair, similar to her own, though hers grew more even, reaching just a little lower. The shackles matched the description too. Kneeling down, she placed her fingers on his neck, checking for a pulse. It seemed he was somehow still alive.

As she stood back up, a small glimmer of gold escaped the cover of her cloak; a Pilgrim's pendant, hanging from the woman's belt. She gave the deer a small scritch on the neck, nodding in approval. "Looks like we found our guy, Dear. Let's go tell the others."

Chapter 40

T HE SMALL BELL chimed as Azazel closed the door to Lamechson's behind him. The angel smiled and waved to the people inside as he did. Though, it would be difficult to tell the man was an angel thanks to the enchanted paper tucked safely inside his jacket, magically hiding his wings. After one final inspection of the small paper bag in his hand, the bag itself tied shut with a decorative bow, he set off.

The angel passed over the canal bridge, listening to the relaxing sound of the water splashing against the stone. He waved to the owner of a nearby café, promising to stop by again soon. He continued on and on, reminding himself not to get distracted.

This was easier said than done once he reached Penemue's Cathedral. Though the courtyard and entrances were still closed off, he could see the handful of Inquisitives outside, on break from the investigation within. The repairs on the shattered window on the far side of the cathedral seemed to be nearly complete, though Azazel still had to take the longer route around to avoid bothering the stonemasons fixing the outer wall.

Eventually, the angel reached his destination. The scent of flowers drifted through the air as he passed the garden surrounding the House of Healing. He stopped for just a moment, staring up at the building with a hand on his hip. Everything he'd done had led to this moment. Hopefully, his friend would be happy to see him.

Inside, the morning sunlight carpeted the wooden floor of the hall. The beams were so strong you could see the dust that filled the air, dancing about as Healers moved to and fro'. Benches lined the walls, along with several doors, some closed, others open. As Azazel counted the door numbers under his breath, he stumbled slightly, knocked to the side by a person rushing through the hall. The man's words came out staggered as he tried to catch his breath.

"Oh heavens, pardon me!" he said.

"Don't worry abo–" Azazel froze for a moment. Had he heard that voice before? Unfortunately, the man continued forward before he could get a good look, darting through a nearby door. Azazel simply watched, realizing he no longer had to count the rooms.

The curtains of the window inside were drawn, though the occasional draft revealed the open shutters, as well as the metal bars behind them. Even on the third story, the bustling sounds of the streets outside made it up to the room, present, but distant enough to simply melt into the background.

Enoch sat quietly in a steel-framed bed. The white sheets were blinding to an unadjusted eye, expertly tucked around the mattress. The Scribe had exchanged his night clothes for a clean, tunic-like shirt. Bandages covered his arms, visible beneath the short sleeves.

Considering how far he'd been carried from the capital, Enoch was surprised to awake in Courciel of all places. The Church had apparently spared no expense tracking him down. Rumors of demons sneaking into the capital had certainly hurt their reputation. Eager to repair the damage they'd asked the Inquisitive Harbesy Serell to lead the search. Through the blood Enoch had left on the library window, the Inquisitive was able to narrow down the search area, until the tracking party finally found him unconscious by the lake. Unfortunately, contradicting the successful hunt depicted in the paper, the Soldiers of Lilith were already long gone before they arrived. Flattering as it was at the time, Enoch knew the goal had been to locate the demons, not a lowly Scribe like himself. Nevertheless, he was happy to be back home, alive and mostly well.

Moving carefully, he flipped the page of his book, nearly at the end. Said ending would have to wait, however, as a familiar man suddenly stumbled into the room. Relief washed over both Enoch and Cyrus as they saw each other. The older Priest fought to hold back tears.

"You're okay!" they said in unison, smiling in embarrassment after the fact. Far less frantic than before, Cyrus walked over, searching for a place to sit.

"I am, yes. And I'm sorry I didn't visit sooner. I wasn't discharged until today." The Priest pulled a chair over to the bed, taking a seat.

"N-No, it's fine," Enoch reassured. "I'm just glad to see you're back to normal."

Now that he had company, Enoch set his book aside, taking note of what page he'd reached. As he did this, Cyrus couldn't help but notice the boy's bandages. The older man stopped mid-movement. Guilt clouded his expression. The Priest finished sitting, now unable to make eye contact.

"Right..." he said softly. "My memory of the incident is still hazy, but from what I've been told..." He glanced over once again, struggling to form the words for a moment. It hurt so badly to see his son in this state. Cyrus let out a sigh, fidgeting with his fingers after folding his hands together. "I know you're wearing those bandages because of me. Enoch, I can't even begin to say how sorry I am. I swore I'd keep you safe, but I hurt you. I–"

"Cyrus, why are *you* apologizing?" Enoch held out his hand to cut the man off, the other held against his own chest. "I'm the one that should be saying sorry."

To Enoch's surprise, Cyrus seemed confused by his response. The Scribe sighed. Now, it was his turn to avert his gaze in guilt. "In the cathedral, you were being affected by the demon's ability. I know you'd never attack me if you weren't. But..." Enoch's mind wandered back to his apartment; to the far more painful fight he'd had with Cyrus; to the look of heartbreak on his mentor's face. "When you came to check on me after I was attacked before. I... I said things that hurt you; things I never should've said. I can't blame that on magic."

Seeking any small comfort that he could, Enoch nervously gripped the bedsheets, distraught by the memory that had fueled his lingering guilt. "This whole time I've been worried that you wouldn't make it. That if I couldn't save you, *that* would be the last thing I ever said to you, and I'd never get to take it back." Each word felt heavier than the last. Tears formed in the Scribe's eyes as he struggled to continue. "And even worse, if I'd done something wrong and you died, then I would've lost the only family I have left."

Ironically, the weight of Cyrus' hand on Enoch's shoulder lightened some of the weight he was carrying. The Scribe had been so caught up in his apology, that he hadn't noticed Cyrus move from his seat to the edge of the bed. Looking over, Enoch saw his mentor, or rather, his family smiling back at him.

"Enoch..." Cyrus said softly. "I care about you more than I care about anything in the Three Realms. There's nothing you could possibly say to change that." The Priest lifted a finger, seeing Enoch taking a breath to argue. "And I'll admit that your words did hurt. But if blaming me for us not being there in Peycile eases your pain, then blame me."

Possibly tighter than intended, Cyrus squeezed Enoch's shoulder. "Even if you hate me for it, I'm glad you survived. I've cherished every moment we've spent together. No matter what you say, or how you feel, I will always love you. So don't apolo–"

A mess of dark curly hair brushed against the side of Cyrus' face as Enoch hugged him close. The older Priest froze, caught off guard. He couldn't remember the last time Enoch had hugged him. Lips curled into a warm smile, Cyrus returned the embrace, listening to Enoch's muffled voice as the Scribe spoke into his shoulder.

"I don't blame you, Cyrus. I never blamed you."

The older Priest's lips tightened for just a moment as he fought back tears. Without a word, he pulled Enoch closer, comforting the boy, as he always tried to do. They held the hug for a while. Were they making up for lost time? Did they fear letting go would end this pleasant dream? Or were they simply so relieved that they didn't even realize how much time had passed? Regardless of the reason, eventually they reluctantly ended the embrace. Once they had, Enoch lifted his arm somewhat, turning his attention to the wrist that had once shimmered in the light. Now, all he could see were the bandages covering the bruises beneath.

"And after everything that's happened, I'm going to work on not blaming myself either," he said. "Doing that won't bring them back."

How many times had he sought comfort in that golden bracelet? How many times had he told himself it was his only shield against the pain of the world; the pain of his past? His experiences without it had hardly been pleasant, but... he couldn't deny that he felt more alive now. In fact, without the bracelet, he could finally see a thread of his own to follow.

For a moment, the curtain swayed in the breeze, a small ray of sunlight reaching the bed as Enoch lowered his hand. "I think that maybe, I survived for a reason," he admitted. For once, the words didn't feel like a lie. "After Peycile, I was afraid, but I can't keep saying my power is a curse. Even I can't deny that I managed to save people in that alley, and at the cathedral." Enoch clenched his fist, his newfound sense of purpose flowing through him like a cool, cleansing river. It felt fragile; terrifying even; but it also felt right. "I may not have been able to save our home, but there are people out there that I *can* help. He glanced over to Cyrus. "I don't know where that goal would bring me though, and I... We only just made things right again, so—"

Once again, Enoch felt the weight of Cyrus' hand on his shoulder. The man's smile beamed with pride. "Enoch, if that's what you want, I'll support you no matter where that path takes you."

"Thank you, Cyrus." Once again, Enoch thought of how much he'd taken the man's love for granted over the years. After a moment, however, Enoch glanced over to the window with a frown. The metal bars appeared behind the drifting curtain for just a second; a second that was more than long than enough for a grim reminder. "But I guess I won't be able to save anyone until the Judicial Inquisitor in charge of my case decides what to do with me." Cyrus' expression mirrored Enoch's, his guilt returning.

"Right. High Inquisitive Foster mentioned you broke quite a few laws to save me," he replied. "I'm sorry for causing so much trouble."

"Don't be. I'm the one that decided to do it in the first place."

On top of the worsening mood in the room, Enoch's stomach twisted at the memory of Inquisitive Foster's visit. The woman had stormed into the treatment room in a rage, several Healers in tow trying to hold her back.

"Actually, the Inquisitor came to see me when I first woke up. She scolded me for a good hour," he said. The Scribe's face softened somewhat as he turned back to Cyrus. "But after she calmed down, she told me that I'd managed to save the lives of fifteen people in the cathedral. She even said that the information I gave about the demons could help the Church catch them sooner."

Enoch forced a smile, the downward shift of the conversation's tone nearly palpable. He shrugged, doing his best to lighten the mood. "So... even if I do get locked away, at least I'll know that you and those people are safe still." An awkward chuckle followed the words, fading into a sigh as his forced optimism quickly dwindled. It seemed that a glass half full mentality wasn't something he could achieve so quickly. Thankfully, a light knock at the door announced the arrival of an expert.

"Y'know, this seems like as good a time as any to hop in," Azazel said cheerfully.

Chapter 41

A T THE TIME, Enoch hadn't considered how strange it was to see Azazel walk through the treatment room door. The act itself was hardly bizarre, as friends often visit when someone they care about is stuck recovering in bed. Instead, the abnormality of the situation came from Enoch's reaction to it. He lit up at the angel's arrival, as if reuniting with an old friend; an old friend he'd only really known for a few days, most of which had been spent bickering. And yet, the sight of the man still brought a smile to his face. Azazel had been known to have that effect on people, so it could have simply been the angel's aura of sheer positivity. However, Enoch would later wonder if he had simply been far lonelier than he'd realized.

"Az–" The Scribe cut himself off before he could finish the name, seeing the angel's eyes widen in panic. Glancing over to Cyrus, Enoch rushed to cover the mistake. "Az–zurpise visitor! How unexpected!"

Even Azazel couldn't help but sigh at the poorly salvaged reaction. Nevertheless, he recovered quickly, properly entering the room. "Yeah... Sorry for dropping by unannounced," he said, stopping next to Cyrus. The Pilgrim held out his hand to the man. "Gregory Veramor. Pilgrim with the Church, and a friend of Enoch's. It's a pleasure to meet you, sir."

At the word friend, Cyrus' eyes went wide in surprise. The shock swiftly switched to glee, and he shook Azazel's hand enthusiastically. "Cyrus Portia. Priest, and Enoch's guardian. I'm so happy to hear he's made a friend!"

The exchange drained the strength from Enoch's posture. His shoulders hunched in embarrassment. The older men were too focused on their handshake to hear the Scribe's muffled mutterings about being too old for Cyrus to react like that to him making friends, even as Azazel finally released the Priest's hand.

"Well, I hope I'm the first of many," he replied with a smile. "But pleasantries aside, I'm actually here on business. I just came from a meeting with the Judicial Inquisitor handling your case."

At the sudden topic change, Enoch and Cyrus exchanged a glance before turning back to Azazel with hesitant curiosity. Azazel's own light-hearted demeanor shifted to fit the serious tone of the topic.

"Your charges were pretty intense," he began, nearly distracted by how similar Enoch and Cyrus' nervous posture was. "But thankfully the final verdict is just a few months of community service!"

The tension visibly released from Enoch and Cyrus' bodies. Relieved and excited, Cyrus patted Enoch on the back with a smile. "That's wonderful! The angels must be watching over you!"

Though he was still facing Cyrus, Enoch's gaze darted to Azazel, seeing the angel smiling at their small celebration. The Scribe wanted to feel relieved, and he undoubtedly was, but he still couldn't help but feel there was more to the situation. Despite this, he mirrored Cyrus' smile. "Yeah, feels like a miracle, that's for sure," he replied. After a moment, Azazel grabbed their attention with a wave.

"I hate to cut the celebration short, but would you mind if I speak to Enoch one on one for a moment, Cyrus?" he asked. The older Priest seemed caught off guard for a second, mind still occupied by the good news. As he realized what Azazel meant, he looked over and nodded.

"Of course! Of course!" he answered. The man stood up, waving to the two of them as he moved over to the door. "I'll come by again later, Enoch. And it was a pleasure meeting you Mr. Veramor."

"You as well," Azazel replied politely, "and Gregory is fine."

Cyrus acknowledged the correction with a nod of his head, and exited the room. Not one to ignore a perfectly good available chair, Azazel took a seat where Cyrus had been before. He placed the small paper bag on his lap.

From the bed, Enoch looked him over, somewhat amused by how their positions had switched. "It looks like your injuries have healed well," he said. Azazel held his arms out, as if to show off the Scribe's healing handiwork.

"They have! Shame I can't say the same about yours just yet. I must've had a better Healer."

The words managed to get a slight smile from Enoch. After a second, however, the Scribe rubbed the back of his neck nervously. "Right. Uh... Sorry, by the way, for just running out before. How'd you manage to find me here?"

The angel leaned back in his chair, his mind wandering back to the last time he'd seen the young Scribe. "Well, after you suddenly woke up and ran off to who knows where, I tried to follow you," he explained. The memory was still clear in his mind. The confusion; the panic; the pain that tore through his body as he tried to get to the door without help. "Thanks to my injuries, I wasn't able to make it far before I had to just trust you could handle yourself." He waved nonchalantly in Enoch's direction. "Based on the result, it seems your handling abilities still need a bit of work."

"Yeah..." Color flushed through Enoch's face as he nodded. "I'll admit I'm probably only alive thanks to dumb luck."

"Hey, luck of any intelligence is a pretty good thing to have on your side." A slight smirk accompanied Azazel's words. He began to play absentmindedly with his heart-shaped earring as he continued. "Luck is also what helped me find you though. Once I could move with a tolerable amount of pain, I went out to look for you. That's when I heard some cathedral gossip about a Scribe stopping a demon attack." Releasing the earring, the angel began to count on his fingers. "Or, that he'd helped organize it. Or that he was an Anti-Church Movement spy. You'll have quite the reputation if your name gets out."

The dread Enoch felt at the thought of his possible infamy weighed his shoulders down, as if subconsciously trying to hide his face. Azazel simply smiled, oblivious to the reaction, leaning back in his seat once again.

"Thankfully, I didn't need a name to figure out you'd gotten dragged into a demon attack again. From there it was easy enough to track you down through my friends and connections in the city."

"That makes sense, I suppose," Enoch replied, managing to untangle the knot the angel's words had tied in his stomach. "But if that's how you found out, then how did you know the verdict for my case? That would be handled by an Inquisitor, not a Pilgrim, right?"

A smug shrug was Azazel's answer as an air of pride enveloped the man. "Who do you think got the sentence lessened in the first place?" he asked. Enoch's eyes went wide, his earlier suspicions confirmed.

"Wait, lessened? What was it before?"

The earlier smug expression vanished as quickly as it appeared. Azazel crossed his arms, able to speak freely now that there was no risk of worrying Cyrus. "I wasn't kidding when I said your charges were intense. They were ready to lock you up and throw away the key before we stepped in."

"We?"

It took a moment for Azazel to reply, the blush in his cheeks far more evident thanks to his pale hair. One of his crossed arms waved about somewhat as he backtracked. "Well... it wasn't *just* me that got the sentence lessened," he admitted. "By the time I found out what was going on, Inquisitive Foster was already fighting for you. I just helped her out a bit by convincing some people to speak on your behalf. The young lady we saved in the alley was more than happy to help. And I even convinced your landlord and his very talented wife to put in a good word or two as well."

As he thought back to visiting Noah and Nammah, Azazel could still smell the warm, chocolatey cookies he'd gotten to try at the time. Then he snapped back to the present, remembering the scent was more than just a memory. He began to untie the bow sealing the bag on his lap as he continued. "Add in the gratitude of the people saved in the cathedral, and the seals of approval of a High Inquisitive and one incredibly handsome Pilgrim, and ta-daa! Jail time becomes community service!" With a flourish, he removed the ribbon from the bag, handing the package to Enoch with a smile. "Oh, and here. I picked these up for you from Lamechson's on the way. You really were right about them being the best in the city."

The sweet, cozy smell caused Enoch's stomach to rumble, far quieter than the angel's had in the past. He pulled a cookie from the bag with a smile. "Thank you... For everything, not just the cookies."

A fluttering feeling filled Azazel's chest at the sight of Enoch's genuine smile. Once again, the boy's demeanor filled him with a painful, yet pleasant nostalgia. He quickly recovered, smiling in return.

"It's the least I could do after how much you helped me. And besides..." The angel pouted and shrugged; the movements made with a lighthearted energy behind them. "I wouldn't be able to relax knowing you were rotting away in a cell somewhere. That kind of guilt just isn't good for your complexion."

"Right..." Enoch replied. He took a bite of the cookie, processing everything he'd just been told. His narrow escape from a life of imprisonment, the fact that so many people had been willing to support him, the possible reputation of being some sort of criminal mastermind... It was a lot to take in. All things considered though, his situation really was the best-case scenario when compared to what could have been.

"Wait..." the Scribe said, remembering exactly what his situation was. He turned to Azazel in confusion. "So, what is my community service anyways?"

As if he'd been waiting for Enoch to ask this question from the beginning, Azazel's lips slowly curled into a smirk.

Chapter 42

"ARE YOU SURE that will be enough?"

Enoch could hardly hear Cyrus' voice through the small bundle of clothes covering the Scribe's face. He lightly kicked his wardrobe door closed, moving over to his bed as Cyrus watched from the table, cocoa in hand.

"Don't really have enough space for more if it isn't," Enoch replied, folding the clothes before placing them into the half-filled suitcase that had belonged to Cyrus until that morning. "But I'm sure there'll be places to wash them."

"That's true, I suppose," Cyrus said. He watched as Enoch tossed two empty journals inside, the case already looking ready to burst without even being closed yet. The Scribe chugged his own cocoa, placing the empty mug on his desk. Cyrus glanced over at the soft *thud*. The shimmering golden metal sitting on top of the desk drew his gaze. He nodded to the magic-suppressing bracelet. "And are you going to take that with you too?" he asked.

Enoch turned back to the desk. He'd asked himself the same question too many times to count since the replacement had arrived. Though he'd decided to try letting himself have his visions, he couldn't deny how tempting the small, golden safety net was. There was also still a bit of space in the suitcase...

Once he was outside, Enoch locked the gate at the bottom of the stairs leading up to his apartment. Unsurprisingly, the thought that he wouldn't unlock it for at least several months gave the action a feeling of greater importance. After savoring the moment a second longer, he moved over to where Noah and Cyrus were chatting, holding the key out to the carpenter. Noah held up his hand, shaking his head before Enoch even had a chance to open his mouth.

"Hold onto it. We'll keep things in order for when ya get back," he said. Enoch nodded in return, sliding the key back into his bag.

"Thanks, Noah," he replied, earning a smile in return from the old man.

Ding Ding! The chiming of the bell above the entrance of Lamechson's rang out as Namaah kicked open the door. A large bag emitting the aroma of freshly baked breads, cookies, muffins and everything in between covered her face, nearly falling over as she tried to approach the group.

"Don't you even think about heading out without these!" she said through the paper. Enoch rushed over to her, taking the bag before it could drop.

"W-Wasn't planning on it," he replied. "Here, let me help with that."

She let him take the bag, admittedly grateful for the help despite her stubborn nature. Her pregnancy seemed to make even the smallest tasks more and more difficult with each passing month. Now that she thought about it, Enoch likely wouldn't be back before the birth. She let out a sigh, still bothered by the suddenness of it all.

"You better take care of yourself out there," she said, looking to where she assumed Enoch's face was behind the large bag.

"I will," Enoch promised.

"And make sure you eat enough. If you come back even thinner than you already are, we aren't going to be able to see you!"

"I'll try my best."

Noah's calloused hand rested gently on his wife's arm, the man sending a concerned smile her way. "Namaah dear, if we keep him here too long, he'll miss the train."

The baker's expression switched from concern to surprise in an instant. "Why didn't you say so!?" she exclaimed. She began to shoo Enoch and Cyrus down the street with her hands. "What're you doing waiting around here? Get a move on!"

The duo stumbled down the street, caught off guard by the sudden shift. As he allowed himself to be moved along, Cyrus reached back to grab the suitcase. After one final wave goodbye to the couple, they rushed to the train station.

The sound of the busy crowds in the station echoed throughout the arched ceiling above. Priests casually patrolled, watching people rush to and fro' to reach their platforms. For the sake of being able to see, Enoch tucked the bag of baked goods under his arm. He followed Cyrus closely through the crowd. "Platform three... platform three... aha!" Cyrus' eyes lit up, and he pointed to the turnoff a short distance ahead.

Their platform was somewhat emptier than the others around it, the dark metallic train already sitting in the station. Towards the large brick archways at the far end of the tracks, Azazel's yellow jacket stood out against the red and brown coloring. The Pilgrim chatted cheerfully with another waiting passenger. Once he noticed the duo had arrived, he smiled and waved enthusiastically. After a quick goodbye to his newest friend, Azazel ran their way.

"You made it! I took care of your ticket already, so we should be good to go!" he said, gesturing to the open train doors. With a nod, Enoch followed the wave of his hand, glancing at the train. Without thinking, his own hand moved to his wrist. The movement went unnoticed by the Scribe, but Cyrus always had been the more observant of the two. The Priest placed a hand on Enoch's shoulder, pulling the boy from his thoughts.

"We'll be here when you get back, I promise," Cyrus reassured with a smile. Enoch gave him one back, though it failed to fully mask the lingering concern in his eyes. Despite the uncertainty, he moved forward, gently pulling Cyrus into a hug.

"I'll be looking forward to a cup of cocoa when I do."

"Of course."

The two pulled away, oblivious to the angel watching with a bright smile. Azazel's second-hand glee found itself overpowered by the large paper bag Enoch had placed on the ground by his luggage. He could feel himself begin to drool.

"Is that—"

"Help yourself," Enoch offered. "There's no way I can eat them all myself."

The Pilgrim's eyes lit up, wasting no time as he crouched down to take a look in the bag. As Enoch and Cyrus watched this, Cyrus' fingers flexed around his cane, his knuckles growing a shade whiter. This time, Enoch placed his hand on the older man's shoulder. The Scribe's reassuring smile was more than enough to put Cyrus at ease.

CHOOOOOOO!!!!!

The train's whistle sounded the approaching end to their time together. Azazel stood back up, bag of baked goods held safely in his arms. The angel spoke through the cookie hanging out of his mouth.

"We fud pwobabwy git goin'," he said? The man waltzed over to the train, climbing aboard. As he disappeared into the compartment, Cyrus and Enoch exchanged an amused glance. Compared to the two of them, Azazel certainly was easy-going.

"Well, Uriel's blessings for your travels," Cyrus said, handing Enoch his suitcase. Enoch nodded.

"Thanks... I'll see you in a few months I suppose. And I'll write when I can until then."

Nodding in return, Cyrus once again nervously gripped his cane as Enoch stepped on board. So many memories flashed through the Priest's mind, and he found himself calling out before even knowing what he wanted to say.

"Enoch..." he said, the Scribe turning to face him, one foot still lingering on the platform. Cyrus smiled. "I love you, and I am so proud of the man you've become."

Just as it had in his brief reencounter with Josephine, Enoch felt his heart stop for a moment. That same sensation of a warm hand reaching out to embrace it. Slowly but surely, the feeling was becoming more and more familiar, and Enoch smiled. "Well, I have a pretty amazing teacher to thank for that," he replied, finally boarding the train. Enoch turned back one more time to face Cyrus on the platform slightly below. "And I love you too, Cyrus. Thank you for everything."

Somewhat moved and somewhat irritated, one of the porters grabbed the train door, looking between the two as they had their moment. Noticing this, Cyrus took a step back, allowing the man to close the door. As the porter moved along the train, the duo waved to each other through the window, and Enoch went to find his seat. Once the Scribe was out of sight, Cyrus let out a sigh, his smile fading ever so slightly.

"Jared, Bereka... Your little boy has grown up," he whispered.

In the train compartment, Enoch's arms strained as he lifted his luggage into the overhead compartment. Azazel brushed some crumbs off his hands from his seat underneath, ready to help. The following *THUD* of the compartment cover closing showed there was no need. The Pilgrim shrugged, looking up at his new ward.

"I guess it's a little too late to change your mind now, but you're sure you're okay doing this with me? Three months is a long time," he said. Enoch sat down across from him, stretching out his wrists after nearly straining them.

"I mean, if I have to spend my community service helping a Pilgrim with their work, it might as well be a Pilgrim I know."

"And here I thought you said yes because you liked spending time with me," Azazel replied with a pout.

CHOOOOOOOO!!!!!

The train whistle blew once again, this time muffled somewhat by the metal of the train. As Enoch looked outside, he noticed Cyrus still standing on the platform. And though Enoch didn't know this at the time, the man remained there long after the train left him behind, this time unable to follow.

In fact, there were many events unknown to the Scribe at that moment. Inquisitive Foster, listening to the reports of her men back at the cathedral, investigating the lingering chariot-sized scuffs on the roof. Josephine blushing as her daughter excitedly shared a painting of a "dog" with the local doctor. Mahway, fleeing through treetops after finally realizing his new friends had lied. Those same three friends, surrounded by other masked demons, planning their next move with their newly obtained information.

High Inquisitor Haven, meeting with a strange winged figure in a small, dark chamber beneath the surface.

These events, set into motion by Enoch's actions, all occurred beyond his knowledge, and his departure occurred beyond theirs. Threads intertwined, yet still singular. As Enoch watched the outer city rush by the window, half listening to Azazel's excited ramblings, he had no clue the true importance of this moment, the ripples and repercussions it would lead to. The fantastical, wonderful, pain filled fate awaiting him.

What is it that decides that fate?

Are we chained to an inescapable plan decided by a higher power? Or are our fates a branching web, our destinies born from the connections we form with others.

The past is set in stone, unchangeable despite the changes it causes in us all. But the future is unwritten. Even if fate guides us towards a chosen purpose or destiny, there are those with the power to break free.

That's what Enoch believed as he dove into that future. In the inky blackness of the unknown, he was gifted a small semblance of light. A light that could help guide others to new paths.

Though, perhaps that chosen purpose was a destiny in and of itself. A thread binding him to a fate that his light couldn't reveal.

The train crossed the outer threshold of the city. This time from the ground, Enoch watched as Courciel merged into the horizon once again. His hand moved to his wrist, and he found himself unable to look away.

The sun shone brightly. The train curved through the surrounding farmland and hills before disappearing into a lush, green forest down the line. Though most of the scenery failed to keep up with the locomotive's speed, Enoch found his gaze drawn to a single bird, somehow managing to match its pace. The creature followed alongside them, fully free; leaving the capital behind. After a moment, it veered away, disappearing past the forest canopy. Enoch smiled, turning to face Azazel, curious as to where this dream would take him.

Perhaps, he truly was bound to some decided fate. Perhaps that train ride had been part of some predetermined plan. But if that fate, that binding thread, could finally give his life a sense of purpose; if it could give him a reason to live...

Perhaps that thread was not a curse, but a lifeline saving him from himself.

Epilogue

SUNLIGHT PIERCED the forest canopy in scattered beams, guiding the small bird as it soared through the trees. Despite these small rays of light, most of the soil below sat in an uneasy shadow. The bird refused to let this frighten it, simply enjoying its freedom without a care.

The small bird landed on a branch next to a clearing, casually preening its feathers until a cry of pain below succeeded where the shadows had failed. It took flight once more, leaving the two noisy figures in the clearing behind.

The first figure laid curled up on his side, the man's blue and gold Priest uniform dotted with dozens of rips and red stains. Currently he held his arm, voice strained as he spoke through gritted teeth. "I swear I'm telling the truth!" he pleaded. "I had nothing to do with the fight with your anti-church buddies!"

The second figure, their body covered almost entirely by a dark gray cloak, pushed the Priest over with their steel-toed boot. The Priest grunted in pain, now pinned on his back. He looked up with shaking eyes at his attacker, listening to the accusatory, spiteful tone of voice.

"I know you didn't," the cloaked figure growled. "You ran off and left your friends to die instead."

"E-Exactly! I didn't attack you!" the Priest replied, desperate for any chance of escape from this torture. "I... I sympathize with what you guys are doing, so– AAAGCK!"

The man's legs kicked and writhed under the increased weight of the attacker's boot on his wounds.

"Don't lie to me," the attacker spat. "I hate dishonest people." The cloaked figure crouched a little lower, raising their hand to the Priest's head. Despite the fact said hand was empty, the Priest still struggled to break free; to move even just a little further away from the approaching limb. His one arm, far redder than the other, refused to move anymore. The second wasn't nearly strong enough to push the attacker's leg off on its own.

"Since you're with the Church, maybe you can answer a question for me," the cloaked figure said, their hand lingering just a short distance from the man's face. "If it's the answer I want, maybe I can look the other way."

This small glimmer of hope halted the man's struggling. He nodded his head fast enough to nearly shake it off. "Y-Yes! Of course! I'll tell you anything you want!"

Leaning in close, the attacker kept their hand aimed at the Priest's head, as if wielding an invisible blade. The Priest's breath fogged the figure's polished metal mask, his breathing getting quicker at the sight of the scarlet eyes glaring through the mask's two narrow slits.

"Do you know a Pilgrim named Gregory Veramor?" the masked attacker asked.

The Priest wracked his brain. What was the correct answer? What did the attacker want to hear? What choice would give him the highest chance of survival!? The man swallowed in a futile attempt to help the dryness of his throat, before shaking his head, tears beginning to form in his eyes.

"No, I don–"

A disgusting squelch sounded out. The Priest's hand clenched reflexively before falling limply to the ground. The masked attacker wiped their small blade off on the man's uniform, the metal retracting back into the cloak once it was clean.

"Well, at least you told the truth," they said, standing up with a slight stretch. "But were you really stupid enough to think I could just let you walk away after seeing our camp?"

Leaving the lifeless body behind, the cloaked figure headed back into the forest, their mask catching some of the light breaking through the canopy.

"Oh well. Maybe the next one will have a better answer."

Glossary

Angel: Immortal denizens of the divine realm Spira. They're known for their large, feathered wings, as well as their high magic capacity. The angels helped humanity fight the demons in the First Surface War, before returning to Spira after their victory. No angels have been seen in Terrael since this ascension. Unlike humans and demons, who are mortal, angels are categorized as beings of magic.

Beast Summoner: One of the nine types of magic abilities. Beast Summoners are able to shape their magic into conjurable beasts. The creature summoned differs from person to person. After it's been separated, the Summoner can absorb it into themselves again if they want to. However, if a summoned creature takes enough damage or moves farther than the Summoner can handle, the magic will disperse and cannot be reabsorbed. The material is entirely made out of the summoner's magic; however, it may take on specific physical attributes. For example, a reptilian creature may have the texture of scales, or a furred creature would feel soft. The amount summoned generally depends on the specific ability, however, most summons follow similar patterns. If a creature is smaller and is made of less magical energy, the Summoner can generally summon several, but if the creature is large, they can usually only summon one. The creatures can either behave like a puppet that simply follows orders, or may have personalities of their own depending on the ability.

Cathedral: Acting as bases for the Church, cathedrals handle many of the Church's responsibilities, usually overseen by a designated Consultant High Inquisitor or Bishop. Religious rites are held in the hall of worship. Information can be found in cathedral libraries. Meetings between Church workers can be held in the meeting rooms, which are also at times used for educational purposes. Pilgrims, Priests and Inquisitors will also pick up their jobs here through the help of a Dispatcher. If someone needs help from the Church, their best option is to find the cathedral that oversees their district. Each cathedral layout is exactly the same, with the circular hall of worship in the center between two rectangular wings; one for employee use, and the other open to the public.

Church: The Church exists to protect humanity. Though it started as a religious group, after the First Surface War and the awakening of magic abilities in humanity, it took on more responsibilities. Now, the Church is the largest military force in Terrael. They handle public safety, education, healthcare, judicial matters, religious rites, and even act as government in a number of cities across the realm. There are some that believe the Church has too much influence, but many are simply grateful that the Church workers are there to protect them from the ever-looming threat of demon attacks.

Church Worker: A general term used to describe people working for the Church. Though it includes titled positions like Priests, Inquisitors, Pilgrims, Healers and Dispatchers, it's more commonly used to describe the employees too low in the hierarchy for proper titles, like trades workers, receptionists and other such roles.

Converter: One of the nine types of magic abilities. A sub-category of Material Shifters. Converters can alter the physical characteristics of materials they come in contact with. Unlike Sculptors, their changes can work on a wider variety of non-living materials. However, the effect they can cause will be specific. For example, a person could cause a stiff plank of wood to become flexible, cause a glass pane to sprout fur, or make a flimsy rolled up piece of paper become as durable as a metal pipe. The affected area and duration of the transformation differs from person to person. If they break physical contact, the effect will end shortly after. It takes magical energy to convert the object, so there is a limit to how long and how much they can convert.

Courciel: The capital city of Terrael. The city is split into two parts, the inner city, and outer city. The inner city is monitored and protected by the Church. In the center is the Grand Cathedral, where the Almighty Voice leads the Church. The cobblestone streets descend from there, with man-made canals lining the more level districts. The inner city is known for its fashion, cleanliness, impressive shops, beautiful canals and peaceful cafes. It's a hub, connecting the various parts of Terrael. The outer city, located beyond the large Holy Wall and moat surrounding the inner city, is less protected, and home to those that rejected, or were rejected by the Church.

Demon: The monstrous denizens of Diapogeum, the demon realm. After the First Surface War, the demons were banished underground by the Archangels. Many of them have been fighting to live on the surface again since. Demons often have jewel-toned skin, horns, tails and sharp claws. Though, the features differ demon to demon. Some also have bat-like wings, able to fly like the angels of Spira. Demons tend to have much stronger magic capacity and tolerance than humans.

Diapogeum: The demon realm. Located underground, Diapogeum is the home of the demons. It was created by the Archangels after the First Surface War to keep the demons and humans separated following the conflict. Though it was meant to be sealed off completely, it's possible to move through Terrael and Diapogeum through the Rifts scattered throughout the two realms.

Healer: The medical specialists of the Church. Though many Healers are recruited due to having magic abilities suited for the job, most are simply individuals trained to treat injuries and illnesses. Healers will primarily be found in houses of healing, but there are some that work as field-medics as well. A Healer's uniform covers their entire body to protect against disease, as well as to remain anonymous. This is because the Archangel Raphael believes those that choose to save lives should not do so for glory or fame, simply because it is the right thing to do. That being said, many do still wear name tags while working to help keep confusion to a minimum.

High Inquisitor: Talented Inquisitors will be promoted to High Inquisitors if they prove themselves worthy. The name itself is more a category than a title, as High Inquisitors have a wide variety of varying responsibilities. Holding the most authority, Consultant High Inquisitors manage cathedrals on behalf of their city or district's Bishop. Judicial High Inquisitors act as judges in court. High Inquisitives handle criminal investigations, usually commanding a team of Inquisitives. Along with issuing orders to their subordinates, High Inquisitors may also be asked to handle jobs deemed too difficult for regular ranked Inquisitors.

High Priest: High Priests delegate orders to the Priests in their squadron. A Priest can become a High Priest if they're chosen by a Bishop and Consultant High Inquisitor. Generally, those chosen are people that showed exceptional strength or leadership skills while fulfilling their duties. One cathedral will usually have multiple High Priests to cover a full patrol schedule. Along with issuing orders to their subordinates, High Priests may also be asked to handle jobs deemed too difficult for regular ranked Priests.

Hijacker: One of the nine types of magic abilities. A subcategory of Beast Manipulators. Hijackers can attach their magic to a living creature if certain requirements are met. Hijackers are able to control the creature bound to their magic. If the requirements are broken, or an ending condition is met, the creature will most likely regain control. What the requirement or freeing condition is depends on the Hijacker's ability. If the Hijacker releases their control willingly, they can regain their magical energy to an extent, but if it's broken by someone else, the magic is lost.

House of Healing: The Church-run medical centers in Terrael. This is where people go to get injuries and illnesses treated, fill prescriptions, get medical advice, etc. A House of Healing will have a main healing wing, and a magical healing wing. They're kept separate to ensure no one with a low tolerance is affected by the magic of a Healers' ability. People will generally be registered with one or two Houses, so that House can have access to their medical records.

Influencer: One of the nine types of magic abilities. A subcategory of Beast Manipulators. Influencers are able to attach their own magic to the magic of other living things. Unlike Hijackers, they gain no control over this other creature. Instead, their magic will affect the creature in some way or another. This can range from causing them to feel certain emotions, to healing, tracking them, or even blocking the use of their magic. This magic generally can't be reabsorbed after it's attached to the creature's magic.

Inquisitors: A faction of the Church that specializes in gathering, analyzing and handling information. There are several branches within the faction, each with their own specialties. Though, many Inquisitors will still have base training in other branches and can assist them if necessary.

Inquisitive: Short for "Investigative Inquisitor". This title was used more commonly when people felt the full title was too long to say. Inquisitives are a branch of the Inquisitor faction in the Church. They specialize in criminal investigation and gathering information.

Judicial Inquisitor: A branch of the Inquisitor faction in the Church. They specialize in handling criminal cases in a court of law, acting as defense and prosecution. To avoid bias, Judicial Inquisitors will alternate between defense and prosecution with each case, but only a trained Judicial High Inquisitor or Bishop can act as judge.

Magic: Magic is the essence of life itself. It flows through every living thing in the Three Realms, and for those lucky enough, its energy can be utilized in the form of magic abilities. However, magic is also quite dangerous to humans and demons. While mortal beings will be unaffected by their own magic, prolonged exposure to foreign magic can cause illness, and eventually death.

Magic Categories: Magic is split into three main categories; Material, Beast, and Special. Material magic users can affect non-living matter with their magic. Beast magic users affect living things. Special covers any abilities that don't fall into the first two categories, or somehow fall under several. Material and Beast are split into three sub-categories, these being Shifter, Summoner and Manipulator. Shifters magic focuses on physical transformation and requires direct contact to work, Summoners magic can be shaped to conjure up magical items or creatures capable of attacking from a distance, and Manipulators can attach their magic to other objects or creatures.

Magic Capacity: Magic capacity is the maximum amount of magic a person naturally has in their body. Using a magic ability won't cause this value to go down, as it's referring to the maximum natural capacity rather than the literal amount of magic that's left. The higher a person's capacity, the more likely it is that they'll have an ability.

Magic Deficiency: Magic deficiency is caused when a person uses more magical energy than they can afford. Magical energy is a person's life energy, and expelling too much will lead to fatigue, shaking, blurred vision, headache, disorientation and numbness in the body. When a person reaches their limit, they'll likely lose consciousness. Currently, the best cure for magic deficiency is sleep. Fresh fruits and vegetables are also known to help to a small degree.

Magical Overflow: Magical overflow is caused when a person is exposed to too much foreign magical energy. When a person uses a magic ability, magical energy radiates from the attack. Prolonged exposure will lead to fever, fatigue, coughing, confusion/disorientation, increased heart-rate and eventually a lack of consciousness. If exposure continues, the fever will rise to dangerous levels and colored marks show up on the skin. These marks will combust after a few hours to a few days. This magical flame-like aura will burn the body, killing the victim. Currently, the best treatment for Magical overflow is isolating the individual from strong sources of magic before they reach the point of no return. However, once the colored marks show up, the exposed person has reached late-stage Magical overflow, and there's no known way to save them.

Magic Tolerance: Unlike beings of magic, humans' and demons' bodies aren't built for magic resistance. Magic tolerance is a person's ability to handle exposure to foreign magical energy. Exceeding your limit for too long will lead to magical overflow, followed by death. Demons have a higher tolerance than humans. As beings of magic, angels are unaffected by foreign magic.

Material Summoner: One of the nine types of magic abilities. Material Summoners are able to shape their magic into conjurable objects. The object summoned differs from person to person. After it's been separated, the Summoner can absorb it into themselves again if they want to. However, if a summoned object takes enough damage or moves farther than the Summoner can handle, the magic will disperse and cannot be reabsorbed. Non-solid summons (i.e. Fire, liquid, electricity) have a tendency to leak more magic, making it very difficult to fully reabsorb without losing some magical energy. The material is entirely made out of the Summoner's magic; however, it may take on specific physical attributes. For example, if someone were to summon magical fire, it would be hot to the touch. If they summoned a shield or bullet, it would feel solid.

Pilgrims: Pilgrims are Church workers that focus on more situational jobs. Pilgrims are essentially professional helpers. They put out fires, they get cats out of trees, they help repair buildings, etc. If a person needs help with something, they'll go to the nearest cathedral and put in a request for help. If a Pilgrim is available and capable of helping in the way that's needed, they'll be sent to assist. Long term requests may be placed on a request board for Pilgrims to take as they like. Sometimes Pilgrims will take street commissions as well, if the client can't make it to a cathedral.

In this case, the client signs a commission form so that the Pilgrim can still receive payment for the job. Though, some Pilgrims will just take jobs under the table to avoid the paperwork.

Priests: The security and soldiers of Terrael. Priests protect the people by patrolling the streets. They act as soldiers in times of crisis. They prevent the use of unlicensed magic, and arrest and detain people that break the law. While they are able to use magic legally, abuse of this power will lead to investigation from an Inquisitor, and possible suspension and detainment. Priests will answer to High Inquisitors, High Priests, or anyone of greater rank than those titles.

Scribe: Bookkeepers, transcribers, authors; Scribes are in charge of the organization and upkeep of Church documents. Scribes are also often left in charge of cathedral libraries, helping people find the resources they need. Before being sent to the Almighty Voice, the daily reports of the Bishops are read through and condensed by the Scribes of the Grand Cathedral. Due to the information they're exposed to, the Scribes of the Grand Cathedral will generally be heavily investigated and must study at Gabriel's Citadel before earning the title.

Sculptor: One of the nine types of magic abilities. A subcategory of Material Shifters. Sculptors are able to use their magic to shape the world around them. Using their magical energy, they can alter the physical shape of the material their magic resonates with. The material differs from person to person, ranging from steel, to wood, or even air. It requires the user to have physical contact with the material, and they must be able to accurately picture the result of their alteration. They can't permanently change the physical characteristics of the material (i.e. make steel soft, or air solid), and cannot alter its mass. The more matter they manipulate, the more magical energy they use.

Seer: Categorized as a "special magic ability type", Seers are people that are especially attuned to the natural magic of the world. This connection gives them glimpses of the future through reading the ebbs and flows of magical energy. If the right actions are taken, the foreseen future can be changed. How the Seer receives these glimpses differs from person to person. Some have visions or hear voices; others are able to have glimpses at will through divination. Due to the source of the visions being more of a sensitivity to magic rather than an ability, not all Seers are able to control when they receive their glimpses. Some Seers are also capable of developing regular magical abilities on top of their ability to read the magic of the world.

Spira: The divine realm, and home to the angels and Archangels. While technically located above Terrael, Spira isn't visible in the sky due to the magic keeping it hidden. Supposedly, the divine realm can only be entered with the permission and assistance of the Archangels, and aside from the Almighty Voice, no human has been openly invited since the Church's founding.

Soldiers of Lilith: A more violent group of demons fighting to claim the surface for themselves. Each member wears a wooden mask that shows their rank. They were behind the Peycile Massacre, where an entire town of people were slaughtered. This tragedy is seen as the starting point of the Second Surface War.

Terrael: The human realm. According to history books, Terrael was created by the archangels long ago. The realm is circular in shape, with the Ring Sea separating its edge from the void surrounding the Three Realms. Most of the cities are connected through railways and roads spread across the land. The realm is also home to many varieties of climates and environments due to the influence of Spira on the weather and biomes. Some of these include the farmlands of central Terrael, Dudael desert in the south, as well as the Northern Mountains. It is possible to pass between Terrael and Diapogeum through the Rifts, but most are locked down by the Church.

The Almighty Voice: The leader of the Church. Elected through the votes of the public and Church members. The Almighty Voice candidates are chosen from among Bishops and High Inquisitors. They act as the face and figurehead of the Church, and have the highest authority within its ranks. Though the candidates are chosen through votes, the ultimate decision of who will fill the position is made by the Archangels within the tower of the Grand Cathedral. The Archangels can call for a re-election if no candidates fit their preferences. The Almighty voice communicates with Spira, manages the Bishops in the Church, and performs rites in Courciel on religious holidays and in times of crisis.